A DANIELLE NOVEL

ALREADY FALLEN

DONNY HUNT

World Castle Publishing, LLC
Pensacola, Florida
Copyright © Donny Hunt 2020
Paperback ISBN: 9781951642877
eBook ISBN: 9781951642884
First Edition World Castle Publishing, LLC, July 20, 2020.
http://www.worldcastlepublishing.com

Licensing Notes

Cover: Karen Fuller
Editor: Maxine Bringenberg

Already Fallen

You look so sad standing there, watching me
As I try to pick up the pieces
I hit hard when I fell, shattered on impact

> You swore you'd always catch me
> Baby didn't you hear me callin'
> By the time you got here
> I'd Already Fallen

Where were you when I was on the street?
Cold and lonely, looking for a home
While I was losing my life
Were you too caught up in your own?

> You swore you'd always catch me
> Baby didn't you hear me callin'
> By the time you got here
> I'd Already Fallen

> > Where do I go from here?
> > Broken, lost and alone
> > I always thought we'd be together
> > Now I'm out here on my own
> > We were going to walk hand-in-hand
> > Can't you see me crawlin'?
> > By the time you came for me
> > I'd Already Fallen

You're burdened by your guilt
I'm tired of wearing my scars
We make quite a pair
We've both fallen so far

> You swore you'd always catch me
> Baby didn't you hear me callin'
> By the time you got here
> I'd Already Fallen

CHAPTER ONE

The alarm went off at six-thirty-five, jarring Danielle Regan out of a deep sleep with the obnoxious tones of a pair of DJs engaging in some mindless banter. Danielle groaned and stretched, feeling every muscle in her six-foot-one-inch frame awakening all at once. As the blood began to flow, she began to make sense of the foolishness that was transpiring on the radio.

"I'm still trying to get used to writing 2009 on my checks," a woman DJ said. "It'll be March before I get used to it."

Her male counterpart chuckled. "You mean it'll be 2010 before you get used to it!" They both chuckled some more.

Danielle groaned again, tossed off her blankets, and swung her long legs off the bed. Her feet hit the cold hardwood floors, and it sent a shiver through her body. She rubbed her eyes before she finally pushed up off the bed and started across the room to kill the alarm. By the time she got to the clock, the DJs had shut up and were replaced by the soft strains of a lonely fiddle.

Danielle froze, her finger hovering centimeters above the button that would silence the alarm clock. Only she couldn't do it. Moments later, George Strait began singing. *"Amarillo by morning, up from San Antone...."*

Her breath caught in her throat as George began to sing. Slowly Danielle backpedaled until she made it back to the bed. She sat gingerly, looking towards the alarm clock, but her eyes were seeing something else, peering beyond the veil of years at another place and another time.

Springtime in Austin. Early evening sunlight was sneaking around the drapes in Danielle's house overlooking Town Lake. She was reclining on one end of her couch, one shapely leg folded underneath her while the other swung slowly. She was cradling a blue Paul Reed Smith guitar in her hands. Her hair was a jumbled brunette frame to her deeply tanned face, and she wore a loose tank top and sports bra with athletic shorts, far from the ideal of a sexy guitar goddess.

On the other end of the couch, her fiancé Kyle Greer sat on the edge of his cushion hunched over a sunburst Yamaha acoustic guitar. From where she sat, Danielle could only see a sliver of his profile: the neatly trimmed beard over a strong jawline and the long blond hair curling just past his neck. Still, Danielle could picture his face—she knew his blue eyes were shut tight in concentration.

Kyle was strumming the main rhythm to "Amarillo By Morning" and doing a credible job of singing, even if his voice was deeper and gruffer than George's. Danielle was playing the fiddle lines on her electric, keeping it subtle and letting Kyle stretch his musical legs. This exercise was for him, not her.

As Kyle reached the end of the song, Danielle launched into a bluesy solo, taking the lonely country song and turning it into something different. She saw Kyle's head snap around and lowered her eyes, focusing on her playing. The more his eyes bored into her, the deeper Danielle pulled into herself, biting her lip to keep from smiling. Despite his disapproving stare, Kyle did not interrupt her, waiting until she finished before speaking.

"King George does not need your showboating," he said as her final note died in the air between them. "You can't improve on perfection."

She kept her head down, but Danielle's eyes flicked up. "Maybe if he had me playing with him, his music wouldn't be so boring."

"Boring? Boring?" He quickly put his guitar aside. "You called King George boring?"

Danielle put her own guitar aside and gathered her feet under her while an impish grin crept onto her face. "King George? More like King Snores."

"Oh you!" Kyle lunged for her, and Danielle skittered over the arm of the couch, giggling like a schoolgirl. "You take that back," Kyle said through a grin of his own.

She stood just beyond his grasp and bent over at the waist. "Make me."

"You bet I will," Kyle answered, and he bounded off the couch after her.

Danielle darted away, leading him up the stairs, though she never quite reached the top. Kyle caught her halfway up, barely catching her around the ankles. She squealed as Kyle turned her over. Her shirt bunched up, exposing her flat stomach. Kyle kissed her softly, slowly working his way up her body. Danielle shivered and moaned as desire began to flick at her soul. Painfully slow, Kyle finally worked his way up to her face. Her fingers snaked through his hair as he hovered just above her.

"Come here, you," Danielle moaned. She clenched his hair in both fists and pulled him down, unable to wait even another second to feel his lips on hers....

"That was King George with 'Amarillo By Morning' here on Wichita's Classic Country KCCZ-FM." Danielle's eyes snapped open at the intrusion. Awareness came suddenly, and Danielle realized that she had been running her hands over her body, a poor substitute for the ones she really wanted. Unwilling to let the memory go, Danielle closed her eyes tight and tried to slip back into the dream. "Up next, let's take a little trip down to 'Austin' with Blake Shelton."

The moment was gone. Danielle sighed and let her hands fall to her sides as she stared at the dusty popcorn ceiling above her. "Oh come on. Now you're pushing it." She waited, hoping, but if her beloved Kyle was out there somewhere, riding on the radio waves, he wasn't showing himself. "Fine, have it your way."

She got up and quickly killed the alarm. Danielle hated country music, but it had been Kyle's passion, so she kept her alarm clock tuned to whatever country station was around in whatever town she happened to be calling home at the moment. This cold January morning found her in an old farmhouse outside the town of Thrasher, Kansas.

Thrasher had been her home for the past nine months, and though it was squarely in the nation's heartland, it felt like the edge of the world to Danielle. She circled her bed and went to the window, parting the dusty blinds with her fingers and looking out into a dark, desolate wasteland. It would be another couple of months before the fields started to grow again, and the landscape began to resemble the way it had looked when she'd pulled in the previous spring.

This spring would mark six years since she left her home and career in Austin, driven away by grief and anger and fear. Danielle Regan—blues guitarist, role model, and cultural icon—had died the previous year in the car crash that had claimed Kyle's life. Once she recovered from her injuries, Danielle took on a new name, changed her look, sold almost everything she owned, and set out to parts unknown. The only thing she kept was a 35th Anniversary edition Camaro that had been gifted to her by the head of General Motors after her '68 model had been totaled in the crash.

The plan was to live the life she never had before. She left Austin with visions of adventure and excitement in her head. Only it didn't turn out that way. No matter where Danielle went, her heartache and loneliness followed. She traversed the country from sea to sea and most points in between, looking for someplace that felt like home, and coming up empty each time.

When she passed through Thrasher the previous April, something about the town's old fashion feel had spoken to her. The city square was alive with people; a farmer's market was going full blast. City hall was at the center of the square, a beautiful old building surrounded with lush, green grass and colorful flowers. It suckered her in. Danielle found a deserted old farmhouse outside of town and rented it, hoping this would be the place she had been searching for.

Beyond the dark and barren fields, Danielle saw the place she needed to go. A place with a lazy river winding through it. A place with a stately capitol building and an iconic tower. A place her soul longed for, and the one place she refused to go.

Danielle let her fingers fall from the blinds and shuffled into the bathroom for a quick shower, stripping her nightshirt as she went and tossing it casually on the bed. It took a moment for her eyes to adjust when she turned on the bathroom light, and longer still for the water to heat up. While she waited, Danielle caught sight of herself in the full-length mirror on the back of the bathroom door.

The woman that looked back at her was but a shadow of what she once was — thin and gaunt, with a scar where they'd taken her spleen and another running up her left leg from the compound fracture she had suffered in the crash. Her hair was just short of her shoulders and dyed bright blonde, but her naturally dark hair was already reclaiming the roots — time for another touch-up.

I used to be pretty.

If she looked hard, Danielle could still see her old self lurking there somewhere, hiding out in her green eyes, looking back at what she'd allowed herself to become with disgust. Her breath got shaky as Danielle felt a crying jag threatening her. She ran her fingers through her hair violently, pulling at it. She wouldn't cry, not for Kyle, and damn sure not for herself. She had made her choices, and that was all there was to it.

Thirty-five minutes later, Danielle emerged into the bitter cold of a Kansas morning dressed in smart black slacks and a white button-down top under a long black coat. A harsh North wind tore at exposed skin as she hurried from her front door to the detached garage on the side of the house.

She opened the garage door where her Camaro sat waiting, the custom red and silver paint job gleaming under the single overhead light. Being in a garage didn't help much — it was as frigid in the car as it was outside. Cursing herself for not having sprung for a remote starter, Danielle started the car. As she shivered, she checked her makeup in the visor mirror as Bon Jovi's "You Give Love A Bad Name" erupted from the radio.

The radio had been her first sign of weakness. For years Danielle had denied herself the joy of music in any way except for the torture of country on her alarm clock. For so long, it had been easy to avoid anything that resembled her old life. She couldn't remember now when that wall had started to crumble, but she could remember grocery shopping somewhere when a Tom Petty song started playing on the overhead speakers. Trapped in the store and in the middle of her shopping, there was no escape. By the time she made it to the register, Danielle was singing along while other customers smiled or laughed.

Her personal Pandora's Box had been cracked, and there was no shutting it again. So Danielle indulged herself. The advent of music streaming made building an impressive music library easy. It had gotten to the point where her daily commutes were the most pleasurable moments of the day.

She knew she was playing with fire. Almost as soon as she let the music back in, Danielle began to feel the pressure to play again. She spent her nights writing lyrics, stuffing one spiral after another with words that withered without the music to bring them to life.

Now she found herself cruising through the small farming community of Thrasher, roughly forty miles northwest of Wichita. The town was already bustling, tight roads congested with work trucks and soccer moms in min-vans taking their kids to school. Along the town square, city workers removed the town's Christmas displays, the holidays now officially over. Thrasher had little geographically in common with her childhood home town of Chaparral in West Texas, but something about the endless rows of fallow fields reminded her of home, which was a warmer memory than it had a right to be.

Once out of town, Danielle put the pedal down, racing along the highway toward Wichita. Several songs later, she pulled into the back parking lot of O'Shay's Sounds, a small music store near Northwest High School. O'Shay's specialized in band and orchestra instruments and sheet music, but also featured a smaller section dedicated to guitars, basses, drums, and the like. Danielle had worked in a similar place when she first moved to Austin. Seventeen years later, that experience had landed her this job, where she had quickly ascended to assistant manager.

She slid in the backdoor and hung her coat on a hook just inside the door next to a blue and gold letter jacket and a beat-up motorcycle jacket. Even from the back storeroom, she could hear the sound of Rhianna pumping through the store's PA system. That would be at the behest of George Pearl, the slightly overweight but gregarious recent grad who opened the store every morning. George lived and breathed marching band and would soon return to college with an eye on becoming a band director.

Danielle paused at the breakroom door, where the smell of cheap coffee wafted into the hall. Danielle debated, then ducked in and poured herself a cup, dosing it with heavy amounts of cream and sugar, before heading onto the floor. She knew she'd never actually drink the coffee, but it was a nice, boss-like accessory, and the process reminded her of Kyle, who had relied on the drink to get his days started.

She stepped swiftly through the swinging door, the heels of her black thigh boots echoing a sharp report. George was standing behind the counter, dancing along to the song, his cheeks red and his straw hair damp with sweat. She tried not to smile as George stopped abruptly, his cheeks flushing red with the embarrassment.

"Morning, Miss Tucker," he huffed, trying too late to be cool. To George as well everyone else she'd met, Danielle Regan was really Renae Tucker. The name still sounded foreign in her ears.

"Morning, George. Would you mind turning it down a little? We might get a customer at some point."

"Sure thing, boss." George whirled and found the volume controls to the store PA. Danielle had a strong feeling that George had a crush on her and used that to get quick results out of him.

"I take it we've had a slow morning?"

"Yes, ma'am," George said. "Couple of old ladies came in looking for some sheet music. They didn't buy anything. It'll probably be dead until lunch."

Danielle walked slowly around the floor, checking over everything, making sure things were where they should be, but she knew they were. George was excellent about keeping the store tidy. It was the afternoon shift that drove her to distraction.

"Probably so," she answered as her eyes drifted to the glass wall that separated the main floor from the guitar section and the pretty guitars that hung on the walls. She could feel the call of the instruments, like planets yearning to pull her into their orbit. "Where's Aldo?" she asked, forcing herself to look away from the temptation. "I saw his jacket hanging in the hall."

"He's sleeping it off in the shop," George said, disgust dripping off the words. "I'm amazed he even made it in at all. He could barely walk."

Danielle picked up a stack of flyers laying on the counter and straightened them up. "I don't figure we'll be needing him for a while. Let him sleep." George huffed, and Danielle gave him an expectant gaze. "Issues?"

He started to speak, stopped, and then started again. "I just don't see why you keep him around. He's lazy, rude, unreliable —"

"He also knows guitars. He relates well to that element, the kids and the wannabes, and the club warriors. He knows how to speak their language. Just like you are in your element talking to band moms."

"I could do what he does," George spurted, planting his fists on his hips as he did. He leaned toward Danielle and lowered his voice. "It's no different than selling some kid his first trumpet. It's all salesmanship." Danielle stared at him silently. George caught it and quickly looked away, shifting uncomfortably, but he did not back down from his claim. "I'll prove it to you if you give me the chance."

Danielle sucked on her bottom lip while she thought about the challenge, then shrugged. "Okay. Next one that comes in is all yours. Even if Aldo wakes up. Let's see what you've got."

"Fine," he said, holding his head up high. "I'll show you."

They waited over an hour, making small talk and doing odd bits of upkeep until George's moment finally arrived in the form of a scruffy looking man who stomped through the door carrying a battered tweed guitar case in one hand. The man instantly reminded Danielle of the oilfield workers that used to fill her old West Texas hometown. His clothes were ragged and stained, his face weathered, his eyes sunken in, and his hands looked like aged leather. His shoulders slumped, and not just because he was cold. He was a man who looked soundly beaten down by the world. He stood just inside the door and let out a long jagged breath, his eyes darting from Danielle to George and back again.

"George?" Danielle said with a slight wave of her hand. "Customer."

"Right," George finally said, coming from around the counter to greet the man. "Welcome to O'Shay's, where every day is a musical day. How can I help you?"

The stranger assessed George quickly and shifted his sights to Danielle. "I wanted to see what I could get for my guitar." He held up the tweed covered case for her to see. "I hear that you make deals sometimes."

"Sometimes," Danielle said coolly. "George, take a look and see what he's got." She kept her arms crossed in front of her, being intentionally standoffish. There was something special in that case. Something that radiated. She felt it stirring long lost feelings deep in her soul. Suddenly she wanted very much for the man to leave. She'd already made up her mind that she wasn't buying, no matter what lurked in the case.

George reached for the case, but the man pulled it back and quickly stepped around him, setting the case down on the counter next to the cash register and opening it. George did a full 360, trying to catch up to the man. When he did, George took one look in the case and laughed out loud. "We're not interested, but thank you for stopping by. You might have better luck at a pawn shop."

"Stuff it, kid," the man snapped. He looked over his shoulder at Danielle, who was still standing several feet, defiantly away. "I want you to look at it."

"I don't do guitars. George is the expert."

"Shit, lady," the man said, his voice scratchy. "This kid wouldn't know his ass from a tube screamer. I want *you* to look at it."

Danielle gave an exaggerated shrug and shuffled over, already practicing her dumb act in her mind, hoping to put a quick end to the entire transaction. Inside the case was a battered Thinline Stratocaster. The Thinlines weren't the most popular Strats, though they had a following. A good one could bring in some money. This one was not good. The vintage blonde paint job was almost all chipped away, revealing every ding and dent in the wood. She could see why George had dismissed it so quickly, but as she well knew, you didn't play guitars with your eyes.

The man knew that too. "Play it."

"Excuse me?" Danielle said, taken aback back his sharp tone.

"I know she doesn't look like much," the man said, softening his tone significantly. "But she plays just fine. That's an Eric Johnson model right there. Eric Johnson was an elite guitar player out of Austin, won a Grammy —"

"I know who Eric Johnson is," Danielle interrupted. She stopped short of adding that she'd played with him on more than one occasion. "Look, Mr...."

"Beck. Sam Beck."

"Mr. Beck, I think George is right. You'd probably have better luck at a pawn shop. This guitar is going to need some work."

"Just play it," he pleaded. "There's a lot of life left in that old guitar. I promise you. If you put a little work in it, you'd make your money back plus some. Just play it."

Danielle looked from Sam Beck to the guitar and again felt its power pulsing in the air. Reluctantly she picked it up and looked it over carefully, taking a long look down the fretboard. "Neck's warped."

"Only slightly," Sam interjected. "Easy fix. You probably got a box of old necks in the back. Play her."

Danielle lowered the guitar. Part of her wanted desperately to play it, but she feared what would happen if she did. Still, she could see no way out of this without at least giving it a halfhearted strum or two. "Fine. Follow me."

She strode into the guitar room, Sam Beck right on her heels, George tagging along sadly in the back. She made her way to a floor model Fender Bullet amp, plugged in, and turned it on. The second the amp started to hum, Danielle felt the stirring deep inside of her, like a great beast awakening after a long winter's sleep. She slowly slipped the weathered old strap over her head and took the neck in her hands. George stepped up and slid a guitar pick into her right hand.

"Thanks," she said sarcastically.

"It still plays," Sam reiterated.

Danielle grabbed a basic G chord, strummed hard, and the guitar sang out, the note floating in the air between them. "So it does," she said coldly.

"She sounds like an angel," Sam added.

Danielle turned to face him. "You seem to love this guitar. Why get rid of it? We have a guy who works on these things. I could work out a payment arrangement for you."

"I wish," Sam said, hangdog eyes focusing on the guitar that now hung around Danielle's neck. "I need the money. I've held on to that thing as long as I could. I got no choice."

Danielle looked away, suddenly uncomfortable seeing the misery in Sam Beck's eyes. She strummed a few more chords but stopped when she realized she was getting into a rhythm. An old man had told her many years earlier that guitars had souls, and when they found the right player, they were locked together. This guitar wanted her. George couldn't see past the paint job and the rusty hardware. He didn't know.

She slipped the guitar off and faced Sam. "I'm sorry, Mr. Beck. I'd like to help you, but it would cost us more to fix it up than we could ever make on it. There's not much market for these old Thinlines. People want a regular Strat." She held it out to him and tried to avoid seeing the defeat that was etched into his face.

He took the guitar from her with a slow nod of his head. "Okay. I understand. Thank you for your time." He slinked out of the room, put the guitar in the case, and headed for the door.

George chuckled as he left the building. "What a piece of shit. And he says that I don't know guitars."

"You wouldn't know a guitar if I shoved one up that fat ass of yours," Danielle mumbled. Her eyes were fixed on the front door.

"What?"

"Nothing," Danielle snapped. "Go straighten something up, would you?"

Outside she heard the low rumble of a truck starting up, and before she had time to think, Danielle was rushing to the door, throwing it open, and running out into the bitter cold and whipping wind. Mr. Beck was at the mouth of the parking lot, waiting for traffic to clear so he could go, moments away from disappearing. Danielle jogged after him, and when she was at the tailgate, she started beating on the side with the palm of her hand. She saw Beck's eyes move in the side mirror and knew that she had his attention.

Beck cranked down the window as she approached the door. She glanced in the backseat of his extended cab and noticed two car seats and an assortment of children's toys strewn about. "How much do you need?"

"I don't want charity, miss."

"I'm not offering charity," Danielle snapped. Now that she had committed to this move, she was in no mood for foolishness. "For the guitar?"

Beck hemmed and hawed, though Danielle didn't buy it. He had already shown his desperation. She knew that he had a number in his head. Finally, after putting on a show, he said "$1,000" with noticeable apprehension.

It wasn't worth it. Danielle knew that you could get a used Thinline in good to excellent condition for $1,500 if you knew where to look. She had at least a half dozen guitars hanging on the wall in the store that were in better shape and much cheaper. Still, the pull of this particular instrument couldn't be denied. "I'll buy it from you."

"I thought you said it would cost more to fix it than it was worth."

"From a business perspective, yes," Danielle said, trying hard not to shiver from the wind that was biting through the thin fabric of her shirt. "I'm buying this for me. Can you come back this afternoon? I'll have the money for you then."

"Yes, ma'am," Sam Beck said as a wide grin broke across his face. "You don't know how much this means to me and to my family. I can get my wife's car fixed—"

"I don't need to know your details," she interrupted. "Come back around two. I'll have your money then. Deal?"

"Deal," Beck said eagerly. The smile on his face touched off a tiny flicker of happiness in her heart. Danielle backed away, but Sam pointed a finger at her. "I knew that there was something about you. A guitar player, a real guitar player, knows another when he sees one."

"You're very perceptive, Mr. Beck. Have a good day now."

"You too," Beck said through his nicotine stained smile.

Danielle stepped back and watched him drive away. She knew deep down in her heart that she had just started something, something she wouldn't be able to control. Something she'd been running away from for far too long. The thought scared her, but it excited her even more.

Beck returned as he promised at two on the dot. Danielle had slipped off at lunch and withdrawn more than the agreed upon price. She couldn't help herself. As she sat in the drive through at the bank, Danielle had flashed on the backseat littered with toys and Happy Meal boxes and thought to herself that if Sam Beck was in that bad of shape, a little extra wouldn't hurt. Thanks to her manager's shrewd business sense and her own frugality, she had more than enough.

When she finally heard the truck rattle into the parking lot, Danielle rushed out from behind the counter and hustled outside. She was at the truck before Beck could even get the car in park. He popped the door with a huge grin on his face. "Well, aren't you the eager beaver? A lot different than this morning, huh?"

His tone instantly turned her off. "Cut the chit chat." She pulled a bank envelope out of one pocket and waved it in the air. "Do you want this or not?"

Beck's eyes got wide. "You know, I do."

"Then where's my guitar?"

"All business, huh? Okay. It's right here." He ducked back into the cab and pulled the battered old guitar case across from the passenger seat. He walked quickly to the front of the truck and plopped the case down and popped the latches.

She lifted the guitar and gave it another once over. One last chance to back out. "All right. Here you go." She slapped the envelope into his hand. "From one guitar player to another. Spend it wisely."

The rest of the day seemed to crawl by. Danielle couldn't wait for the store to close. She had ideas and couldn't wait to get started. Once the store closed, cleanup seemed to take even longer, just more mundane details to get in her way.

She finally hustled her afternoon crew out the door and locked up behind them. There were still more tedious manager chores to delay her further. She quickly totaled the day's receipts, then triple counted the money in the drawers. She would deposit the funds on her way home, then take a little detour. Before she could play with her new toy, a shopping trip was in order.

CHAPTER TWO

AxeMasters was heaven on earth for musical gearheads. Danielle had never been that hung up on gear, usually preferring a simple set-up. For Danielle, less was definitely more. Still, if AxeMasters didn't have it, you probably didn't need it.

The store was located in a newly built strip mall and still smelled like fresh timber and paint. There was a room for keyboards, a room for drums, a room for basses, and a room for recording equipment and other necessities, as well as practice rooms if you wanted to take lessons there. The main room, though, was reserved for guitars, and they were everywhere, hung on the walls all the way to the ceiling, scattered around the floor on stands next to the wide variety of amps that were available. They had every type of guitar you could imagine, and throughout the store, music of various types and qualities filled the air as people tried out instruments.

Danielle stepped inside and brushed the hair out of her eyes. She was distracted, thinking only about her shopping list as she rounded the checkout counter only to suddenly find herself face to face with a ghost. Her ghost. A near life-sized cardboard display of a much younger Danielle, smiling and holding a red Strat that looked a lot like her first one, but not quite. Danielle gasped and froze, staring at the image from the past, looking down into its face because it wasn't quite tall enough.

"Can I help you, miss?" Danielle turned to find a sales associate in a bright yellow polo standing behind her. His name tag told her that his name was Scott.

"Huh? No, no. I just wasn't expecting…her when I came around the corner," Danielle said, trying not to sound flustered. With a growing sense of dread, Danielle realized she was standing right next to herself. Would he recognize her? She was ready to bolt if he did.

"Yeah, that just dropped today. I hear she plays like a beast," Scott the salesman said genially. "You want to try it? We got one up on the wall." He nodded, and Danielle turned, following his gaze to a candy apple red Strat hanging from a peg high up on the wall. It was a beautiful guitar.

"No," she said firmly, turning back to the salesman. "No, I just came for a set of strings and some new tuning pegs. And I want to look at your amps."

"I get ya," he agreed. "What're you playing now?"

Danielle started to answer and then stopped. She could feel her cardboard ghost looking over her shoulder, and it made her nervous. "Actually, before I do anything, do you have a bathroom?"

"Sure. In the back over there by the practice rooms. When you get done, I'll be out here waiting for you."

Danielle excused herself and wound her way through the stacks of amplifiers to the back and hurried into the bathroom.

Locking the door behind her, Danielle braced herself on the sink and tried to gather her wits. When she'd been performing, having her own signature Strat had been a goal. Now it had come true, and she hadn't even known about it. For a split second, she wanted to be angry at her manager for it, but it passed as quickly as it came. She had left him in charge with full authority to do whatever he wanted.

Danielle splashed some cold water on her face, straightened up, and prepared to go back out, reminding herself not to get distracted. She was there to get what she came for and get out. No more, no less.

She stepped out of the bathroom, noticed a water fountain, and stopped to take a drink. The water was nice and cool, and she drank deeply while her eyes absentmindedly scanned the bulletin board above the fountain. It was jammed full of ads: musicians looking for bands, bands looking for musicians, upcoming shows, and all the usual stuff.

Danielle finished her drink and wiped water away from her lips when she spotted a familiar name among the flyers — Colin Nix. She pushed aside some overlapping flyers, and there he was. Colin Nix live at Brett's Brewery in Kansas City for one week only. Only one or two of the little tabs at the bottom of the poster had been pulled away. She snatched one for herself while she studied the poster more closely. His engagement started in a week, and Kansas City was only a couple of hours away. A road trip couldn't hurt, could it? Danielle stuffed the tab in her coat pocket and returned to the front of the store, where Scott in the yellow polo was trying not to look impatient.

"Ah, there she is," he said when he noticed her approach. "Now, what can I do you for?"

Danielle looked him in the eye. "I need two packs of Ernie Ball's, nickel wound, and that Fender Hot Rod amp."

Scott's eyes lit up. "Yes, ma'am. Anything else while you're here?"

She started to say no and then stopped. "Well, do you carry home studios?"

"Yes, ma'am. I'd be happy to show them to you. We've got a really nice 4 track on sale right back here."

Danielle wound up getting a lot more than planned, but she was just thinking of things she might need. Dollar signs danced in Scott's eyes with each new item she mentioned. They were at the checkout when she caught another glimpse of Cardboard Danielle. Her eyes tracked from the cutout up the wall to the shiny guitar on the way above. "You said I could try that out?"

The salesman followed her eyes. "The Danielle? Yeah, if you'd like." He looked at the impressive number of things she'd already bought.

"Get it down."

Scott made his way to the wall and retrieved a long, hook-like instrument. He used it to grab the guitar and gently lowered it into Danielle's hands. Without meaning too, she muttered, "Oh wow," as she took possession of it.

The instrument was a world lighter than the one it was modeled after, but it felt good in her hands. As she admired the feel, Scott subtly plugged the guitar into a nearby amp and switched it on. The amp began to hum, and it sounded like the call of angels in her ears.

With a toe, Scott drug a stool over to her. "Give it a spin."

Danielle glanced over at him, smiled, and eased down onto the stool. Soon she was floating on air as her fingers danced along the fretboard. She ran the gamut of her box of tricks, slides and bends, hammer-owns, and pull-offs. She played with no care or concept of how much time was passing. Only when she finally stopped did Danielle become aware that the entire store was watching her. Curiously, several people seemed to be pointing their cellphones at her.

Most of the customers had shocked expressions on their faces, but Scott simply smiled down at her smugly. "So, can I carry that to the checkout for you?"

Danielle's hands and fingers burned. She handed the guitar back to him and rubbed her hands. "No, but you can hang it back up."

As the rest of the store went back about their business, it was Scott's turn to be awestruck. Danielle started to gather her equipment while Scott stumbled for a response. "But you really seemed to like it."

"Doesn't mean I want to buy it." As Scott took the guitar, her eyes found the price tag. "I just bought one anyway."

Scott resigned and replaced the guitar, no doubt calculating the commission on a three thousand dollar guitar. Danielle wrapped up their business quickly and hurried out of the store. On the drive home, she chastised herself. She could feel herself being pulled down a rabbit hole, and the thought didn't scare her as much as it should have.

CHAPTER THREE

The next morning, Danielle stood in front of her closet in nothing but a towel, facing a moral dilemma she'd never anticipated. All of her business clothes hung neatly in front of her, but the thought of slipping into another business suit made her skin crawl. On the other end of the closet rod, her jeans hung casual and inviting, mainly neglected since she'd started her job. The part of her that tried hard to be Renae Tucker told her to dress appropriately. The rest of her wanted no part of it. She chewed on her bottom lip while she drip dried and debated her move.

Since Danielle was essentially the boss, she could wear whatever she wanted, but if she dared to go casual and indulge that side of her, could she put the horse back in the barn? With the clock ticking, Danielle finally decided to split the difference, selecting her nicest pair of black jeans and pairing it with a sheer jade blouse that she loved because of how it made her eyes stand out.

Without thinking, Danielle bypassed her long wool coat for her black leather bomber jacket on the way out the door. It was another miserable, cold Kansas morning. It was the type of day when it was actually too cold to snow, the north wind like jagged teeth tearing at exposed skin, but Danielle never entertained switching coats. She hurried to the garage.

On the highway headed into town, she blasted the radio and let the Camaro out, certain that no cop was going to be interested in getting out in the cold for a mere speeding ticket. Despite the frigid weather, she felt a warmth growing inside her, and it wasn't from the heater. The closer she got to being herself again, the more right it felt.

As the asphalt passed under her wheels, Danielle's thoughts drifted to Austin, where the weather was probably much nicer, and the town was — well, it was Austin. It was home. There was no place in the world like Austin, which was why no place she'd chosen to hang her hat had been home. You couldn't replace the irreplaceable.

For the millionth time in the last seven years, that little voice started up in Danielle's head. The one that said that she should go home. Don't give two weeks' notice, don't leave a note, pack up only what you need, and hit the road. Right now. If she made good time, she could grab dinner on Sixth and take in some music.

The Wichita City Limits drew closer, and Danielle shoved the insidious thoughts away with a deep breath. No. She would indulge this new direction only so far. The entire point of embracing her inner Danielle was with the hopes that it would ease the urge to go back, not increase it. She had responsibilities here, a sense of purpose and direction that had been lacking in her previous stops. She couldn't leave.

Only that wasn't true. No matter how much Danielle tried to pretend that she was just a regular working person, it was a lie.

She was sitting on a small fortune, and with one phone call, she could double it. There was nothing to hold her in Wichita other than a misplaced sense of loyalty to a man she hardly knew.

She batted those thoughts around her head until the glow of brake lights ahead forced her to snap to attention. Morning traffic jam, the bane of her existence. She stopped and sighed. Normally Danielle would have missed this, but she'd taken far too long debating her clothes, admiring herself in the mirror, and simply dragging her feet. She was less than a mile from her store, but probably a good half hour or more from getting there.

She sat and steamed about her predicament until the song on the radio caught her attention, and not in a good way. She'd been listening to the city's lone classic rock station, and nothing had really struck her until "Come On Eileen" filled her car. She desperately fumbled for the SCAN button. "What the fuck," she snarled to no one in particular. "That's classic rock? Jesus." Mercifully she sent the radio on the hunt for a new station, but the damage was done. It would take a truly great song to keep that from getting stuck in her head.

Almost all the way around the horn, the search went as the traffic barely kept forward. Lots of Top 40 and Rap and Country to be had, very little else. At least until the strains of Hootie And The Blowfish's "Hold My Hand" caught her ear. Hootie was a band that had come up and hit it big during Danielle's senior year of high school, and she'd been a fan of the song. She stopped the scan and settled back in her seat, happy to let the song take her back to a time that she now remembered more fondly than it deserved.

Danielle's childhood had always been a mixed bag of bittersweet memories and outright nightmares, but her senior year had also been touched by death, which seemed to walk beside Danielle like a stubborn stray dog. Yet Danielle knew that had her guardian, a gentle old man named Kel, not died, she probably never would have set out for Austin and would have settled for a meager life in the West Texas desert. Of all the deaths that had impacted Danielle's life, Kel's was the one that haunted her the least, yet it was probably the most important.

The song faded into a new song, and Danielle's fingers wrapped around her steering wheel like a python. She recognized this song, too, because it was her own. "Blessed Poison," regarded by most as her signature song, began with an ominous guitar riff before a much younger Danielle's husky voice started up. For this song, she'd intentionally made her voice deeper during the verses. She had imagined the effect on the listener would be like lulling them into a sense of security before she shook them when the choruses kicked in, and her voice shot up like a scream. She was never sure if anyone ever felt that way, but it was one of her most successful songs, so whatever she had done, people liked it.

The traffic continued to limp along, and Danielle was finally able to see the flashing lights of emergency vehicles ahead, signifying an accident scene. No wonder traffic was going nowhere. She was almost past the site when "Blessed Poison" faded, replaced by the obnoxious voice of a DJ who was trying way too hard to sound like a 50s game show host.

"That was 'Blessed Poison' by Danielle Regan on 90s Radio Wichita, KNTS. Remember when she used to be so cool? Me neither," he snickered. "I keep waiting to see her pop on the shopping channel hocking the latest Guitar Hero game. Guess it truly is better to burn out than to fade away, huh kids?"

Danielle punched off the radio and glared at it, imaging the

DJ's face where the radio face was. "Fuck you, you fat little turd. You won't be laughing when I shove that microphone up your ass, will you?"

The radio stayed silent, but the DJ's words kept echoing in her head. She suddenly felt sick and bit her lip to keep tears from creeping into her eyes. She had never considered how she would be remembered. It never mattered, but she had never anticipated becoming a joke. That realization was too much to bear.

Finally, mercifully, the congestion passed the accident site, and the lanes opened up. Danielle hit the gas and went flying through traffic, weaving from one lane to the next. She wasn't worried about how late she was for work. She was trying to outrun the smug little DJ and his smarmy comments. It wasn't working.

By the time she finally parked behind the store and jumped out, Danielle was a half-step short of a full-fledged meltdown. Her wounded pride wanted revenge, wanted to come charging back, and make him eat his words. The other half, the vulnerable side that had never recovered from the tragedy that had driven her away to begin with, viewed his derision as the exact reason why she should never go back. Why subject yourself to that kind of scrutiny if you didn't have to?

Danielle hustled in the back door, which slammed behind her thanks to a strong push from the wind. She hustled into the break room, where she hung her coat and clocked in and stepped into the bathroom long enough to fix the damage the wind had done to her hair before making her way to the sales floor.

"Morning, Miss Tucker," George said, jovial as always. "Going casual today, huh?"

Danielle hardly noticed. Her head was still filled with the

petty insults from the DJ. She took a long, slow look around the room. "George," muttered. "Do you ever wonder what you're doing with your life?"

"No, not really. I have a plan. You know that. We talk about it."

"Yeah, I guess you're right."

"Everything okay, boss?"

"Not really." She strolled the floor, looking like she was checking on the status of things, but in reality, her mind was racing. George had a plan, a very clear one. He knew what he wanted out of life. Danielle had nothing. She was merely existing from one day to the next. For so long, it had been enough, but now she found herself craving more. She turned quickly to George. "What would you do if something happened and your plan got blown up? Completely destroyed. What would you do then if being a band director was out of the question?"

George put a finger to his lip as he thought. He finally shrugged. "I'm not sure, but I know I would find a way, some way, to be involved in band. That's where my heart is. I couldn't live without it."

"Huh." Danielle studied the young man and saw the sincerity in him. He was just a kid still, but he had a clear vision of who he was and what he wanted. Danielle realized at that moment that she did too. She was just too stubborn to embrace it. "Hey, hold down the fort for me, please. I'll be right back."

Danielle hustled into the back office, where she took out a pen and a piece of paper and scribbled a quick letter of resignation to Mr. O'Shay, shoved it in an envelope, and sealed it. Reaching in a desk drawer, she found the list of employees and began calling until she found another assistant manager who would answer the phone. "Leonard? This is Renae at the store. I hate to bother you on short notice, but I've had a family emergency, and I need to leave. Can you come in and cover the store for me?"

"I suppose," Leonard said. "What happened?"

Danielle fumbled for an excuse. When she finally came up with one, she fought hard to keep a smile off her face. "My mom died. I'm headed back home to make the arrangements. I'll let the old man know that I'll be gone for a while if you can come in."

"Oh man, I hate to hear that. Yeah, I'll be there in fifteen minutes. I'm sorry."

"Thank you. I appreciate that. George will man the store alone until you get here. Thanks again."

She came back to the floor to find a nervous George pacing behind the counter. She joined him behind the counter and laid the envelope on the cash register. "George, no matter what, don't lose sight of your dreams, okay?" George was clearly confused and started to answer, but Danielle stopped him by giving him a light peck on the lips. "Take care of yourself."

Feeling lighter on her feet than she had in ages, Danielle headed for the back door. George called out after her, but she kept walking. He was fully capable of handling the store. She couldn't stand the thought of wasting even one more minute there.

CHAPTER FOUR

Danielle pulled out of Thrasher a week later, headed for Kansas City. She took her time on the drive. She hadn't gone on any sort of road trip since deciding to settle in Thrasher. It felt good to be out on the road again.

In the week since she'd quit the store, Danielle had barely emerged from the house. Her life revolved around her new guitar. Working in the shed and using YouTube videos for guidance, Danielle set about restoring the old instrument. She took it apart, stripped it, and rebuilt the guitar from the ground up. She replaced the warped neck with a new one, put on gold hardware, and completely rewired the pickups, knobs, and selector switch. When it was all done, she gave the body a metallic purple paint job and a pearlized pickguard. The battered old Thinline was now a one-of-a-kind Danielle Regan original. She had made her own signature guitar for a lot less than $3,000.

With the guitar now in playing shape, Danielle set about getting herself back into shape. She was surprised at how quickly the muscle memory returned. The stamina would take a bit longer, but on the records she made, the improvement from one day to the other was apparent.

Another nice thing was that the cold snap had broken, and the winds had died down. By mid-afternoon, the temperature had climbed into the mid-40s, and the skies were clear. It was the first moderately nice day Danielle had experienced in two weeks, and it brightened her mood considerably.

She pulled into Kansas City just before three, and immediately set the location of Brett's Brewery before finding a decent hotel not too far away and checking in. Once that was taken care of, she set out to find some of the famed KC barbecue she'd heard so much about, and found it almost, but not quite, as good as the stuff back home. After her early dinner, she cruised the streets, taking in the sites of yet another town she had visited often but never had the time to actually see.

Soon enough, it was time to head back to Brett's, and she got there early enough to scope out a decent parking spot in a small lot in the back of the building. Brett's proudly boasted that it was Kansas City's newest and best microbrewery. Danielle had never been in a microbrewery before, so strike up another new life experience.

It was set in an old tire warehouse in what had once been an industrial neighborhood but was now being rehabbed into an entertainment district. The building had a warm feel to it, with soft yellow lighting and deeply stained wood furniture. The brewery equipment was visible through a glass wall on the west side of the building, big stainless steel tanks and piping that clashed with the rest of the motif.

The hostess seated Danielle at a table for two in the middle of the room. She decided to be adventurous and ordered one of the

house special beers and settled in, expecting a long wait before
showtime.

The crowd filed in slowly, mainly in twos and fours, though
there was a larger group that forced the staff to combine tables
along the east wall. The growing crowd created a low murmur
that filled the quiet awkwardness Danielle had felt when she was
one of the first customers in the place. She took her first sip of
custom brewed beer and determined that it tasted like beer and
pushed it aside. Perhaps she was just an unsophisticated small
town Texas girl, but she didn't get beer and doubted that she ever
would. Custom brewed or commercial, it all tasted like horse piss
to her.

At preciously eight o'clock, the overhead lights dimmed, and
a curtain was pulled in front of the glass walls of the brewery as
the soft hum of a single amp started. She doubted anyone else in
the bar even heard it, but Danielle did. That sound immediately
took Danielle back to any one of the hundreds of nights when she
had stood on a stage, not unlike this one, that almost unnoticeable
hum leading her into yet another concert. Her pulse quickened at
the very thought.

Now the only light came from the tiny tea light candles
on each table, as all attention should have turned to the stage.
However, most of the customers seemed oblivious to what was
about to start.

Danielle wriggled in her seat, anxious for her first glimpse
of Colin Nix in thirteen years. Back then, he had been scruffy
and charming, a well-regarded Scottish actor who had journeyed
to America with his side band to experience life as a rock'n'roll
singer. They had clashed at first. Danielle thought he was doing
it as a joke and disliked the unprofessionalism he and his band

had displayed. He learned, and they bonded. It could have gone further, but an old flame had called him out of the blue, and Colin dropped her like a bad habit. The rejection had stung, but Danielle had long since moved past it. They wouldn't have made it and allowing the relationship to progress further would only have intensified the pain when everything finally crashed.

A young woman stepped up to the microphone. "Ladies and gentlemen, thank you for coming out to Brett's. Tonight and all week long, we have a special treat for you. Some of you may be aware of his work on the Silver Screen, but tonight he's going to wow you with his voice. All the way from Aberdeen, Scotland, please welcome to the stage, Colin Nix!"

There was a smattering of applause as Colin took the stage. The years had not been kind. His light brown hair had grayed, and his hairline had receded significantly. He had put on enough weight to officially qualify as pudgy. He was far from the suave leading man he had been when she'd known him.

Colin came out with nothing but an acoustic guitar, wearing a white dress shirt open at the collar and black jeans. He pulled up a stool and sat down in front of the single microphone. "Good evening, Kansas City," he purred, his voice still as smooth as ever with a touch of a Scottish accent he'd never learned to cover up. "Thank you for being here and letting me provide your entertainment this evening. Let's get on with the show." There was another round of lukewarm applause, and Danielle caught the flicker of disappointment on Colin's face. When he'd first come to America in the spring of 1996, he'd come with a full band and entourage and played big clubs. Now here he was, a one man show playing a microbrewery in Kansas City. It was a long drop.

As Colin began to play, Danielle was soon surprised by

more than just the changes in his appearance. His voice was far different, stronger now, more defined than in that initial tour in '96. Instead of booming loud rock songs about sex and indulgence and prancing around the stage, most of his songs were introspective. As the show wound on, he sang a lot about the sea, painting himself as an old pirate yearning for a return to the open water. Had his songs been more upbeat, she would have accused him of listening to too much Jimmy Buffett, a crime that was damn near unforgivable. However, his songs were far more soulful and bluesy, leading Danielle to wonder if she had influenced him, at least a small bit.

Throughout the show, Colin tried to engage the audience with inconsistent results. Her heart broke for Colin as he would pour himself into a song, losing himself in the performance, only to be greeted with minimal response. She hoped that this wasn't the way all of his concerts were received.

After an hour and a half, Colin stood, pushed the stool away, and removed his acoustic guitar, trading it for a simple black and white Stratocaster, not all that different from the red and white one she had learned on. The hum of the amp got louder with the switch in guitars.

"Thank you so much for coming out tonight. I appreciate your kindness." He paused and again received minimal applause and a couple of woots. "For my last song of the evening, I want to perform a song that means a great deal to me. I wrote this song a long time ago for someone very special, someone that I didn't treat right. You know people, sometimes you only get one chance to be the person you need to be, that you should be and that the people around you need you to be. There's no guarantee of a second chance. So my advice to you is, if you have a special someone in your life, let them know every day. I never got a second chance with this young lady, and it haunts me still."

The murmurs in the audience stopped, and for the first time all night, he had their undivided attention. Danielle smiled as she looked around the room and saw the crowd in rapt attention. Good for Colin to finally reel them in.

"I've been performing this song every show for about ten years now. Every night I imagine that she's out there somewhere, sitting in the dark in the back of the theater and that she hears my song. That's what I hope for." He paused again, just a heartbeat, and the murmurs of the audience now were louder in response.

He had roped her in too. Danielle knew the girl that he spoke of. She was the one Colin had left her for, a high school sweetheart that had suddenly popped back into his life. He left Danielle, both professionally and personally, at the drop of a hat and ran back to her. She could only guess from Colin's tale of woe that it hadn't worked out for him.

Colin looked like he blinked tears out of his eyes, and for a split second, Danielle thought it was legit, but then she remembered he was a professionally trained actor. This was all an act. For all she knew, his old flame was backstage in the dressing room waiting for him.

He held the guitar in front of him. "This young lady is the reason why I'm here tonight. She taught me how to be a singer, a performer, to reach inside myself for something more. She taught me to quit being an actor and to be real. She taught me how to play this thing. So you can blame her for tonight."

The crowd laughed except Danielle. He wasn't talking about his old flame at all. Her blood ran cold at the realization. *He was talking about her.*

"I hope you'll love this song as much as I love playing it. It's called 'Siren Of The Strings.'"

With that, he backed away from the mic and started to play. Sitting slack-jawed, Danielle watched in amazement as Colin began playing a slow, wailing blues intro on the guitar. She had no idea he'd learned to play so well.

Colin began singing another heartfelt tale of loss and longing, but this time his voice rang out with so much more depth, and Danielle could almost count the tears that fell as he sang the song. It was a stunning performance, one that moved her in a way no one else had moved her before. She pushed away from the table gently and meandered her way through the staggered tables, her eyes still locked on Colin, whose own eyes were latched shut as he belted out the lyrics.

She made it to the front of the stage, close enough that she stood just outside the circle of the spotlight that focused on Colin. He quit singing, stepped back, and ripped into another solo, giving away a corner of a satisfied grin as he hit the first piercing notes and let them hang in the air. The crowd hollered in excitement, and he grinned bigger, hamming it up now for the audience that he had fought so hard to win over. As Colin's eyes swept the crowd, Danielle stepped forward out of the shadows.

He saw her in an instant. She wasn't sure if he'd recognize her after all the years and with her new look, but he did, almost instantly. They locked eyes, and then Danielle smiled up at him and bowed slightly as a sign of respect before slinking back into the shadows and out of sight.

For a moment, Danielle thought about leaving, but she still needed to pay for her drink, and she also wondered if he might come out after the show looking for her. It didn't get that far. As

"Siren Of The Strings" finally wound down, Colin stepped to the mic again. He was grinning ear to ear as the crowd stood and applauded.

"Thank you so much. I appreciate it. You know, sometimes things work out in ways you couldn't imagine. I've been blessed to be here tonight to perform for all of you, and you get to be treated to a little something extra." This sat well with the crowd, which roared their approval. Danielle's stomach dropped as she realized what he was doing. "The young lady I spoke about, the one that I've dreamed of seeing again for over a decade, is sitting out there with you all right now. I'm wondering if you make a real big racket if she might jump up here and join me for a song."

The spotlight swung over the crowd until it settled on Danielle. The crowd erupted, and Danielle suddenly found herself trapped. Strange hands reached out for her, pushing her in the back or grabbing her arm. Part of her wanted to run right then, to dart out the door, but another part desperately wanted to climb up on that stage.

"Come on, my darling," Colin called from the stage. "Just one time. For old times' sake."

Danielle yanked her arm away from one overzealous fan, but the others succeeded in pushing her to the side of the stage where Colin now squatted, holding a hand out for her. She hesitated, then took the hand and allowed him to pull her up, much to the delight of the crowd. She barely had a chance to stand up straight before he swallowed her in a bear hug.

"I've waited so long for this night," he whispered in her ear.

"Don't say my name," she whispered in return. Colin pushed her away, an unspoken question on his face. "Please," Danielle whispered.

"As you wish." He bowed, then removed the Strat, and pushed it into her hands. "Do you still remember that song 'Nobody's Children'? We used to play it together."

"I should. I wrote it."

"Let's do that."

Standing there on the stage together, seeing Colin's toothy grin, Danielle felt like she'd been transported back in time. She felt the years, and the scars pull off her as she adjusted the tuning on the guitar and got ready.

"Whenever you're ready," she told him with a wink.

"Go for it."

They wound up playing three songs that night, one from Colin's first album and then a cover of an obscure Stones' song called "Sway," before they called it a night. As soon as the curtain dropped, Colin latched onto Danielle's arm and pulled her to his dressing room. He was giggling like a schoolgirl as he slammed the door, wrapping her in another big hug. He smelled of high priced cologne and sweat, with a trace of cigarette smoke underneath. His skin was still wet and clammy from the show.

After what seemed an eternity, Colin relaxed his grip and held Danielle away from him. "Blonde is not your color, my dear."

"Yeah, I know," she answered, reactively reaching up and twirling a strand of hair around her finger. "You look...."

"Fat and bald, I know. Time waits for no one, as the song goes. But it has been kind to you, a bit skinny though. Come, sit with me." Like the gentleman he was, he took Danielle gently by the hand and led her to the loveseat. She sat tentatively on the edge of the cushion as Colin settled next to her.

He stared at her like he had all those years ago, back when she thought he might have been her One True Love. "After all these years, you finally walk back into my life. I want you to know," he said, wagging a finger at her. "That story I told was not bullshit."

"I didn't think—"

"Yes, you did," Colin said through a toothy grin. "I know you better than that, Danielle Regan. You always could see through my bullshit, and never hesitated to call me on it. There may be a lot of water under our respective bridges, but I know how you think."

Danielle held his gaze for a second before a slow smile crossed her face. "Okay, I may have thought that it was a little bullshit." Colin kept staring at her. "Okay, a lot of bullshit."

"I would expect no less," he relented.

"I have to say I'm surprised," Danielle said. "I figured after you left me, you ran off and never looked back. When I came here tonight, I didn't expect to be the central character of your grand finale."

Colin sighed and popped up off the couch. He walked over to a small fridge and took out a water bottle. "No, nothing could be further from the truth." He seemed to struggle, but he finally managed to look back at her. "I thought of you every day for a long while, and you've never been far from my mind. Especially when I put on my music hat."

Colin sat back down and reached out for Danielle's hands. "What I did was probably the worst thing I'd ever done. I never doubted I was doing the right thing as far as giving Sarah and I another chance. I had to do that for myself and my own peace of mind. It was *how* I did it. I was a coward. I thought of looking into your eyes. You were still so young and innocent, and to see the heartbreak...I just couldn't face it. I was a true and honest asshole."

"That you were," Danielle responded, but she did it with a smile. "It probably hurt a lot worse the way you did it. I would have preferred that you look me in the eyes."

"I know," Colin said, dropping his head in shame. "So often, I've wished I could have that moment over." He let a maudlin silence hang in the air between them for too long. "But you want to know the worst part of it all?"

"What's that?"

"It wound up being a huge mistake. Sarah and I, we just didn't work for one another. No matter how hard we tried or how badly we wanted it. The more we pushed it, the worse things got." He stood and circled the table, looking at the blank, recently plastered walls. "I left you for her, and things starting going south soon after. So we got married, and things got worse. We had a child, and things got worse. We tried counseling, had a trial separation, really left no stone unturned, and everything failed. We both wanted it, but sometimes two souls don't fit together the way they should." He turned on a heel and took Danielle in from across the room. "Do you know what I mean?"

"Oh yeah." She thought back on her first fiancé, Adam, and her tumultuous relationship with him. He had been to her what Sarah had been to Colin, and she had almost made the same mistakes. "I know very well." As they looked across the small room at each other, an uncomfortable thought came to Danielle. She stood but kept the coffee table between them. "You know, I didn't come here to try and rekindle anything. I just wanted to catch up, see how things had turned out...."

"Oh goodness!" Colin exclaimed. "Oh no. I'm sorry if something I said led you to believe that. I thought...oh no." He came to her and took her hands in his. "Please understand, I have moved on in my life, as I'm sure you have with yours."

Danielle pulled her hands away. "Of course I have. That was a long time ago. I just didn't want you to think…."

Colin let out a hearty belly laugh. "Oh good. Whew, that is a relief." He edged by her, sat back down, and patted the cushion next to him. When Danielle sat, he continued. "No, things are great for me now, and I think they'll be even better after tonight. How I treated you has been a cross that I have borne for too long a time. Being able to say this to you, to come clean, takes that cross from me. But no, I have no desire to restart anything with you." He breathed in sharply, which caused Danielle to recoil a tad. "Not to intimate that I wouldn't want to. You're still very beautiful and all."

It was Danielle's turn to laugh now. She patted him on the knee. "It's okay. You didn't offend me. You said things were going great for you?"

"Oh yes," Colin said with obvious relief. "I have a beautiful partner back home. We've both been through the wringer and come out the other side. She has a career, I have a career, and we both understand our careers come first. It's a perfect arrangement that allows two very selfish people to remain selfish without feeling guilty about it, and still have someone to come home to."

The mood in the room changed suddenly, and Colin edged closer to her. "I…heard about your fiancé and the accident. I am so sorry for your loss."

Danielle breathed in sharply and turned away in case a tear tried to escape. She hadn't spoken openly about Kyle's death in years. In fact, thinking back, she'd never really spoken about it at all, choosing instead to avoid the subject altogether.

When she was sure that she had her composure, Danielle turned back. "It's behind me." She wondered if it sounded as hollow to Colin as it felt coming out of her mouth. "I moved on the best way I could."

"By changing your appearance and dropping out of sight? I've followed your career with interest, and I know you have neither released new material nor made a public appearance since the accident."

Danielle had to remind herself that as far as the public knew, that's exactly what it was, an accident. Amazingly, the true details of the wreck had remained hidden, and she was thankful for that. The last thing she wanted was to have Kyle's death drug out in the tabloids again. She'd missed most of the initial press coverage due to her own injuries.

"My heart wasn't in it anymore. So I decided to do other things instead. I've traveled, seen some things, and just lived an ordinary life."

"But no one to share it with?"

"No," Danielle said sharply. "That part of my life is over. When Kyle died, he took my heart with him. You can't get that back."

"I see." Colin stood and walked to a small fridge on the other side of the room, opened it, pulled out another bottle of water, and tossed it to Danielle.

"Thank you," she said, somewhat confused.

"The least I can do. It dawns on me that I didn't offer you a drink. I am a poor host sometimes. I think it also proper that I offer you a drink before I call you on your own bullshit."

"Oh really?" Danielle twisted the lid off the water bottle, took a long drink, and settled back in her seat. "Please enlighten me."

"So you are how old now? About thirty?"

"Almost thirty-four. What does that have to do with anything?"

"Lots of people have lost the ones they love and gone on to find happiness and companionship. There's no such thing as One True Love. Souls can connect on so many different levels, and it is foolish to believe that because your fiancé died, you have to live the rest of your life alone. You deserve better than that."

Danielle smirked and shook her head, but Colin wasn't about to give her the floor yet.

"It's written all over your face. The sadness. The loneliness. It makes you look ten years older. There used to be a spark in your eyes that is gone. It is devastating to see you like this."

"Well, I'm sorry," Danielle snapped. She leaned forward. "I came to grips a long time ago with the fact that I'm not meant to be with anyone. Every relationship I ever had was a disaster in one way or another. I'm okay. I'm over it. Some people are destined to live their lives alone. Doesn't make me special."

Colin grunted and turned away, forcing Danielle to stifle a laugh. She'd seen that same response in almost everyone at one point or another. She was keenly aware of just how big of a pain in the ass she could be. She watched as Colin fumbled around in a drawer, took out a pack of cigarettes of a brand she didn't recognize, lit one up, and slowly took the first drag.

"Listen," he said in a carefully measured tone. "There is no destiny. No one is meant for this or that. We all make choices in our lives. You *choose* not to let anyone near you. You *chose* to abandon everything that you once held dear. I don't know if it's some sort of convoluted punishment or what it is, but whatever you call it, it still totals up to bullshit."

"I can't—"

"You won't," he interrupted sharply enough to give Danielle a start. "Even if you chose to never let anyone in again, what about your music? I know how much your music meant to you. Don't try to tell me you don't miss it. I saw you up there tonight, how much fun you had. Don't try to deny it."

"I've started to miss it, the last little bit." She continued looking anywhere but directly at Colin. "Just playing around. For fun, not with any intentions."

"What was it that prompted this sudden change?"

"I don't know." She tossed the water bottle onto the cushion and stood, tucking her hands into her jean pockets. "It just started building."

"Then Danielle," Colin said softly, "Take that skill and go to the place where you can do something with it. There's still brilliance in you. Don't deprive the world of your gifts, and quit denying yourself the pleasure."

"Easier said than done."

"No, it's not. It's as easy to go back as it was to leave. You just pack your car…and go. You know the way." He approached her slowly and took Danielle softly by the shoulders. "The world needs another Danielle Regan record. The world needs more Danielle Regans, period. Go home."

"I burned a lot of bridges."

"They can be rebuilt. It may take time and work, but bridges can be rebuilt." Colin leaned up on his tiptoes, pulled Danielle in, and gave her a soft kiss on the forehead. Pulling away, he held her at arm's length. "Stop looking for excuses and just go home."

CHAPTER FIVE

The next morning, Danielle pulled out of Kansas City with a lot on her mind. Usually, the open road offered a haven for her, a chance to clear her head. She often did her best thinking behind the wheel of a car. This time, the road was a big part of what was bothering her.

The thought of returning to Thrasher and spending another night in the dark, drafty farmhouse was almost unbearable. She was tired of cold and wind and barren fields. The life of a nomad was wearing her down, and Danielle was ready to put an end to it.

Then she thought of Austin. Could it be home again? Could she handle the pressure and the expectations? Could she stand it when there was a memory lurking around every corner? What of those she left behind? She would have to face them, and she didn't know if she could do it.

As the miles rolled on, clarity never came. Colin's words ran through her mind on repeat. He was so insistent that she go back, Danielle began to wonder if Colin didn't have ulterior motives.

She hated to think that, but it had to be considered.

She drew closer to home, and still, Danielle had no idea of what she wanted to do next. To take her mind off things, she flipped on the radio and scanned the stations, looking for decent music. It helped the miles pass as she jumped from one station to the next, occasionally hitting on a great song.

By the time she pulled into the outskirts of Thrasher, Danielle still hadn't found any answers, and her confusion had been augmented by a ravenous hunger. Danielle spotted Kristie's Diner on the side of the road and made the impromptu decision to pull in and grab some takeout.

Kristie's had originally been an old gas station, and the owners had repurposed as much of the original gas station for the décor as possible. The place was a little drafty, but no one seemed to mind much. The place was largely deserted at midday on a Sunday, except for a pair of old timers in overalls and John Deere hats who sat at the end of the counter watching a replay of the latest Kansas Jayhawks basketball game on a small TV on the wall.

As soon as Danielle stepped in, Kristie saw her. She was tall and stout with black-rimmed glasses, dark hair, and an infectious spirit. "Girl, it's about time you popped back in here," Kristie called out in a voice that betrayed one too many cigarettes.

Months of eating most of her meals here had enabled Danielle to learn all about Kristie's story. A local product who went on to become a decorated athlete at the University of Kansas before returning home to save the family business from ruin, Kristie was a local hero in more ways than one.

"Where you been keeping yourself lately? I haven't seen you in nearly a month."

Danielle thought about protesting, certain that it had only been a couple of weeks, but Kristie had shown to have a remarkable memory for her customers, so Danielle let it pass to avoid any potential embarrassment. "I've been around," she said as she hopped onto a chrome and vinyl barstool. "I just got back into town as a matter of fact. Spent a couple of days up in Kansas City."

"Well, that's good," Kristie answered. "Nice to see you getting out. I hate to think of you wasting away out there all alone in that old house." Kristie leaned across the counter. "Did you meet any men in KC?"

Danielle shook her head with a laugh. "No. At least not in that way."

She playfully swatted Danielle's arm. "Ah. Well, if you're interested, word around town is that Stevie Roth, who owns the hardware store, is on the outs with his wife. He'd be quite the catch. Got a successful business and most of his hair still. A girl could do worse."

"Thanks for the tip. If I ever get over to the hardware store, I'll scope him out and see what I think." She had no desire but knew well that Kristie would stay on the subject until she got the answer she was looking for. "In the meantime, can I get a grilled chicken salad to go please?"

Kristie's face fell. "You don't want to stay and eat?"

"Not tonight. I've still got to unpack. I just want to put on my bum clothes and sit around and watch some TV."

"All right. Coming up." Kristie shuffled away to place the order and tend to her customers at the other end of the counter. Danielle listened to them nitpick the game on TV. Danielle watched with little interest. She'd never been much of a sports fan, despite having been an athlete in high school. They held no interest to her, and this particular basketball game was no danger to change that.

Kristie returned a few minutes later with a white plastic bag in her hands. "One grilled chicken salad with extra ranch for you." She placed the bag on the counter in front of Danielle, eye checking the men at the end of the bar, and leaned in. "I threw in a slice of chocolate cake for dessert, my treat," she whispered. "We need to put some weight on you."

"Well, thank you," Danielle said, both touched and somewhat annoyed at the gesture. She dug a twenty out of her pocket and handed it across. "Keep the change."

Kristie took a quick glance and saw the generous tip Danielle was giving her. With a grin, she gave Danielle a quick hug. "Did I ever tell you that you're my favorite customer?"

"Once or twice," Danielle answered.

~*~

Danielle was relieved to finally make it home. She unpacked quickly, put her salad on a plate, and sat on the couch in front of the TV for something to stare at while she ate. She flew through the channels until a familiar face caught her eye.

Adam Quisenberry was on her TV screen, his eyes looking through the screen right into hers. It gave Danielle a start, which turned into a chuckle moments later. He was an actor, it was a movie. As insidious as Adam could be, she was fairly certain he hadn't perfected an ability to infiltrate her television.

She sat back on the couch and watched the movie unfold. She didn't recognize the film at all, which was a take on an old '40s detective story titled *Old Wounds*. She studied Adam's face on the screen, and he looked different, older, and more weathered. Had he aged that much, or was it make up? Danielle couldn't tell, but she knew that this was a recent movie. The last she had heard, Adam had moved to Wyoming and gotten married. It looked like his new leaf hadn't lasted long, not that she was the least bit surprised by that.

As the movie progressed, she got into it. It was one of Adam's better movies, and that was saying something because, for all his personal flaws, he had a knack for selecting the right projects. As the movie wound towards its climax, Adam and his love interest had to sneak out a second-story window to escape the bad guys. Adam's character made it easily, but the woman fell, because of course, she did, and Adam had to catch her. The stunned woman looked at Adam with big doe eyes. "You know I'll always be there to catch you," Adam said as he put her down.

"Don't buy it," Danielle said, jabbing a fork full of lettuce at the TV. "He told me that too. But where was he when I fell?"

The question rolled around in Danielle's head. *Where were you when I fell?* Danielle put her plate aside and rifled through the mess on her coffee table until she found a note pad and pen. The words began spilling out of her as if she had opened a vein. Danielle had always done her best work when inspiration hit, and as she bled ink onto the page, she knew in her heart that she had a great song on her hands.

When she was done, Danielle sat back and read through her new lyrics twice, making slight adjustments each time, before reaching for her guitar. The music flowed just as freely as the words had, and soon night had fallen, and she was still banging away, overlaying tracks on her home studio, building a new masterpiece.

By the time she was done, a new day was already dawning.

She listened to the new song on repeat, letting it all sink it. There was still work to be done, but Danielle could hear the finished product in her heart. The problem was, she'd done all she could do from here. She needed a real studio and a band to finish the song.

After a dozen listens, Danielle shut off the music, sat back, and stared at her mess of equipment and notes. She was wasting her time and her talents here, and if nothing else, the day's events had proven to her that her music was the path to the happiness she kept chasing. Once she made that simple admission to herself, everything else fell into place. She was wasting her time in Thrasher. It was foolish to resist any longer. It was time to go home.

Still too wired to sleep, Danielle began straightening up the house and packing. Years of traveling light and moving often had made the art of packing second nature to her, and everything was ready by late morning. She stacked her belongings by the door and made a final sweep of the house to make sure everything was cleaned up and in good order.

Danielle toyed with the idea of leaving then, but exhaustion was overtaking her, and she knew it would be a bad decision. She decided to sleep the rest of the day and leave early the next morning.

On her way to the bedroom, she passed the phone on the kitchen wall and picked it up. She knew the number by memory but hesitated to dial it. The phone started beeping at her, so she hung up. No need to call Steve, she decided. She'd surprise him. Austin was a full day's drive away, but as Danielle finally drifted off to sleep, she did so with the knowledge that the next sunset she saw would be over the Colorado River.

The next morning, Danielle was back on the road before sunrise. She had taken the time to write a brief note to the landlord, then put the keys and a check for six months' worth of rent in an envelope. She came back through town one last time. She found her way to the landlord's house and left the car idling at the curb as she quickly ran up and deposited the envelope in his mailbox. Then she was gone, driving as fast as she dared, eager to put Kansas, and to a great extent the last six years of her life, in her rearview mirror.

Danielle was starving by the time she hit the city of Edmond on the northern outskirts of Oklahoma City. She'd seen a billboard for a local place named Teddy's and decided to give it a try. She found the place not far off the interstate.

Teddy's was a mom-and-pop joint located in an old convenience store and was designed to emulate an old country store with antique appliances and authentic metal signs everywhere. The old fashioned décor was offset by a large poster behind the counter that read **Oklahoma City Welcomes The Thunder** with several basketball players under it. The tables were arranged in neat rows, and there was a counter running the length of the place. A TV mounted above the counter was tuned to Fox News, where the discussion was all about Barack Obama's upcoming inauguration.

Danielle took a seat at the counter, and a young woman in a Thunder T-shirt and jeans slid her a menu. Danielle decided on a club sandwich and a glass of sweet tea and turned her attention to the TV while she waited. Fox was just coming back from commercial when the waitress plopped the sandwich and a basket of fries in front of her. She started to devour it as a pretty blonde began introducing an in-studio guest, some woman hawking a book about dealing with her "tragedy." Danielle didn't care enough to pay attention.

Onto the screen popped a stunningly average woman who looked to be about fifty. She was blonde with glasses, a little too heavy but not fat, with a thick North Woods accent. The host and the woman bantered pleasantly while Danielle ate, providing nothing more than background noise, not much different from the sounds coming from the kitchen.

Until the name Sean Alec Moore was dropped. Danielle put her sandwich down and looked up to the TV. Why did she know that name? Danielle had never been a follower of current events, especially not since her accident, but she knew the name. Something was buzzing at the back of her mind. Something insistent, but she couldn't put her finger on it.

The pudgy woman was talking about their life together in upper Wisconsin, and on cue came a picture of the two of them, the woman looking much younger, at a football game, both wearing red and white clothes with a large W on them. More pictures: her husband with their kids, working in the yard, playing in the snow. As she talked, the woman began to choke up, eliciting empathy from the host.

"Let's talk about that night," the leggy host said as the camera came back to them. She leaned forward and patted the older woman on the thigh. "How did you hear about the accident?"

Accident. Her brain was buzzing again, louder this time. What accident?

"I didn't hear until the next morning," the woman said, choking back tears. "I woke up to the state police pounding on my door. I was confused, I didn't know what was going on, but I knew. The second I saw them, I knew something terrible had happened to my Sean."

Danielle found herself riveted. She literally moved to the edge of the stool she was sitting on, her lunch now completely forgotten.

"Your husband was out of town, right?" The host asked.

"Yes," the woman answered, dabbing at her eyes with a tissue. "He had told me that he going to a leadership conference in Austin. It was supposed to be a three day symposium, and then he'd be back. It was going to help him get a promotion at work. He showed me the tickets and hotel reservations. I had no reason to believe...." She broke into full-fledged sobbing.

Austin. Sean Alec Moore. Accident. Danielle's head was swirling. Had something happened while she was gone? She began to worry that one of her friends might have been involved. Suddenly the pressure to go back home intensified. If one of her friends had been injured or died, while she was gone.... Danielle shuddered at the very thought.

On the screen, a new picture came up. A nasty car crash. It was late at night, but the scene was lit brightly by the lights of emergency vehicles. A huge Dodge truck was sitting at an angle, the front smashed, the windshield shattered. The driver had been going the wrong way on the highway.

It took a moment for Danielle to notice the other car, a black Camaro convertible. The Camaro had taken the impact on the front left corner, and the huge truck had obliterated the front end. The white seats were stained red with blood.

Then, with horror, Danielle realized that it was her car. Her body started to shake as she remembered waking up in a hospital bed days later, her body broken, her spirit destroyed. Steve was there at her bedside, and he had told her the news.

"…accident," the woman was saying. "He'd drifted over into oncoming traffic. They thought he might have fallen asleep or…." She took a deep breath, trying to get herself under control. "Or had a heart attack. They didn't know much at the time."

"It wasn't an accident," Danielle muttered. Steve had told her that.

"But it wasn't an accident, was it? Tell us, Nicole, what really happened that night seven years ago."

"He had a…he…." Nicole was having a hard time spitting it out. "He had…targeted the car."

"It was an assassination," Danielle whispered under her breath. He'd been waiting, watching. He sped up when the car came into view. It came back to her now in flashes. She should have been driving, she always drove, but Kyle had been pestering her. She wanted to show him that she could loosen up and not be such a control freak, so she gave Kyle the keys.

He was driving slow and careful because he didn't want to screw up. Danielle was in the passenger seat dreaming. They would be married soon, and everything was going to be right in her world. She had her head back, loving the feel of the wind in her hair. She had been aware of lights, bright lights on her face, and then….

The hospital. Everything between them driving and then were just stray moments. Impressions really. Sensations. Everything had changed in an instant; everything had been taken from her, and Danielle never knew, never had a chance to brace, to say anything.

"Obsessed," Nicole was saying on the TV. "I went down into the basement…." She shuddered. The host started to speak, but Nicole cut her off. "She had bewitched him. Turned his mind around."

"You're talking about Danielle Regan, the singer?" A young publicity photo of Danielle popped up. She was wearing a light purple jacket over a darker corset top and a black miniskirt, staring into the camera with a look Steve had dubbed The Smolder.

"Yes," Nicole affirmed. "That woman had entranced my sweet Alec with her devil music and her…booty shaking."

"Entranced?" Danielle hissed at the TV. "Booty shaking? Are you kidding me?"

Someone off to the side gasped, and Danielle turned to find the entire wait staff staring at the TV and whispering amongst themselves. She rolled her eyes and turned back to the TV. The host was holding up Nicole's book. "You can learn more about Nicole's ordeal right here in *The Seduction Of Alec*, which will be out in stores this Tuesday."

Danielle had heard enough. She pushed away from the counter so violently that the stool skidded across the floor, turned over, and bounced into a nearby table. She dug a twenty out of her pocket, threw it on the counter, and all but ran out the door.

Danielle's hands were vises on the steering wheel as she guided the Camaro back up on to the interstate, still thinking about the woman. Her husband, her loser husband, had been obsessed and tried to kill two people out of some bizarre jealousy, and now this woman was trying to make Danielle the bad guy?

Of course, the national media would eat it up — any chance to knock a celebrity down a few pegs, even if they were only former celebrities. Danielle could just picture the circus when she finally rolled back into town, and people knew. The press would be all over her. As if she didn't have enough to deal with, now Danielle had to face up to this.

She was winding her way through the thickening Oklahoma City traffic when Danielle suddenly began to feel sick. She would have to relive that terrible night, over and over again. She'd have to answer for what he, this Alec Moore, had done to her. The press would bring up every incident of her past, every moment of bad behavior, and throw it in her face. Danielle thought she might throw up.

What had started out as a pleasant journey had taken a nasty turn for the worse. Danielle began to feel the pressure in the back of her mind—the desire to turn around, to shoot off somewhere else, to hide away from it all again. The junction of I-40 and I-35 loomed just ahead. With one simple turn, she could jet off to the west and avoid it all. It wouldn't be so hard to find another little town far off the beaten path and start over again. She was used to it.

"No," Danielle muttered between clenched teeth. She was tired of running. Why should this Nicole Moore have the only say? She might be the darling of the press for the moment, but Danielle had spent a good chunk of her life in the spotlight. She knew how to play the media game as well as anyone. She'd all but destroyed a man's career with a publicity stunt. She'd have her say.

She rolled past the I-40 exit and kept running south. As the car churned on and the miles rolled by, Danielle put a final dagger in the heart of Renae Tucker and all the fears and doubts that had led to her creation. Danielle Regan was coming back, all the way back. She wasn't just going to slink in under cover of darkness. No, she would come back breathing fire, and heaven help anyone who didn't get out of her way.

Chapter Six

After nine hours on the road, Danielle was weary and restless. Night had fallen, and she'd been counting off the town names as she went, but Austin didn't seem to be getting any closer. Her eyes scanned the horizon, waiting for the skyline to come into view. She wondered if Austin had missed her as much as she'd missed it. Was it possible for a town to miss someone? If it were, Austin would be the place.

Then slowly, the landmarks came into view. The University Tower and the Capitol Dome, shining like stars in the night—runway lights bringing her in on the final approach. Danielle felt the smile breaking across her face. She'd driven into this town more times than she cared to count, but it felt special every time.

She remembered the first time, in the spring of 1993, fresh out of high school with a chip on her shoulder and a guitar on her back, and not much else. She'd been driving a beat-to-shit Ford truck with no air conditioning, and engine noise so loud she didn't even bother turning on the radio. It was daytime then, rush hour traffic backing up all the way out to Georgetown, the heat from the cars, and the asphalt almost unbearable. Yet Danielle knew she was where she was supposed to be. She knew it as an eighteen-year-old. Now she asked herself if she had known how the next ten years would unfold, would she have still completed the drive.

Yes, she would have finished it. Teenage Danielle didn't back down from anything. She didn't run away. She had picked up that trait afterward.

Here she was, pulling into the northern city limits as a thirty-four-year-old, hoping there was enough teenage Danielle still inside to make this work. It felt the same, though, like the world was stacked against her, and the only weapon she had was her guitar, just like it was supposed to be all along.

She spotted a Hampton Inn off the interstate that looked fairly nice and pulled in, thankful to get off the road. She checked in for two nights under the name Renae Tucker, then carted her gear up to the room with every intention of being in for the night. When she was finished lugging all her worldly possessions up to her room, she collapsed on the bed, which was thankfully soft and inviting, and it pulled her down into sleep.

She awoke with a start later, feeling panicked and confused. Danielle violently rubbed the sleep out of her eyes and located the clock. It was 9:42, and she'd been asleep for two and a half hours. She sat on the edge of the bed, her elbows on her knees, and debated her next move. More sleep was inviting and well deserved, but she was hungry, and it was early as far as things went in Austin.

She walked to the window and looked out, but her room was on the back side of the hotel and faced east, so she couldn't see the familiar landmarks. Danielle touched her left hand to the cold glass. She stared off into a darkness punctuated by city lights that could have belonged to any decent sized town in America, but these were Austin lights, and they were calling her out.

Decision made, Danielle splashed some cold water on her face, changed clothes, and set out again, ready to begin a homecoming too long delayed already.

Soon she was shooting down I-35 heading toward downtown, the traffic blissfully light. She peeled off and found downtown to be quiet. She guided the Camaro into a street side parking spot on 6th Street, locked the car, buried her hands in the pockets of her jacket, and started walking west toward Congress. Even though it was dead, it was still 6th; various forms of music still bled out of the nearby bars, and the air was still fused with fresh pizza, car exhaust, and the smells of the nearby river. People still bounced from place to place, most in groups, but there were some couples and the occasional lone wolf as well. The taxis prowled the streets looking for fares, as did the rickshaws. The cops made their presence known, but stayed to the side, for the most part, just keeping an eye on things.

As Danielle walked, she saw not just the present but the past. She stopped and lingered on the corner where she had once played for spare change, which was also the corner where she had met Adam Quisenberry. She walked on, past bars she used to play, all now with new names, and past the Buffalo Billiards where she'd spent a lot of money shooting pool in her downtime.

She reached Congress Street and turned right, making her way down to the wide sidewalks toward the capitol, which stood majestically bathed in light. She stood for several minutes at the corner of Congress and 11th, just staring at the grand old building, with the UT Tower standing in the background, trying to commit it all to memory. Only when the chill and the hunger began to overtake her did Danielle finally move, walking back the way she'd come, back to the car, and the warmth of the heater.

Dinner was in order, but she had one more stop to make first. She drove up to Congress but turned left this time, over the river, and then into a parking lot just on the other side at Auditorium Shores. She parked again and hopped out. Late night joggers were working their way along the river's edge, while a few erstwhile folks fished from the banks. Danielle worked her way west along the river until she came to the statue of Stevie Ray Vaughan in his familiar hat and boots, guitar in hand, gazing as always to the south toward the building where Austin City Limits was filmed.

Danielle stood in front of the statue and remembered the man. She had met him when she was young, and he was nobody. Her parents used to host parties that would rage into the early morning hours, and he was sometimes there, always playing his guitar and singing. She'd called him The Funny Looking Man back then. She couldn't even remember now when she had realized that he'd gone on to fame and fortune. After leaving Austin, her mother had banned her from listening to music, sheltered her from so much. He had died before she ever had a chance to return here, nothing but a ghost on the periphery of her life.

Yet he always felt like a companion to her, a force at her back, urging her onward, perhaps to complete what he had never been able to do. "Hey, Stevie," she said softly. "Sorry I've been gone so long. Had some things to sort out, but I guess you knew that." She looked around, aware that some of the people taking leisurely strolls were staring at her. "The place looks good. I see a lot of new buildings, but feels the same." She stepped closer until she was right at the base of the statue. "You wouldn't know him, but if you meet a guy named Kyle Greer up there, tell him I love him, and that I'm sorry. Let Dad know too. I'm sure he's hanging around up there somewhere." Danielle felt tears threaten to break loose and bit her lip, determined to hold them at bay. "Anyway, I'm back now, and I'm going to do things right this time."

She stood a while longer, not knowing what else to say, hoping for some sort of subtle sign that having a conversation with a statue didn't make her crazy. She didn't get the validation she was hoping for.

Finally, Danielle moved on and soon found herself at a Denny's that she had once frequented. She saw the very booth where Adam had jumped on a table, spouting some weird artistic shit about movies. A redneck had almost kicked his ass that night. She laughed at the memory but took a seat at the counter instead. Adam wasn't a ghost. He was still very real, and they had a connection she didn't fully understand. But they both felt it, and Danielle didn't want to set off any cosmic warning bells that Adam might hear.

She chowed down that night on a bacon cheeseburger and a Coke, a meal she hadn't allowed herself to indulge in since the accident. She found that she couldn't finish it, but it was good, nonetheless, and finally, Danielle decided to call it a night. In the morning, she would seek out Steve, and once she did that, there was no turning back.

As Danielle slipped into bed later that night, she asked herself one last time if she was sure this was what she wanted. Six years of anonymity had spoiled her. Could she handle it when everybody recognized her? She might have questioned it further, but she was too far gone, and soon sleep pulled her under.

CHAPTER SEVEN

Danielle slept until ten, then took her sweet time in the shower. She was in no particular hurry, in part because she was giving herself as long as possible to change her mind. Yet, as nervous as she was getting about coming back, Danielle was even more excited. She decided to dress up for the occasion, hoping that presenting a professional look might alleviate some of the concerns Steve was certain to have.

As Danielle checked herself in the mirror before leaving the hotel, she wished that she could do more. She was so pale and thin, and she'd come to hate the blonde dye job. Wouldn't take much to do away with it, she reasoned. Finding a beauty shop that took walk-ins would take some time, more time to reconsider. Then again, if she wasn't fully ready to jump back into being Danielle, the blonde might still serve a purpose. She chose to leave it, and instead searched out a restaurant where she could grab a late breakfast.

After she was done with breakfast, Danielle took the Camaro through a car wash to get the months of winter and road gunk off the car. She went through twice, getting the cheap wash the first time and then the works the second. She figured it needed both for as long as it had been. When it was done, she parked and did a quick inspection, quite pleased with how the custom paint job now sparkled with a wash and a wax.

Soon she was at the automated gate to the parking garage under the Metcalf Building. Danielle had no reason to believe her code would still work but figured it would be fun to try anyway. Surprisingly the gate went up for her, and Danielle rolled on into the garage and soon found her way to what had been her reserved spot. There was a silver Lexus in what had been Steve's spot, but there was no guarantee it was still his. If it was, she reasoned that the empty spot to the right was still hers and pulled in. If it wasn't, tough luck to the other guy.

The elevators dinged open on the 13th floor, and Danielle stepped out into the foyer. A pair of double glass doors in front of her bore the name Reckless Roads Inc. The Reckless came from the name of Danielle's backup band, Reckless Passions, and was chosen specifically to give the band members a sense of belonging. Roads because they were always on the road back in the day, as well as a nod to Danielle's penchant for taking impromptu road trips when she got stressed.

She walked through the doors and into an office that was both familiar and alien all at once. The layout of the lobby was the same, but it had clearly been redone with a more modern look. Framed posters of acts she'd never heard of hung on the walls, and there was a glass trophy case stuffed to the gills with memorabilia from Danielle's past: gold and platinum records, awards, magazine covers. She had left it all to Steve when she left, and he had, in turn, created a shrine. She imagined that any young artist who came up here to negotiate with Steve would find it terribly impressive.

In the lobby, a nervous, scruffy looking young man in dusty jeans and a denim hoodie sat bouncing his leg and looking around furtively. Behind a fancy receptionist desk, a cute young woman in purple framed glasses and a nameplate that read Baylee watched her with a skeptical eye. Danielle walked up to her.

"Hey, is the big guy in?"

"Mr. Redus is busy. Do you have an appointment?"

"No, I'm afraid I don't," Danielle said. She could tell by Baylee's demeanor that this was going to be a fight, and Danielle was ready to play. It would be a short fight. "Just buzz him and tell him that his prodigal child has returned."

She wasn't having any of it. "Mr. Redus only sees people by appointment. If you'd like to make an appointment, I can see what's available."

Danielle leaned across the desk and looked Baylee in the eye. "Just buzz him and tell him. I promise you, he'll want to see me." She reached across the desk. "It's just that little button right there."

Baylee swatted her hand. "Quit that. Mr. Redus is busy at the moment. If you would like to have a seat and wait, I will tell him when he becomes available."

Danielle pulled her hand back and smiled. "Good enough. I'll just go have a seat then." Baylee shooed her away, and Danielle took a seat next to the nervous young man. "How're you doing?"

The man glanced up at her quickly, then back down to the floor. "Fine." Heartbeats passed, and then he looked up again. "I wish I had your confidence. To just come in here and announce yourself as someone's meal ticket. That's ballsy."

"Ah, it's nothing." She checked Baylee and saw that the receptionist wasn't paying attention to her. She leaned in closer to the young man. "You really want to see ballsy? Watch this."

Danielle stood and approached the desk again, carefully eyeing a poster that hung to her left that looked like a book cover. "Excuse me, that poster there. Is that for a book?"

Baylee turned and glanced at the poster in question. "Yes, it is. That's Mr. Townsend's most recent novel. It just dropped last month and is doing quite well."

"That's odd. I didn't know he was working as a literary agent. I thought Steve only did musical acts."

"He's branching out," Baylee said.

"I guess his inexperience explains how he missed that glaringly obvious misprint in the title. I'm amazed a guy like Steve Redus would want that hanging in his office."

"What?" Baylee turned all the way around, giving Danielle what she needed. She darted to her right, turning the corner of the desk. Baylee, caught flat-footed, tried to jump up after her, but it was too late. Danielle was at the office door and threw it open.

As Baylee's hand clamped down on Danielle's arm, Steve looked up from his desk with a start, what looked to be a Reuben sandwich in one hand and a Judith White novel in the other. His brown suit jacket was thrown over the back of his chair, his shirt sleeves were up, and his tie hung loosely around his neck. His eyes got wide.

"Dani?"

Baylee yanked back on Danielle's arm. "Mr. Redus, I'm so sorry—she just burst in. I tried to stop her."

Danielle pulled her arm free from Baylee's grip and held

them out beside her. "I'm back."

Steve threw down the sandwich and the novel and sprang out of his chair. "Dani, my God! I can't believe it!"

Steve, who was even bigger than Danielle remembered, engulfed her in a monstrous hug that stole her breath out of her chest. He finally let go and held her away from him.

"Um, sir...," Baylee called from behind Danielle.

"You're fine. Go back to your desk," he told her. His attention never left Danielle. "After all these years." He paused to take a good look at her. "You look like shit."

"Thanks," Danielle answered. "I missed you too." His face turned green, and he started to apologize, but Danielle cut him off. "It's okay," she said as she slapped him on the shoulder. "I know I look like shit. I see it in the mirror every day."

Steve invited her to sit, and she did so as he retreated behind his desk. He started to pick up his sandwich, then put it back down to peer across the desk at her. "So, is this just a social visit or...?"

"Or have I come back for good so you can strap a saddle on me and start riding?" She shrugged and slouched back in the chair, resting her right foot on her left knee. "Oh, I don't know. I've had so many adventures. I don't know if I could settle back down into a boring old job again."

"Oh," Steve said. "Well, I'm glad you stopped by to see me, though. Just passing through?"

"Yep," Danielle said. "Just thought I'd stop by and say hi on my way to the next stop. I'm headed down to the coast. Gonna do some deep sea fishing in the Gulf."

"You're shitting me," Steve scowled.

Danielle laughed in response. "Yeah, I am." She dropped her

foot to the floor. "Truth is, I'm bored, and I'm tired of running. It was finally time to come home. And if you would still have me, then yes, I would like to go back to work."

"Would I?" Steve pushed the sandwich aside. "You have no idea." He stood and circled the desk, Danielle following with her eyes as he worked his way to the back of the room and his personal wall of fame. "See all of these pictures? Not a damn one of them can sell albums. I've tried everything: country acts, hip-hop acts. I've even got one client on the World Music scene who shares many of your less redeeming characteristics, but I can't find a hit. Not even a minor one. So if you're ready to come back, then yes, I will have you. As a matter of fact, your timing couldn't have been better."

"How so?"

"Because Rico Cardenas has been breathing down my neck for months now wanting a new album of original material. You left me a lot of things when you left, but you didn't leave me any music, except for the one song."

"I remember," Danielle whispered. "I destroyed everything else. I had tons, too, in various stages of development. I even destroyed some stuff Kyle and I had worked on, and I really regret that. I wasn't real smart about that."

"You were in mourning, I understand. But I do wish you would have reached out for some help. I would have been there for you. Trish and Ty, Randy, and Teri. We all would have been there for you."

Danielle sighed and stood, ambling over to the window behind Steve's desk. She opened the blinds and stared out over downtown. "I never doubted that y'all would have been there. In fact, that's exactly why I didn't reach out. I didn't want anybody to be there. All I wanted was to be left alone." She turned away from the window to see that Steve had crossed the room and was just a few feet away from her. "If I had stayed, y'all would have stayed on me and wouldn't have let me wallow in self-pity. So I had to leave."

"It took you six years to get the pity out of your system?"

"No. It only took me a few months to do that. It took me six years to work up the courage to come back. Turns out that once you start running, it's really hard to stop. You turn on yourself. It's kind of weird. I was going by this assumed name, and there was a time when I feared I was on the verge of developing some sort of split personality. Got pretty dark for a while."

"Well, none of that matters now," Steve said, still keeping a respectful distance. "So, have you still been playing or —?"

"Yes, I have. Been working pretty hard at it for a little bit. I don't think I'm the same as I used to be, maybe not as fast."

"Well then, I guess I should start working on putting a band together for you." Steve edged by Danielle and slid into his chair. "I'll hit the phones."

Danielle pushed aside some papers and sat on the edge of the desk. "What about the band I used to have? Are they not on the table?" Steve looked up at her, and she saw everything she needed in that glance. "I guess not."

Steve swung his chair around toward her. "You have to understand, it's been nearly six years. Life goes on. You said that you weren't coming back, so they moved on. Garrett owns a bar, Trish is a teacher, Ty runs Randy's old place. DeShon is doing session work — he's all over the place."

"I get it," Danielle said defensively. "I'm assuming those aren't going to be pleasant conversations."

"When you go to see them? No, they won't. So do me a favor and don't do that yet. Let's get you settled in first. Where are you staying?"

"Right now at a Hampton on North 35. I'll find a better place, but it'll do for now."

"I have an apartment west of here, faces downtown—beautiful view, especially at night. I'll talk to the manager and see if there are any openings. I think you'd like it."

"In the same building with you? I don't know about that. Kind of like moving back in with your parents."

"You are starting over," Steve reminded her. "Just let me check, no obligation. If you want, I can get you a room in one of the nice places down on the river, where you'll be closer to the action."

Danielle stood. "Nah, I'm good. I think it's kind of a good idea to have a little space. I got used to it out there. I don't know how I'll do living in a city again." They locked eyes, and Danielle knew there were so many things that still needed to be discussed, but she was beginning to feel claustrophobic. "Listen, I know you're busy, and now you're going to be even busier, so I'm going to get out of here. I'll check back with you in a couple of days." She started for the door but stopped with her hand on the knob. "Don't forget that there's some kid waiting for you out here."

"Ah crap," Steve moaned. "That's Calvin." He glanced up at Danielle. "Poor kid thinks he's the second coming of Bob Dylan."

"He's not?"

"Hell. He's not even Jacob Dylan."

"Hey," Danielle said sharply. "I really liked The Wallflowers."

"So did everybody else, in 1996," Steve said, holding out his arms. "The world's changed since then. Have you heard anything from Jacob Dylan lately?" Danielle didn't have a response. "Exactly." He sighed heavily. "Send him in on your way out."

Danielle nodded and opened the door, paused, and pushed it closed quietly. She turned to see Steve staring at her expectantly. "Do you think the world really wants a new Danielle Regan album?"

"Maybe not," he said. "But, we'll make 'em want one."

CHAPTER EIGHT

Danielle left the Metcalf Building and headed west out of Austin toward Town Lake. It had turned into a beautiful day with temperatures in the low sixties, a marked change from the extended cold of Kansas in winter. She opened the car up on the MOPAC, slicing through traffic and loving the rush.

Soon she found the area she was looking for. What had once upon a time been a new housing development had blossomed into a full-scale neighborhood. She navigated the streets with ease, finally climbing a hill that ended in a cul-de-sac. The last time she had been here, the house stood alone, as the surrounding lots had intentionally been left undeveloped. Now the house was surrounded on all sides.

Danielle edged her car to the side and parked, staring longingly at the two-story red brick home that had once seemed so large and impressive. Now several houses on the street dwarfed the one that had once been hers. She'd bought the land out from under Adam, who had shown her the plot originally, but her ship had come in before his. She'd designed the house, complete with a full working studio in the basement and a balcony outside the second-story bedroom that looked out on the lake below.

The newer owners had done a lot of work, mainly landscaping, adding lots of bushes and flower beds, and plenty of outdoor furniture, most of it with a Texas motif. She thought she could see part of a Backyard Adventure playground lurking in the back over a privacy fence that had been added after she had sold the property.

Danielle sat with the driver's side window down and tried to picture the area the way it had been when she'd had the entire block to herself, but she had a hard time plugging in the details. She hadn't spent much time outside the house. In fact, she realized with sadness, she had wasted the house, only at the very end filling it with the love and life it deserved. It appeared that whoever held the house now had rectified that, though they had also added neighbors to the mix.

She sat and wondered. If she found a realtor and made a crazy offer, could she buy the house back? Surely she could make an offer that would make finding a new home easy, but would they sell? Who knew what kind of memories the new residents had made in the house?

No, it was no longer hers, and that was the way it should be. She needed a fresh start, and pushing someone out of their family home wasn't the way to do it. She drove away, hoping the urge to buy it back would dissipate as she got further away. Finally, winding her way back to the MOPAC, Danielle paused. The Capital of Texas highway wasn't far away. Did she want to revisit the site of the crash? After a lengthy internal debate, Danielle turned left instead, almost running from the temptation. There was nothing to be gained by going back to that stretch of highway.

Back in town, Danielle drove aimlessly, fighting through the increasingly terrible Austin traffic on her own personal sightseeing tour. She stuck to the pleasant places: the pharmacy/restaurant where a UT baseball player had taken her on a spur of the moment lunch date, the eastside club where she'd made her debut, the music store she had once worked at. She remembered Steve mentioning that her former band member Ty Woods ran the place, which was now called Austin Soundsource. Danielle was tempted to slip in, but Steve had warned her to stay away, so Danielle drove on by. There was a strong possibility that Ty wouldn't be happy to see her, and Danielle wasn't quite ready to face that yet.

Steve had not warned her against seeing Randy and Teri Holder. Randy had been a friend of her dad's and had taken Danielle in upon her arrival in Austin. She had worked in his store and lived over his garage for two years while Randy had acted as her first manager. Danielle remembered Randy as ever-keeled and gregarious, giving her reason to hope that seeing him might turn out all right.

The Holders lived on a narrow, tree-lined street full of small, aging houses. The neighborhood was made up of low income young families, college students, and older couples who'd been there forever. Teri and Randy fell in the last category

Randy's had been the sight of some good times for Danielle, which was why her heart sank when she pulled up in front of the house. The white picket fence was twisted and broken in places, the paint badly chipping all around. The sidewalk in front of the house was jutting up, and the yard was overgrown with weeds. There was a green and silver full size Ford van in driveway affixed with a wheelchair lift, and she noticed a ramp where the porch stairs once were.

Danielle approached slowly, a feeling of dread gnawing at her gut. She paused at the warped old gate, thought about turning around, then decided against it. The latch was rusted and hung up, but she finally fought it loose and stepped into the yard. What had once been well-trimmed hedges that ran along the front porch, flanking the porch steps, now just looked like giant snarled tumbleweeds.

Danielle stepped carefully up warped boards to the front door and rang the doorbell. The chimes inside rang loudly. She waited patiently, and soon enough, she heard rumblings on the other side of the door. She prepared herself as latches were thrown, and the storm door finally opened.

Randy Holder was sitting on a motorized wheelchair, his features obscured by the thick old screen of his rickety screen door. "Can I help you, miss?" He sounded the same, his voice deep and gruff, though with a little more edge than it used to have.

Danielle took ahold of the handle and pulled gently. The screen swung open, and she looked down at Randy. He hadn't changed much at all. His gray hair was still long and flowing, his arms and neck still thick. He had put on some weight, but not a lot. She pushed her hair behind her ears and smiled pensively. "Got a minute to visit with an old friend?"

"Who...?" Randy stopped and peered up at her. Eyesight must have slipped, she thought. She crouched down in front of him.

"Hiya, Randy."

"Dani?" She smiled bigger and nodded. "Danielle Elizabeth

Regan. You get your scrawny little ass in this house right now."
He backed up his wheelchair, and Danielle stepped into a
darkened front room that smelled of menthol-rub, tobacco, and
cabbage. "Follow me," Randy said, suddenly sounding like his
lively old self. "Ain't nothing in this living room anymore, so no
worries about tripping over shit."

She followed him through the living room and a short hallway
into a tiny kitchen that was bright with natural light. It was a
cramped little room, and all the appliances were on the wrong
side of twenty — as was the linoleum on the floor, the tablecloth,
and the curtains over the east facing windows. Yet the room was
tidy and clean.

"Teri! Teri! Look who just came knocking on our door."

Teri Holder was standing on the opposite end of the room,
her back to the doorway, and hunched over something on the
counter. When Randy called out to her, she turned, a knife in
hand, and Danielle saw that she was making sandwiches. Like
Randy, she hadn't changed much: a few more pounds and a lot
more gray hair. They both seemed to be in decent enough shape.

"Hey," Danielle said timidly.

Randy had always been completely in Danielle's corner,
but she and Teri had a couple of run-ins behind them. She had a
naturally harsh look, and for a moment, Danielle braced herself
for the worst. Instead, Teri tossed the knife on the counter and
wiped her hands on a flower-print apron that was tied along her
waist.

"Well, I'll be. Danielle, is that you, honey?"

"In the flesh."

Teri crossed the room quickly and enveloped Danielle in her
arms. Danielle accepted and returned the hug, and they both

held on longer than they needed to.

"Hey, don't I get one of those?" Randy called from her side. Danielle laughed, leaned over, and hugged Randy around the neck.

When she stood, Teri was appraising her and flicked a strand of her hair with a meaty finger. "What is this? You look dreadful. Blonde is not your color." She continued to finger Danielle's hair. "You always had such beautiful brown hair. Don't know why you'd want to hide it."

"I was incognito. You should have seen me when I had the red pixie cut."

"Oh lord, no. You didn't. With your body type and bone structure? You must've looked like a thirteen-year-old boy."

"It wasn't a great look," Danielle agreed.

"Well, come in here and take a seat. I was just fixin' us some sandwiches. You want one?" Teri was already headed back to her work. Randy rolled past Danielle and pulled up to the kitchen table. Danielle pulled out a chair to his left that was slightly wobbly. "No thank you." She turned to Randy. "What's with the wheels?"

"Ah, I had a knee replacement a couple of years ago. Damn thing got all infected and fucked up. I was on my back for weeks. Finally got it all healed up, but I'm so heavy that my old knees just can't hold the weight. So I'm stuck rolling around in this thing."

"Just for a while," Teri interrupted as she brought two plates to the table. She slid one to Randy and sat hers down opposite. "We're going to lose weight and get you back on your feet. Don't fret about that."

Randy rolled his eyes. "I'd rather just stuff my face and roll around. I'm getting too old to worry about watching my weight."

Danielle looked over his wheelchair. "I don't know, might not be so bad. Get you a flame job on it, maybe some custom wheels, some chrome. You could spend the rest of your days riding around in style. The ladies love the chrome, you know."

"Don't encourage him," Teri snapped.

"Or, I was going to say, you could quit being stupid and lose some weight. You may be getting old, but you're too young to be tooling around in one of these."

"Says the girl who packed up her shit and went into hiding for six years," Randy fired back. He meant it as a good-natured rub, and Danielle knew it, but the way the words came out struck a nerve. She pulled back. "Oh Dani, I'm sorry," Randy said softly. "I didn't mean—"

"Don't sweat it," Danielle said, trying to be flippant. "I deserved that." She looked from Randy to Teri and back, meeting them both in the eyes. "I'm sorry I just left like that, and that I didn't say goodbye to anyone. I was a mess. It felt like the walls were closing in around me, and...he was everywhere I looked. I needed to get away."

"Well, at least you came back," Teri said. "Are you back for good, or just passing through?"

"The plan is for good. According to Steve, the label is putting some serious pressure on him, on me, to release some fresh material. So I guess I'm going to work."

"You got a place to stay?" Randy asked. "'Cause if you need, we haven't touched the apartment over the garage since you left. I'm sure it needs a good cleanin', but you're welcome to use it."

"Talk about coming full circle," Danielle laughed. "I'm in a hotel right now."

"Then check out and get over here. Even if you're only in

town for a few weeks, better havin' a home to come home to than some stuffy old hotel. Teri's still a great cook. We'll put some meat on those skinny old bones of yours."

The deal was actually appealing, and Danielle could see the symmetry in it. "Is it all right with you?" She asked Teri. Teri agreed. "Okay. I'll check out tomorrow. I'm already registered for two nights, might as well get my money's worth. You know, I drove by the store earlier. Almost stopped in for a look around."

Randy licked his lips nervously. "Ty…wasn't real happy about you leaving. Neither was Trish. I think you cut 'em both pretty deep when you took off. I'm not sure how they'll take it when you come strolling in."

"Steve had warned me that I should probably steer clear for a few days, which is why I didn't go in. Was it really that bad?"

"The whole circumstance was strange," Teri said as she forced down a bite. "We all knew you were struggling, and there wasn't much we could do. It wasn't a bad idea to leave for a little while. Steve told everyone that you weren't planning on coming back, but I don't think anybody really believed that. That's what you did. You'd go lose yourself for a while, but you always came back, and usually better than when you left. We all waited for you to pop back up, and when it became clear that you weren't, it was hard."

Danielle was fiddling with the salt and pepper shakers on the table as a way to avoid looking either of them in the eye. "I could have handled it better. There's no roadmap for how to deal with something like that. I tried to hold it together. I really did."

Randy patted her on the arm. "Tried too hard. You should have let go. Be honest with me here." Randy locked eyes with her. "How many times did you cry over Kyle?"

Danielle felt herself go hard all over. "Once. The night I decided to leave. That was it."

"You sound proud of that," Teri said.

"It was all I needed. After that, it was time to focus on what needed to be done. I had a goal to focus on. It helped keep my mind off of things." Randy and Teri eyed each other across the table, and Danielle knew what they were thinking. "I don't need to cry over something over and over again. That's not who I am. I said my goodbyes, I did my mourning, and I moved on."

"I hope you're right," Randy said solemnly.

"Enough of this," said Teri. "Danielle, if you would like to stay in the apartment, could I bother you to help me straighten it up some? I don't navigate stairs as well as I used to."

"I'd be happy to."

Teri put her plate in the sink and led Danielle to the garage and up the outside stairs to the apartment. True to their word, nothing had changed since Danielle had called the little apartment home over a decade earlier. Everything was covered in dust and cobwebs, but otherwise undisturbed.

They spent over an hour cleaning up. The nostalgia in the room was palpable, and Danielle found herself constantly interrupted by one memory or another. While cleaning the window that overlooked the driveway, Danielle swore she could see Adam strolling up the driveway, young and cocky in baggy shorts and no shirt. The thought brought a smile to her face.

They finally finished, and Teri was clearly worn out, so Danielle said her goodbyes but promised she would return the next day with her stuff. Dinner was overdue, but she needed a shower first, so Danielle returned to the hotel. The woman at the front desk caught her on the way by to tell her that she had a message.

Curious, Danielle returned to the desk to find a note and a small package waiting for her. She signed for it and retreated upstairs, tossing the package on the bed so she could start the shower. As she waited for the water to heat up, she stripped away her dirty clothes, almost forgetting about the package.

She sat on the bed and opened the letter and instantly recognized Steve's precise handwriting. *Dinner at Matt's tonight. 8 p.m. Be nice and don't forget your present.* She knew that Matt's meant Matt's El Rancho, one of Austin's most famous Tex-Mex restaurants. Tex-Mex sounded like a good idea — leave it to Steve.

She turned her attention to the small box, wrapped in festive red and green Christmas paper. "Just a few weeks late," she said to the package before ripping it open. She found a small rectangular box and popped it open to find a cellphone inside with an attached note. *It's already programmed. Keep it on you at all times.* The "at all times" was underlined three times.

She took the phone out, studied it briefly, then put it back in the box and stowed in her suitcase. Cellphones were an accessory she had no use for. Steve was just going to have to deal with that.

She was starting to run out of time, so Danielle hustled to the shower. Steve had something else up his sleeve, and she was anxious to see what it was.

Chapter Nine

Danielle spotted Steve's silver Lexus almost as soon as she pulled into the parking lot at Matt's. Even through rolled-up windows, she could hear the music bleeding out into the night. The place just exuded fun in a way that nothing in Kansas could ever hope to do. Danielle sat in her car as it idled, just taking in the sight of people as they came and went, the glow of neon lights clear through the windows.

As she made her way into the restaurant, Danielle watched the faces of the people as she passed, watching for any indication that someone recognized her. She didn't see any as she wound her way through the throng of humanity. She told the hostess that she was meeting someone and was told to look around.

It was not Steve that caught her attention first, but the stunning blonde that sat across from him. She wore a salmon colored strapless dress that hugged her every curve, and her eyes flashed in the dark. She stood off to the side, watching them talk. Steve had never had a relationship as long as they'd known each other, and in watching them talk, she didn't strike Danielle as a girlfriend, but more like a client. Finally, she approached the table.

"Steve? Did I make a mistake? I thought you wanted to meet at eight."

They both looked up. The blonde looked confused but soon turned her eyes on Steve, burning holes in him from across the table. Steve looked off-balance, something that Danielle had never witnessed. He fumbled for his words. "No, no mistake at all. Have a seat, and I'll order you a drink."

Danielle pulled out the seat to Steve's right and sat down gently. She glanced at the blonde out of the corner of her eye. "Maybe I missed something in your note, but I thought this was a you-and-me dinner, not a group thing."

"Yes, well—" Steve started.

The blonde shot up out of her seat and thrust her hand across the table. "Shannon Henderson, since Steve can't seem to find it in himself to introduce us." Danielle took the handshake but froze up on the introduction, which seemed to amuse the other girl. "So, do you have a name, or are you just Um?"

Danielle dropped her hand. "Charming girl," Danielle said to Steve. "I'm not sure how you want to play this. Are we keeping things under wraps, or...?"

"Yes, for the moment, but Shannon here can relate. She performs under the name Rikka Olausson. She's had three Top Twenty hits on the World Music Charts." He shifted his attention to the blonde. "Shannon, may I introduce you to Danielle Regan."

"Really?" Shannon withdrew her hand slowly and eased back into her seat, her gaze locked on Danielle. "I didn't know you were back in town. Last I heard you were retired."

"Retirement is boring. I decided it was time to get back in the game."

"Oh, and you choose now to come back." Her eyes dropped to the floor. "Lucky me."

Steve decided to step in. "Shannon, this doesn't change anything regarding your album. You are still my number one priority at the moment. I just found out that Danielle was back in town this morning. Now, as I was saying—"

"But I won't be your priority for long, will I? The Golden Girl has returned. If you've got her, why do you even need someone like me? I'm just going to be a distraction for you."

The waitress brought margaritas for Shannon and Steve while Danielle ordered water. Steve waved her away. "You are not going to be a distraction," he assured Shannon as the waitress disappeared into the crowd.

Danielle saw him struggling and decided to throw him a lifeline. "Listen, I'm not looking to mess things up for anybody. This was all very spur of the moment. I don't even have a band yet, so I have no problem laying low and staying out of the way." To Steve, she said, "Take care of your other clients. I don't expect you to drop everything for me."

"That's big of you," Shannon said, but Danielle caught the sarcasm in her voice.

"I'm trying to be nice," Danielle said, leaning her elbows on the table. "Don't take an attitude with me. You won't like how that turns out. I don't tolerate diva shit."

"Ladies, please," Steve begged, trying to re-establish some form of control over the proceedings.

Shannon copied Danielle's actions. "I don't tolerate people swooping in and trying to steal my thunder."

"Ladies," Steve bellowed with enough authority that those

seated near them turned to look. He took a deep breath and straightened his tie, and two sets of eyes turned their fire on him. "Now, if you would please allow me to talk, I believe I can straighten everything out. " Both women slumped back in their chairs and crossed their arms, almost in unison. "Thank you. Now, let me take you through this and explain my vision here."

The girls waited, neither appearing too pleased with the situation.

"Shannon, as I was saying, I talked to Rico today, and he is making your album a top priority. He says it is vital that we deliver him something he can get on the radio. They're going to fast track this *if* we can give them what they want."

He turned to his right. "Danielle, Rico is extremely pleased that you're back, and he's anxious to get you back in the studio, but I was able to cool him off a bit, which is good because we have a lot of things to work out first. If you're working on demos or anything, that's great. Just keep writing and getting down ideas and settle in."

"That's all I wanted to do," Danielle answered defensively. "Then, the princess here started giving me lip."

"You can't blame me for being worried," Shannon fired back. "You're his star. He has a shrine to you in his office."

Danielle smirked. "I saw it. Give Steve four consecutive platinum albums, and you might get one too."

Steve jumped in. "It's not a shrine. Focus, girls." He leaned in to Danielle. "And actually it was five. The one you and Kyle did right before the wreck went platinum too, but you were a little preoccupied." Steve straightened up, either missing or ignoring the go-to-hell look Shannon had for him. "I had a thought, and I wanted your take on it. Now, I know what your first reactions are going to be, but just hear me out for a minute. Shannon, you know that the label thinks you need some help. Danielle, you've been gone a long time, and you can't just jump back in. So what if the two of you work together?"

Both women started to react, but Steve started talking again before they had an opportunity to protest.

"If you will stop and think about this for a moment you'll see the wisdom in this. Danielle, you can help Shannon with her songwriting, help her make her songs a little more radio friendly, and find a unique voice—you excel at that. Plus, it gives you something to do and a way to dip your toes in the water before you jump in. Shannon, we have to do something. You don't want to work with a hired gun, and that's fine, but this type of situation is more like two peers bouncing ideas off one another. Danielle doesn't even need to be credited on the album if you don't want. She can strictly be behind the scenes. But Danielle is an encyclopedia of music. Take advantage of the opportunity."

Shannon swallowed her protest and leaned back, chewing her lip as she pondered the idea. "Strictly behind the scenes?"

Steve risked a quick sideways glance at Danielle, who was watching him. "I think we could arrange that." He tensed up, waiting for some sort of revolt from Danielle. After a few precious moments without one, he looked again.

Danielle shrugged. "Doesn't sound like such a bad idea. Last thing I want to do is sit around for two months waiting to get started. I don't need the validation of being credited anywhere." She turned to Shannon and jabbed a finger at her. "But you can't pull any diva shit with me, or I'll kick your scrawny ass back to Fargo."

Shannon rolled her eyes. "I'm from Minnesota."

"I been to both places," Danielle answered. "There's no difference."

Steve sensed another verbal joust coming. "Well then, ladies, I'm glad we could come to an understanding. Let's order and enjoy our dinner."

He waved the waitress over, and they all ordered. Steve was so proud of himself he ordered a second margarita in celebration.

Shannon and Danielle sat in silence, sizing each other up across the table. After an unbearable silence, Shannon finally spoke up. "So Danielle, how long have you been gone now? Ten years?"

"Almost six," Danielle answered in monotone.

"Tell me," Shannon continued, oblivious to the fact that she was dancing at the mouth of a volcano. "What does a retired rock star do for six years? Did you travel to exotic places or doing exciting things?"

The question was innocent enough—it was Shannon's tone that was questionable. "I learned how to shoot guns and live off the grid in preparation for the coming government take over and inevitable civil war." She said it so matter-of-factly she almost believed it herself.

Across the way, Shannon's eyes got wide. "Oh…really?"

"Yeah," Danielle said with all seriousness before turning to Steve. "Where did you get this girl? Were they having a clearance sale at Dipshits R Us?"

"I am not a dipshit," Shannon fired back. "I'm trying to engage in some polite conversation."

"You're being a snarky little brat is what you're doing. I see through you easier than that flimsy excuse for a dress you're wearing."

"Maybe I am. I don't particularly care for some washed-up has-been elbowing her way into my project, much less trying to take my manager out from under me. You had your time in the spotlight. Why don't you crawl back under the rock you've been hiding beneath and let somebody else have their turn?"

"This wasn't my idea, sweetie." Danielle shot up out of her chair. "Steve, I can't believe you did this to me. What happened to you?"

Steve swallowed nervously as he took Danielle's hand. "I had to grow the business. I couldn't keep things going, just managing your legacy. Please sit down and let's fix this thing."

"I don't think I want to. Tits McGee over here has a point. I stroll into town, and you're trying to pair us up? Doesn't make sense. Something isn't right, and I'm not going to be the bad guy."

"There doesn't have to be a bad guy," Steve pleaded. "I'm just doing what I think is in the best interests of my two best clients." He looked from Danielle to Shannon and back again. "Collaboration is the name of the game now. Crossing musical borders, mashing genres, that's what it's all about. That's how you get people's attention. Danielle, you've already done this when you went to Nashville. That album was ahead of its time, and people have only just begun to discover that. Now you can use that experience to help someone who's still trying to get some traction."

"Nashville was my idea. This is not her idea. You're forcing it on her and trying to coerce me into it, and I'm not playing that game." She stepped away from the table. "Rikka, Shannon, whatever your name is, I'm sorry about this. You don't have to worry. I'm out."

"Danielle, wait," Steve begged. "At least stay for dinner."

"I'll get drive-through on the way home."

She stormed off, feeling like an idiot for believing she could just come back and things would be back to normal. She couldn't get away from there fast enough.

CHAPTER TEN

Danielle sat at a red light, blocks from the restaurant, fuming as she tapped the fingers of her right hand on the knob of the gear shift. She breathed heavily as she tried to rein in her thoughts. What Steve had done felt like a betrayal, and though she knew he was only doing what he thought was best, she couldn't absolve it.

As the wait continued, the thought started bouncing around in her head that she should leave again. That this was the sign she needed to tell her that this was not the way. Almost instinctively, Danielle started running through potential destinations if she did decide to bolt. Perhaps it was time to leave the country altogether. People had told her that Australia was a lot like Texas—maybe it was worth checking out.

Finally, the light turned green, and Danielle sped away. The hotel was a good distance from the restaurant, giving her plenty of time to think about her next step as she navigated the winding streets. The inescapable truth was that Danielle was where she wanted to be, and she knew it, but that didn't necessarily mean she had to resume her old life. Her band mates had all gone on to other things. Why couldn't she?

The answer to that was just as simple. She'd spent the better part of six years trying to find something else that satisfied her, and she had come up with nothing. She was a musician, and nothing else in the world filled the void. Danielle simply couldn't see herself doing anything else.

Steve could go. As she drew nearer to the interstate, that thought began to germinate. She had been with Steve for a long time, and he had always done right by her, but times change, and he had changed with them. Perhaps they were no longer compatible. New leadership might be just what she needed.

The problem with that was that Steve had earned her trust over all the years and challenges. Considering how deep her trust issues already ran, Danielle couldn't see a way that she'd be able to put her faith in anyone else. The business was so full of scumbags. The chances of finding another gem like Steve were few.

By the time she got to the hotel, Danielle was deeply confused, irritated, and exhausted. There was no way she could make any sort of a rational decision. Instead, she turned on the TV, slipped into her nightshirt, and decided to turn her brain off for a while. She thumbed through the channels until finally settling on a movie about two brothers on the run from a crazed truck driver and settled in, hoping the film would provide her some sort of much needed escape.

Danielle wasn't even aware she had fallen asleep until a knock on the door woke her up. She lifted her head and tried to shake the cobwebs away as the knock persisted, a soft, almost hesitant sound. Danielle's eyes finally focused on the TV. Her movie was over, and now they were showing some sci-fi creature movie.

She rubbed the sleep out of her eyes and fumbled for the remote to kill the TV. The alarm clock told her it wasn't even ten yet, far too early for her to be this sleepy. The knock persisted as Danielle padded across the carpet barefoot. She took a look out of the peephole to see Shannon standing on the other side.

"Jesus," she muttered as Danielle undid the locks and opened the door. The woman standing on the other side of the door looked very little like the cocky diva she'd tried to have dinner with two hours earlier.

"Hi. I...." Shannon looked Danielle over and noticed the nightshirt. "I'm sorry. I didn't realize you had already gone to sleep. I can come back."

Danielle pushed her hair away from her face. "I'm awake now. What do you want?"

Shannon tried a sheepish grin, but it melted almost immediately. "To talk. We got off on the wrong foot, and I know that's my fault. I was hoping we could try again. Steve and I had a long conversation and.... Maybe things will go better in a less hectic environment."

Danielle sighed and wanted to slam the door in Shannon's face, but she held off. "If Steve sent you — "

"No, he didn't," she interjected. "In fact, he warned me against coming here. Said you would eat me alive. I'm here because I need to be. Can I come in?"

Danielle stared her down, then with an exaggerated eye roll, and a jerk of her head indicated that Shannon could come in. The other woman slid by her and settled on the corner of the bed. Danielle shut the door, trudged back to the bed, and plopped down, sitting with her back against the headrest. Shannon shifted to look at her bed.

"That nightshirt doesn't do much for you," Shannon said with a twinkle in her eye. "Hides your figure too much. Very high school."

"Are you mocking my choice of sleepwear?"

"No, not at all," Shannon answered defensively. "Just making conversation. What it does do is show off those legs." Shannon's eyes danced over Danielle's outstretched legs, which she crossed at the ankles, and eventually settled on the long scar where the bone had broken skin. "Wow," she muttered, running her fingers over the area. "That's some scar you've got there. Must have hurt like hell."

"Didn't feel good," Danielle answered in monotone. "Is there a point to this?"

Shannon looked away from the scar but kept running her fingers lightly over Danielle's leg. "I didn't handle myself very well at dinner, and I apologize for that." She quit rubbing and gave Danielle's calf a subtle squeeze.

Danielle responded by pulling her legs up closer to her body. "Fine. You're excused. Anything else, or did you just come here to feel me up?"

"Oh honey, that's hardly my idea of feeling somebody up." Shannon paused, but when Danielle responded with a dead-eye stare, she moved on. "I kind of feel like Steve messed up tonight, just throwing us together like that. I know I didn't handle it well. I got defensive and rebelled, and I probably shouldn't have. It's not the best first impression I've ever made."

Danielle stifled a yawn, stretched, and ran both hands through her hair. "This is all fine. Yes, Steve fucked up. It's all on him. I probably would have reacted the same way if I were in your shoes. Whatever forgiveness you're looking for, consider it granted. Now please leave."

"It's not just that." Shannon's eyes left Danielle and focused on the hardshell guitar case that rested on a table by the window. "Despite everything that went wrong tonight, I think Steve was right. I do need help. I don't know what the label wants, but they haven't liked anything I've given them. You're a pro at this. A star, a legend. I shouldn't have been so quick to disregard your help."

Danielle shifted, sitting up on her knees. "So you're asking for my help now? After all of that drama earlier, why should I?"

Shannon leaned forward until they were face to face, their noses almost touching. "Because you remember what it was like to be a struggling young artist and you want to help. And because, even though you don't want to, you're starting to like me."

Danielle leaned back, putting a little distance between them. "What gives you that idea?"

"I know people," Shannon smirked. She jumped up off the bed and made her way to the table, where she popped the latched on the guitar case and took out Danielle's beat up Strat. "Nice guitar. Very bohemian." She looked over her shoulder at Danielle, who was watching her carefully. Shannon did a full turn, then tossed the guitar at Danielle, who caught the neck with one hand. "Play something for me."

Danielle sat the guitar next to her on the bed. "I don't play on command."

Shannon ignored her and started humming a tune that Danielle instantly recognized. Before she could say anything,

Shannon started softly singing. *"There's a lady who's sure, all that glitters in gold."* She was slowly working her way back to the bed, her eyes locked on Danielle's. *"And she's buying a stairway to heaven."*

Danielle chuckled. "You think I'm just going to pick up the guitar and start playing 'Stairway' because you sing a couple of bars? For all you know, I might not even know that song."

"Actually, I know you do," Shannon said as she settled back on the bed. "January 14, 2000. Target Center in Minneapolis. You did that song as one of the encores. You actually did a duet with your keyboard player, and it was really pretty. She had a great voice, and you harmonized so well together. There's actually a copy of that performance on YouTube."

"So you're a fan."

"Not really," Shannon answered quickly. "I only went because a friend wanted to go. But I could see, even then, that you weren't just a rock star. You were a musician, a true artist, and that's what I wanted to be. That was a moment for me. I know for you it was just another song in another concert on another tour, but I've been chasing a moment like that my whole life."

"If that's the case, why were you being such a bitch earlier?"

"Because I was threatened. You don't see the way Steve looks when he talks about you. You don't see how his eyes keep going to your picture on the wall when he's supposed to be having a meeting. I'm convinced he just signed me because he thought I could be another you. I think that's why he tried to put us together so fast."

"You were threatened by me?" Danielle laughed. "Look at you. You're a Greek goddess, and you were threatened by me?"

Shannon smiled at the compliment. "Well, I'm glad you

noticed." Quickly her mood turned sour. "But we're not talking about a beauty pageant here. When it comes to music, you're the goddess, and I'm...nothing."

"So you're afraid you're going to get lost in the weeds. I get that, but all you had to do was say no. You didn't need to poke at me like you did. That's never going to get you very far with me."

"So I have discovered."

They both went silent, and Danielle reached over for the guitar and pulled it into her lap. "For the record, 'Stairway' wasn't my idea. I always thought that song was overrated. My other guitar player wanted us to do it. He's the one who thought Trish and I would sound amazing doing it together. We only played it, like, four times, maybe."

Shannon crawled across the bed and sat beside Danielle. "I have a much better voice than she did. So can you arrange a song for me like that? Maybe even help me write one?"

Danielle had started fiddling with the guitar, automatically picking out random notes, fingerpicking them as they talked. "I'll think about it. I'll have to hear what you've got so far, see what I've got to work with. I'm not making any promises."

Shannon edged closer to her. "That's all I can ask for."

Danielle was beginning to get the impression that Shannon's interest in her might not just be musical, and it was making her edgy. "I'll sleep on it and get back to you. Deal?"

"Deal," Shannon answered with a glimmer of satisfaction. "Want any company while you sleep?"

"Go home. I'll call Steve in a couple of days."

"Fine," Shannon huffed. She scurried off the bed toward the door but stopped just short. "You know, it strikes me that I didn't have dinner tonight. Wanna go somewhere and grab a bite?"

"Goodnight, Shannon," Danielle said firmly, ignoring her own welling hunger. "Close the door on the way out.

Shannon pouted but did as asked, leaving Danielle alone to fiddle with the guitar some more. She thought about Shannon as she doodled. There was a definite hunger in Shannon, but Danielle doubted how serious she really was. There was a flightiness in her demeanor that bugged Danielle. She was honestly undecided about what to do about the invitation. She hadn't come all this way to play second fiddle, but the idea had appeal.

She finally decided to wait until she could talk to Steve again. Perhaps in the morning, things would be clearer. She laid the guitar gently on the pillow next to her, ducked under the covers, and went back to sleep, mainly just so she could quit thinking about it.

CHAPTER ELEVEN

Danielle pulled into a gravel parking lot behind The Hard Charger, a nondescript building a stone's throw from the Colorado River. The most impressive thing about the brown brick building was the sign over the door featuring a muscled up, anthropomorphic stallion snarling and playing guitar. The artistry was top notch.

Inside it could have been any one of a hundred bars in Texas alone: dimly lit with beer signs hanging on every available surface, jukebox in one corner, a rough stage at one end, and a long, polished bar of black wood. When she strolled in, Garrett Hardesty was wiping down that bar while a pair of grizzled old men sat at one end nursing Coors longnecks. A stocky middle-aged woman in a too-short denim skirt skittered from table to table, wiping everything down.

In their days touring together, Garrett had been a scrawny kid with punk rock hair and a couple of tattoos. He was no longer scrawny—and not all of the weight was muscle—the tattoos had more than doubled, the hair was gone, and he had added a dangly earring in one lobe. She approached the bar hesitantly, feeling the eyes of the old men at the other end, and knew that she was out of her element.

Garrett looked up with weary eyes and said, "I was wondering when you were going to show up."

Danielle edged down onto a barstool. "You were expecting me?"

"People been telling me that you were in town. I talked to a couple of girls in Steve's office this morning, and they confirmed it. They say that the Big Guy is running around with a twelve-foot boner since you got back in town. Apparently, everybody thinks you're going to save 'em."

"Don't know where they got that idea."

"Me neither. I learned a long time ago, not to count on you." He turned, pulled a Coors out of the fridge, popped the lid, and set it down in front of her. Danielle looked at it like some sort of poisonous animal. "Ah, still playing Snow White, are we?" He snatched up the bottle and took a long tug. "If you're gonna sit in my bar, you're gonna drink. Here." Garrett snapped up a short glass, filled it with ice, some liquor, and poured Coke on top of it, then dropped in a plastic stirrer and gave it a couple of swirls. "Try this."

Danielle took a sip, licked her lips, and smiled. "Not bad. Tastes like a vanilla Coke."

"Spiced rum. So from now on, when you're in adult company, and you don't want to be a complete prude, you can drink. You're welcome."

She held up her glass. "Great. Thanks." Garrett touched his beer to it in a mock toast, and she took another drink. "It looks like you've done pretty well for yourself. Steve said the place is pretty decent."

He took a somber look around. "It pays the bills and keeps me from getting a real job. Get a fairly decent selection of girls on show nights, so the scenery's not bad. Keeps me in the game a little bit. Not like DeShon, though. Lucky bastard is still playing, the only one of the four of us that is. I might jump in every once in a while when a band comes through, but nothing like it used to be."

"Yeah, I'm sorry about that."

"No, you're not," he said sharply enough that Danielle rocked back on her stool. "You never liked me. I was there because I was DeShon's friend." Garrett put his hands up. "It's okay. I never liked you that much either. Thought you were a prima donna. Still, we made some great music together. I miss that."

"That we did," Danielle said as she took another sip of her drink. "I miss it, too, if it's any consolation."

"But you didn't have to quit. That was your choice. Ty and Trish and I, we didn't have a choice." He looked away from Danielle, his eyes focusing on something unseen far past the walls of the bar. Danielle waited for him to come back to her. "You're just a kid, and one day you run off and join the circus. It's all fun, but nobody ever tells you that sooner or later, you gotta grow up. You didn't have to, but the rest of us did. It's okay now, but it sucked at the time."

Danielle didn't know what to say, so she changed the subject. "That's a cool sign you've got out front. Did you design that?"

"Yeah, I did," he said with pride. "I've had that image in my head since middle school. I designed a whole band of animals, but the horse always looked the best."

"I never knew you were an artist. It's very impressive."

"You never took the time to get to know me," Garrett said as he picked up his bottle and came around the bar, settling on the stool next to Danielle and surveying his place. "Looking back on those days is such a weird thing. People ask me what it was like, and at first, I say it was boring. I used to dream of an audience full of girls flashing their titties at me, groupies servicing me backstage during a show, all of that shit. I go off and join a band backing a chick, and there's no girls, no groupies. Hell, you wouldn't even let the celebrities backstage. I don't have any of those cool experiences that a lot of rockers do because you cockblocked everybody."

Danielle swiveled on her stool so that she was also looking out over the bar. "I'm not sorry for that. Those may sound like fun stories, but a lot of bad stuff comes from deals like that too. Lot of lives have been ruined by the excesses of the rock lifestyle."

"I know. That's what's so weird about it. Despite not having all that stuff, it was still awesome. Being able to walk out onto the stage every night, playing drums for a living—and a good one at that. It was really pretty cool. I didn't appreciate the good things until they were gone. All I could care about at first was that I never got the girls and the attention."

They went silent. Danielle was debating her next move. She drained her glass, turned, and sat it down on the bar. "You wanna take another run at it?"

Garret chuckled. "Shit."

"Seriously. I'm getting back in, and I need a band. We play well together, and it would be nice having at least one familiar face with me. I think enough time has passed, and we've both grown up enough that it would be better the second time around."

Garrett looked over at her, but his eyes were looking beyond her. She waited, chewing on her lip while he thought it over. "Nah," he finally said with a smirk. "It's tempting, but I got a good thing here. I had my time, but I've moved past it now. Besides, I hear that the Big Guy is putting you with a band already."

"I haven't heard that." Garrett gave her a disbelieving look, and Danielle quickly relented. "He probably is, but I reserve the right to put my own group together. There's a place for you if you want it. I feel I owe you that. I know I was a bitch to you a lot."

"Hedging your bets, huh? I thought the Big Guy was infallible."

"I never said that." She looked down at the floor. "He's not the same—he's changed a lot."

"We all have." Garrett studied her, then shrugged. "I respect you coming here and trying to put things right, but I'll pass. Wouldn't be the same without everybody. Thanks for the offer, though. Next time I see DeShon, I'll tell him to give you a ring."

Danielle got excited. Of all the people in her life she owed an apology to, he was at the top of the list. "How often do you see him?"

Garrett smiled behind the mouth of his bottle. "I don't."

~*~

Amazingly, Danielle located Trish and Ty in the phone book. She doubted that they would be listed, but figured it was worth a try. They now lived in the suburb of Buda. Danielle killed time by going shopping for some needed accessories and some new clothes. Once evening came, she made her way to the house and pulled up to the curb. It was a solid, middle-class house in a Cape Cod style, painted a soft blue with white trim. The yard was yellowed for the winter, but she could easily see it being lush in the summer. The attached two car garage was closed, but Danielle saw light peeking from around the drapes in the front window.

Danielle hopped out and hustled up to the front door. It took her a solid minute to work up the nerve to ring the doorbell. There was a rustling inside, and soon the porch light flickered on, followed soon by the turning of locks, and then the door opened. Trish's breath caught in her throat as she realized who was standing at her door. She was no longer the nubile youngster Danielle remembered. Her red hair was darker and thrown up in a messy bun, but she still had the same pale, china doll complexion, and was as scrawny as the day they met.

"Hi," Danielle said awkwardly as Trish studied her in the light.

Trish turned and shouted back into the house. "You're not going to believe who's standing on our doorstep."

Ty shuffled to Trish's side moments later. He had filled out some, but the extra weight looked good on him. His hair was now cut short, and he had grown out a full beard. He was wearing a Texas Longhorns sweatshirt over gray athletic shorts. "Oh my God. It can't be."

They stared at each other through the screen door until Danielle finally spoke. "So does a girl get invited in, or should I leave?" Trish and Ty exchanged looks, Ty shrugged his shoulders, and Trish popped open the door. "Thanks," Danielle said as she stepped inside.

The house was warm and inviting, decorated in earthy tones, and resplendent with family pictures and assorted artifacts. The floor was littered with dolls and their accessories. There was no indication of their previous lives as award-winning musicians.

The smell of home cooking was thick in the air.

"Well, come on back," Ty said gruffly, and he turned and headed toward the back of the house.

She followed Ty through the living room and into the kitchen, with Trish right behind her. The dining room table was set, and at one end, a precocious little girl sat in a booster seat, picking at a plastic plate full of peas and carrots and what looked like grilled chicken.

"Isn't she precious?" Danielle said, the words sounding strange coming out of her mouth. She'd never had much interest in kids.

Ty sat at the girl's side. "This is Catelyn," he said. "She's five."

"Oh wow. So y'all must have had her not long after I left," Danielle said, just trying to strike up some sort of polite conversation.

"Yeah," Trish said as she made her way to the stove to stir something. "I had just found out." She did her stirring, then turned around. "I was excited to tell my best friend." As she stood leaning against the stove, Trish wiped a stray tear from her cheek. "I went over to the house to tell you, but the place was empty, and there was a For Sale sign in front, so I went up to the office. Steve told me that you were gone and you weren't planning on coming back. Didn't even have the balls to say goodbye. So once again, the selfishness of Danielle Regan trumps everybody else's joy. Some best friend, huh?"

The obvious pain behind Trish's words hit heavy. "I'm sorry," was all she could think to say, though she knew in her heart she needed to say so much more.

"Save your sorrys for someone who cares," Trish snapped

before turning back to her stove.

Danielle shifted her focus to Ty. She tucked her hands in her jeans pockets and leaned against the door frame. "I know I hurt y'all when I left. You're right, I was selfish. I'm not here to ask for forgiveness or to make excuses for what I did. I've had a lot of time to think over the last six years and believe me, I've dissected everything in minute detail."

Trish whirled and stomped up to the table. "Then, why are you here? Why come back now?"

"Because I got tired of running." Danielle forced herself away from the wall and moved to the table but did not sit. "I guess I finally punished myself enough, and I got lonely. This is home. All those years I was gone, I tried so hard to find a new home, and nothing ever fit."

Ty smirked at her. "I could have told you that. If you had just talked to us, told us what you were thinking, we could've saved you a lot of time and trouble."

"Oh, I know. That's what I was afraid of. I knew if I told anybody ahead of time, somebody would talk me out of it. Once I made the decision, I had to act fast to avoid that." Danielle put both hands on the back of a chair and slowly pulled it out. Ty didn't say anything, so she sat gingerly. "I was messed up."

The little girl, distracted by Danielle, accidentally spilled a spoonful of carrots, and Ty plucked a napkin off the table and shoveled the mess into it. "We know you were messed up, and you were hurting. You asked for space, and we gave it to you. We deserved something."

"It was just so stupid," Trish said as she slammed down the spoon, she was stirring with. She whirled around and found Danielle. "You always took off on your little road trips when you needed to clear your head, and it was fine, and when you came back, you had something brilliant. I don't know why you couldn't have just done that. To sell everything you owned and change your name and move away was just…retarded. I hate using that word, but that's what it was."

"I did it because I didn't want to be me anymore. I wished that I had died in that crash. I just couldn't see any way I could live again."

Ty was studying her intently across the table. After a long deliberation, he finally asked her the question. "Did you think about killing yourself?"

"No," Danielle answered firmly. "I would never. I just don't believe in that. Doesn't mean I couldn't wish I was dead, though."

He seemed relieved as he slumped back into his chair.

"It was still stupid," Trish said, anchored to the stove. "You needed grief counseling. Your dumb ass always wanted to do everything on your own, and you never wanted anybody's help. You just never listen. And I still can't figure out why you're here if you aren't looking for forgiveness."

"I'm not exactly sure myself," Danielle said, trying to laugh it off but getting nothing in return from either of them. "I knew I couldn't come back here and not come to see you. Hell, I probably would have come back sooner, but the thought of having to face all the people I left behind terrified me."

Ty helped his daughter scoop up another spoonful of peas. "I don't know what to say to you. It hurt when you left, but we've moved on. You were our friend, but you've been gone so long I don't feel any sort of connection to you anymore. I don't need to chew you out or anything. As far as I'm concerned, you're just a fragment of our youth, a piece of the past that's better left there."

"Fair enough." Danielle stood and stepped lightly towards Trish. "Is that how you feel too?"

"I don't know how I feel right now. You blindsided me." After a brief pause, Trish started back up. "Where are you staying? Maybe I can swing by in a couple of days when I've had a chance to process things, and we could talk."

Danielle took that as a victory and smiled at her. "I'd like that. You remember Randy Holder? I'm back at his house, living above his garage."

Any semblance of softness melted away from Trish's face. "You went to see Randy? You moved into Randy's house? And you're just now coming to see us? Who else have you seen?"

Danielle took a step back, her head lowering. "Steve. Garrett."

"Garrett?" Trish's voice pierced the air, and Danielle shied away from her. "You went to see Garrett before you came to us? Are you fucking kidding me?"

"I knew y'all were at work, and I had plenty of time to kill. I mean, if I had done things Steve's way, I probably wouldn't be here now. He told me to wait."

"Because Saint Steve always knows what he's doing. The one person in this whole goddamn world you'll listen to. Unbelievable."

"Well, I figured this would be the most uncomfortable meeting, and it's the one I feel the worst about. I thought I'd save it for last."

"Because we mean that little to you," Trish snarled. Danielle heard a chair push back and felt Ty stand behind her.

"Well hon, I get what Dani's saying here. It makes sense."

"Nothing she does ever makes sense," Trish said, snapping off each word. "All she does is spread chaos and heartbreak everywhere she goes." Trish's eyes never left Danielle's as she spoke. "Get out of my house and don't come back. I don't want to see you again."

Danielle felt her heart breaking. She began to wonder if this was why Steve had asked her to wait. Was he going to try and soften things up for her first? "Trish, please. Take a couple of days, and let's talk."

"I'm through talking. Get out."

Danielle swallowed hard, fighting her hardest to hold on and to keep her emotions in check. "Okay, fine," she said with difficulty. "I'll go."

She hurried to the door, winding her way through the minefield of toys in the living room to the door, and was in the process of letting herself out when a shuffling noise caught her attention. Trish was steaming towards her, pure rage burning in her eyes. Danielle saw the right hand loaded up but could do nothing to stop it. Trish slapped her with more force than Danielle would have given her credit for, and she felt the tears immediately welling in her eyes.

At the moment Trish's hand struck her cheek, Danielle felt herself racing backward through time to her mother's house in her old hometown of Chaparral. It was a hot, dusty summer day, and her mother was the one delivering the blow. She felt the tingle on her cheek just as she had that day. Danielle's fingers curled into fists, and she felt her jaw tighten like a steel trap as her guilt instantly transformed into rage.

Ty was there in an instant, pushing between them and shoving Trish back. "Enough."

"You were my sister," Trish screamed. "I loved you. I would have done anything for you. I would have been there. I was there.

We both were. We never left your side, and you just threw us out. Why couldn't you love me the way I loved you?"

As instantly as it flashed, Danielle's anger evaporated. It took her a moment to realize it wasn't her mother who had delivered the blow, and that this one was probably deserved. Still breathing heavily, Danielle groped for something to say. "Trish…." She reached for her friend.

"Don't touch me," Trish snarled, pulling further away. "You had your chances. I'm through mourning for you. You wanted to die? Well, to us, you are dead. I hope it's all you thought it would be."

A million words flooded through Danielle's mind at that moment. She thought about telling Trish that she did love them, more deeply than she'd ever shown. She thought about apologizing, about begging for forgiveness. She thought about a lot of things. But, be it defeat or pride or even arrogance, Danielle swallowed all of those words, ducked her head, and stepped out into the cool night air. Ty slammed the door behind her and turned out the porch light.

Danielle shuffled back to the car, the sting of Trish's slap still lingering on her cheek. Her mother was there on the edge of Danielle's mind, telling her what a bad person she was. A reminder of how anyone who got close to her got hurt. Danielle sat in the car and pounded on the steering wheel with both hands. "Get out of my head," she screamed. "Get out, get out, get out."

She felt herself ripping apart. Her hands locked on the steering wheel, and she held on so tight her knuckles turned white from the effort. She was aware there were strange sounds coming out of her throat, but in the moment, she was powerless to stop them. Her mother's face floated in front of her, and Danielle shut her eyes tight to make it go away.

After several long minutes, she felt herself slowly relax. Her breathing slowed, and her body unwound. Danielle forced her eyes open, and thankfully saw nothing but a generic middle-class neighborhood. Her cheek no longer stung, and her mother was nowhere and nothing, just as she had been for the last sixteen years of Danielle's life.

"Oh my God," she finally managed to mutter in a trembling voice. "That was so much worse than I thought it would be." With shaky hands, she plucked her keys out of her pocket and started the car. She had no plan, nowhere to go and nothing to do, but she did suddenly have an urge for another of Garrett's rum and Cokes.

Danielle barely made her way back into town. At one point, she was sure her mother was in the backseat, and she almost ran off the road before realizing it was all in her head.

The Hard Charger was different by night. The parking lot was filled, and cars spilled out onto the street. She circled the block twice before someone finally left, and she was able to swipe a parking spot. The music was bleeding out of the building, a hard rock song she didn't recognize. Several people loitered around the door puffing on cigarettes.

Her legs felt like rubber as Danielle worked her way to the door. Some of the men outside watched her approach—she felt their hungry eyes on her, and she prayed they wouldn't try anything. In her youth, Danielle feared no one and had often held her own against bigger, stronger men. That was when she was basically an athlete. Now she was skin and bones, weak and emotionally frazzled. She was in no shape to fight off a would-be attacker, and she knew it.

Luckily she passed with only a few murmured come-ons that she didn't even comprehend, and pushed through the crowd to the bar. The bartender, a stork-like girl with bright purple hair, noticed her and moved to take her order.

"Rum and Coke, please," Danielle barely managed to say. Like everything else in the world, Danielle felt she had no control over her own voice, which lilted as she spoke. The bartender went to work and put the glass in front of her.

"Three fifty, hon."

Danielle took her wallet out of her front pocket, snatched a twenty, and slammed it down on the bar. "I'm gonna need another one."

"No, you're not." With a great effort, she turned her head to the right to see Garrett standing there, towel drying a tall beer mug. He shifted the mug to one hand, scooped up her drink, and swallowed it in one shot. "You need to go home."

Danielle swallowed, hoping to bring some strength into her voice. "I have no home."

"You went to see Trish, didn't you?" Garrett looked down at her with pity in his eyes. "That probably wasn't a very good idea. Let me drive you back to your hotel."

Danielle stepped back, wobbled slightly, and then straightened up. "I can drive. I drove here. Besides…." Her voice went soft. "Last time I rode shotgun, somebody died."

Garrett didn't answer. He came around the bar, wrapped an arm around Danielle's waist, and pulled her toward the door. "You try to drive in this condition, and you'll die. I've seen you like this before, you know. It never ends well."

With the arm around her waist, Garrett gently probed Danielle's front pocket until he found her keys and yanked them free. Danielle leaned into him. "Nothing ever ends well if I'm involved. I wreck everything sooner or later."

Garrett passed the keys from one hand to the other before pushing Danielle's head onto his shoulder. "You need a good night's sleep. Things will be better in the morning." She let him guide her to the car and gave somewhat coherent directions to Randy's house. She pressed her forehead to the glass as he drove, focusing on the lights. Trish's words kept echoing in her ears, and she felt the slap over and over again. Her mother kept tapping her on the shoulder, desperately trying to get Danielle to turn around and see her. The entire time she waited for a pair of headlights to suddenly veer over in their direction.

With a solid jolt, Garrett pulled the Camaro into Randy's driveway and killed the engine. "In the house or over the garage?"

"Garage," she mumbled. "I can do it from here."

"I don't think so," Garrett came around the back of the car and helped Danielle out of the passenger seat and up the metal stairs to her apartment. When he went to unlock the door, Danielle snatched the keys away.

"I can do it." Her hands were still shaking, and Garrett put his over hers to steady it. Danielle glanced over her shoulder at him. "Thanks." She worked the lock and stepped into the darkened room, fumbling before she finally found the light switch.

"You'll be good from here, right? I don't have to babysit you?"

Danielle took a deep breath and let it out slowly. It finally felt like things were returning to normal, and she felt in control again. She turned slowly. "Yes, I'm fine. It's over now." Garrett stood in her doorway, studying her until it became uncomfortable. "Do you need something?"

"Just making sure you're not lying to me."

"I'm fine," she repeated, and this time she felt like she was telling the truth. "Thank you for bringing me home."

"That was some breakdown," Garrett answered. "You don't go half-assed. I'll give you that." He turned, stopped, and turned back. "Things will get better if you give it time. You'll be okay."

Danielle wanted to go to him and hug him, but she planted her feet instead. "Thank you. I needed to hear that."

"Yeah, I know. Goodnight, Danielle."

He pulled the door closed behind him. She heard his feet pounding down the stairs and soon enough heard him talking to someone. She peeked out the window and watched him walk down the driveway, cell phone pressed to his ear. She watched from her catbird seat as he leaned on the back corner of the Camaro and waited. Eventually, a taxi came, and Garrett hopped in.

Danielle looked over at the main house, hoping to see a light on, but all was dark. She shivered, feeling the same cold loneliness that had finally driven her out of Kansas. As she moved to the door to lock up and kill the lights, Danielle again began to doubt the wisdom of her return. She peeled her clothes off and slid into bed, the doubts still dancing around her brain until she finally, mercifully, fell asleep.

CHAPTER TWELVE

"Are you hungover?"

Randy had rolled up to the kitchen table, a tall glass of orange juice in front of him, while Teri stood at the stove frying up eggs and bacon, when Danielle managed to drag herself into the main house the next morning. His normally gregarious demeanor turned on a dime as she walked in.

"No, but not for the lack of trying," Danielle said as she toed a chair over next to him and immediately laid her head on the table. "The jerk bartender wouldn't let me drink. Goody two-shoes."

"Is that who brought you home last night?" Randy asked.

Before Danielle could lift her head to answer, Teri interrupted. "If you didn't drink, why are you acting like this? You certainly seem hungover."

Danielle lifted her head and gave Teri a weak smile. "Would you buy a massive panic attack or near total mental breakdown as reasons?" She laid her head back down. "I feel like I've been run through a meat grinder."

She felt Randy's heavy hand land on her back, and he started rubbing just as gently as he was able to.

"You went to see everybody, huh? I warned you it wouldn't go well," Randy said.

Danielle simply grunted in response.

Teri slid two plates onto the table in front of them and poured Danielle a glass of juice. "Have some breakfast. You'll feel better." Danielle didn't respond. "Do you want to talk about it?

"Oh God, no," she finally answered. Danielle lifted her head off the table and sipped at her juice. "No, it's over now. I held on, and that's the main thing. I didn't lose my shit. Came close, but I didn't, and I didn't pack up and run off either. I figure it'll be easier from here on out."

She caught the look Randy and Teri shared with each other. They doubted her, and probably with good reason. Instead of arguing with them about it, she started eating instead.

Finally, Randy asked, "What's the plan now that you've seen everybody?"

"Good question," she answered around a bite of fried egg. "I haven't thought it out that far. Go upstairs and start writing, I guess. Got lots of new inspiration to work with."

"What about Steve?" Teri asked. "Doesn't he have something for you? I figured he'd be working you like a mule by now."

"I haven't talked to him since dinner the other night, and that didn't go very well either." She waved a flimsy piece of bacon in Teri's direction. "He's got this big-titted Scandinavian pop tart that he's managing now, and he wants me to help her out because, apparently, she sucks. But he didn't say anything to me, or her—he just invited both of us to dinner and expected us to instantly bond or some sort of dumb shit. "

"Uh oh," Teri moaned.

"Damn right. She came to my hotel that night and tried to make things right, but I don't know. I've been thinking that maybe I need to move on from Steve, find a new manager. He's different now. The old Steve never would have pulled a bush league move like that."

"Well now, sweetie," Teri said. "He's had to adapt and adjust over the years. He's got a lot on his plate. Besides, maybe he's not the only one who's changed."

Danielle rolled her eyes to Randy, who sat nodding his head. "She does it to me too." He pointed his beefy index finger at Teri. "Instant bullshit detector right there."

"I get that he's got other clients. I'm talking about how he just springs this idea on both of us without even introducing us. It was like a shock tactic. I'm not sure what he was thinking would happen."

"Maybe he counted on that old Danielle Regan professionalism boiling to the surface," Teri answered. "For all of your warts, the music always came first. He was probably banking on that. You should call him."

"I will after breakfast," Danielle conceded. "He bought me a stupid cellphone." She patted her jeans pockets, but the phone was nowhere. "Ah crap. What did I do with it?"

"Shoulda tossed it out the window on 35," Randy snorted. "Hate those damn things. Everybody always got their nose in 'em. Listenin' to music on 'em. You can't listen to music on a phone. Sounds like shit. You gotta have a stereo, man. That's still the only proper way to listen to music."

"I haven't thrown it out the window yet," Danielle said as she wracked her brain. "I wanted to. I'm sure it's in the apartment somewhere. Like I said, I'll deal with it after breakfast."

They ate in silence until Randy broke the tension. "I'd have given a hundred bucks to see Danielle Regan shit-faced drunk, though. That would have been great. The only thing less likely to happen than that is the pope making a sex tape."

"Randy!" Teri scolded him, but Danielle laughed.

"Well, you can blame Garrett Hardesty for costing you that opportunity. "

"Little asshole," Randy snarled.

"Right," Danielle agreed.

~*~

Back in the apartment after breakfast and a shower, Danielle finally located Steve's cell stuffed in the side pocket of a duffle bag in the bottom of her closet. There were only fifteen missed messages over the preceding thirty-six hours. She fumbled around with the phone until she figured out how to call him back.

After two rings, Steve snapped into the phone. "Where the hell have you been?"

Danielle hung up, sat the phone on her nightstand, and waited. Promptly it rang again. She let it ring four times before she answered without saying a word.

Steve was quiet for two beats. "Danielle, glad you could call me back. Can we get together and talk?"

"That's better," she said. "A girl leaves town for a couple of years, and you go and lose your manners. What would your momma say?"

"My mother was a rude bitch," Steve responded. "I'm going to text you an address. Bring your gear and meet me there this afternoon."

"What's going on?"

"I squeezed you and Shannon in some studio time. I want to let you play around and see what you can come up with. Clock is ticking, we have to get moving."

Danielle felt her blood begin to boil and took a slow breath to calm herself. "Steve," she said in a carefully measured tone. "I never agreed to work with her. I'm still on the fence about that. I really don't care for how you keep assuming I'm going to go along with your little plan." With each word, she felt her composure start to crack. She clenched her left fingers into a fist, letting her nails dig into the palm of her hand.

"Dani, I really need you to do this for me. I finally managed to get Shannon to see the wisdom in it. Please don't make it a fight. After everything I've done for you over the years, I think you owe me this."

"I *owe* you?" Danielle clenched harder. "Whose talent did you piggyback on to get that big fancy office of yours? I worked my ass off for you. Everything you have you have because of me, and you're going to say that I owe you?"

There was a pause on the other end, and Danielle could imagine that Steve was carefully calculating a response. "Yes, your music is what got us here. But I also put up with a lot of things for you, Danielle. I dealt with a lot of headaches, put out a ton of fires, and fought a bunch of battles for you. And who did you leave in charge of your business when you decided to run off? Me. Five and a half years of cobbling together whatever I could, making excuses for where you were. We are a team, and I need you to be a good teammate for me now."

Steve's logic pierced through Danielle's anger and left a bad taste in her mouth. She looked out the window at a sky full of puffy white clouds and tried to find some answer there. She saw nothing. "Send me the address and the time," Danielle said. "But I'm not making any promises. I still don't know about this, and I feel like I'm being bullied into it."

"I'm not bullying you. I'm—"

"I know what you're doing," Danielle snapped. Again she had to strain to reel her emotions in. "I still don't like how you're handling this. I just…." She tried to pick the right words out of all the thoughts swirling in her head. "I'm having second thoughts about this thing. It wasn't supposed to be this hard."

"You didn't think you could just pop back up after all this time, and things would instantly be like they were, did you?" Steve didn't wait for Danielle to answer. "What was I supposed to do when you said you were never coming back? Was I supposed to just wait by the window and pray for you to change your mind? Now you're back, I'm supposed to drop all my other clients and cater to your every whim again? I can't do that, and I won't do that. This is the new reality, and you're going to have to get used to it."

"I didn't think anything, I just did it." Danielle's pride was wounded. Steve had a way of dressing her down, and she hated it when he did it. "Maybe I don't like the new reality. Nothing is going right, and I'm just wondering if this whole thing is a mistake."

"Don't think like that."

"I'll think however I damn well want," she fired back. "I need…."

"What? What do you need?"

Danielle heard Steve instantly switch from overbearing parent to do-everything manager in a heartbeat. That was the Steve she knew and loved, the one she had yet to meet in her return. "I need…." She thought about it. She needed a lot. "I need someone to talk to — an uninterested third party. I don't have any friends. Randy and Teri have their own problems, and I know what you want me to do."

"I'm afraid I can't help you with that. There's a price to be paid for burning bridges. I'm sorry. I truly am. I don't envy the position you're in, and I do understand. I know I haven't handled things the best, but my back's to the wall here, more than you could even know. All I can say to you is this. You're here, and you came back for a reason. The music and me are all you have left. Best advice I can give you is work. It'll give you something to focus on. The rest will sort itself out if you just give it time."

The last vestiges of Danielle's sudden resentment flitted away, but she wasn't ready to surrender quite yet. "Send me the address."

She ended the call and dropped the phone onto the bed. Moments later, it buzzed as Steve's text came in. She ignored it, choosing instead to continue staring out the window as her thoughts raced. Morning slowly faded to afternoon before an idea finally came to her.

Danielle scooped up her phone and car keys and pounded down the stairs. She burst into the kitchen, where Randy and Teri were huddled around a small TV on the counter, watching some inane afternoon talk show. They both jumped when Danielle threw the door open.

"Is Ryan Gregson still around?"

The startled pair exchanged a glance. Teri scolded Danielle for her entrance, but Randy was stroking his beard in thought. "I think so. He left KABJ a while back, but I think he's on…. Oh, where is he?" Danielle stood in the doorway, hanging on his every movement. "I think he went over to KRWP. It's this little mom-and-pop station, one of the last of its kind. Their studios are out by the airport somewhere."

"KRWP? Great. Thank you."

Danielle rushed back out and hopped in the car. She struggled again to figure out the phone but ultimately was able to locate a number for KRWP. When the receptionist answered, she identified herself as Steve's secretary, and the other woman was quick to confirm that not only was Ryan working, but he was already in the office.

Once Danielle figured out how to work the GPS, she had the address and set off. Twenty minutes later, she angled into a parking spot in front of a '60s era building that wouldn't have passed for a radio station were it not for the three huge satellite arrays on the side of the building. The building was a low slung, single story affair with tinted glass walls.

Danielle walked into a building decorated with genuine redwood paneling everywhere. The receptionist, a pleasant but plump lady with long silver hair, smiled warmly from behind a desk covered in papers and assorted office paraphernalia.

"I was hoping to speak with Ryan Gregson. I'm an old friend from his KABJ days."

"Absolutely," the receptionist said. "He's back in the offices. I'll page him for you."

Ryan Gregson had been the first DJ in Austin to play Danielle's music and had been a strong advocate for her throughout. When Danielle's career took off, she repaid the favor by being a frequent guest on his show and usually bringing some new or rare pieces for him to debut. She had learned later that when she was lying in the hospital after the crash, Ryan had taken to the airwaves, pumping out non-stop Danielle music until she was out of the woods.

He emerged from a room in the back, looking remarkably similar to how she remembered him: short and scrawny, with a sharp widow's peak and glasses. He dressed like a bookworm in khakis and sweaters. He had his hands in his pockets as he walked up the short hallway, and at first, Danielle could tell that he had no idea who she was, so she moved toward him quickly.

The realization dawned on him, and Ryan broke out in a huge smile. "God as my witness is that...?"

"It's your old friend Renae," Danielle said, swallowing him up in a big hug. "I'm keeping a low profile," she whispered in his ear.

"Gotcha," Ryan whispered back. They broke the embrace, and Ryan immediately played the game. "Well, Renae, it feels like forever since we've seen each other." He put an arm around her waist, since he was too short to get it around her shoulders, and turned her around. "Come on back here with me, and let's catch up. Man, it's good to see you again."

Ryan led her first into an open office area where several people she assumed to be salespeople sat at desks looking busy. No one looked up as they made their way through and down a narrow hallway with two closed rooms. Ryan directed her to the last room.

The production room was unspectacular—a soundboard, a pair of microphones, some recording equipment, and several big binders full of CDs stacked haphazardly on a counter. Ryan closed the door behind them and hopped up on a stool. Danielle took another one.

"So what brings Danielle Regan back to Austin after all these years? What is it…? Let me see." Ryan put a finger to his chin and looked up at the ceiling. "Spring 2003, right? So almost six years?"

"Very good."

Ryan seemed pleased with himself. "So are you back back or just passing through? Steve told me that you had gone on walkabout."

"Walkabout? What the hell is that? And Steve told you I left? He wasn't supposed to broadcast it."

"He confided in me. We have a very close working relationship. He feeds me new tunes and the occasional bit of industry speculation, and I make sure his clients get a healthy dose of airplay when they've got a new single coming out. It's a win-win. But don't worry, he swore me to secrecy, and I never said a word."

"Okay, good. So what is this walkabout business?"

Ryan seemed genuinely surprised. "From that movie *Crocodile Dundee*. You know? The one about the guy from the Australian outback who comes to New York, and at the end of the movie he's about to go wander about the country before the girl finds him and confesses her love. Don't tell me you didn't see it. It was huge when we were kids."

"I've never been big into movies," Danielle said, still having no clue what he was talking about. "Anyway. The plan is… was…maybe still is…to stay and go back to work, but I'm having second thoughts and was hoping maybe I could bounce some things off of you. Strictly off the record."

"Anything for Dani, you know that." He rested his elbows on the counter between them and his chin on his hand. "So tell me, what's going on? Why are you having doubts?"

Danielle placed her hands flat on the counter and drummed nervously as she talked. "Lots of things. For one, Steve seems different. The way he's acted—I don't know. I just don't like it. He's being kind of weird."

"I bet he is."

"What do you mean by that?"

"Well," Ryan said, adjusting his glasses. "Word has it that your old label is teetering on the brink of bankruptcy. They need a new star. Steve's company is in the same boat. He's thrown a bunch of money around and signed a bunch of people, but his eye for talent isn't so great. The people he's been signing aren't for shit. Everybody is about to lose their shirt."

"Crap," Danielle muttered, feeling instantly guilty for the way she'd treated him. "He said something about his back being against the wall. Now that makes more sense." She decided to shift gears. "He's got this new girl he's working with, some blonde. Shannon, something."

"Shannon? I don't know...." Ryan snapped his fingers. "I bet you're talking about Rikka Olausson. That's her stage name. Kind of moderately big on the World Music scene, Europop stuff. Writes most of her songs about fairies and dragons, stuff like that. Imagine mid-years Led Zeppelin on wuss. But she's built like a brick shithouse."

Danielle laughed. "You know, I never really understood that phrase, a brick shithouse."

"Well," Ryan said, sounding professorial. "She's got the body of a goddess. Long legs, little hips, big—"

"I know what she looks like," Danielle said. "I've met her. The saying is just weird. Anyway. Steve has this massive hard-on for us to work together. He's really insistent, but I'm not sure

I want to do it. I never wanted to work with hired guns, and certainly never intended to be one."

"Um, I see." Ryan leaned back and drummed on his thighs. "I see where Steve's going with this, though, if he could pull it off. You see, Rikka—Shannon—whatever her name is, has near operatic range, and she knows how to use it. Plus, she's got sex appeal and charisma for days. If he could get you to be her Jimmy Page and toughen up her sound a little, build up her lyrics, it could be massive. It would, at the least, be unique. But, I see why you wouldn't want to do it. She's got an ego, and her work ethic is only so-so. And you didn't come here to work on other people's stuff." He looked over at her with a sideways glance. "You getting the gang back together?"

"No. The gang has gone on to other things. Trish and Ty have a kid and real jobs, and none of them were too happy to see me."

"Ah, so you gotta put a new band together too. That's going to take some time." Ryan sighed. "I can't tell you if you should do it or not—only you can make that choice—but I don't think it's a bad idea. Let me tell you something, though." Again he leaned over like he was about to reveal some deep secret. "Don't let him push you off as a side player. If he's going for what I think he's going for, it's going to be as much your album as it is hers. It should be like a partnership, and you should at least get equal billing."

"No, I don't want that. I'm just going to be helping out."

Ryan chuckled as he spun around on his stool. "That's a laugh. I've heard her music. He says it's just to help, but I promise you as sure as we're sitting here if you get involved, it's going to morph into a whole new project. I promise."

Danielle looked away as she thought about it. "That doesn't

help me at all."

"Sorry. I wish I could do more for you, but I can't tell you what to do."

"I know." Danielle stood with a heavy sigh and started for the door, but stopped with her hand on the knob and turned. "Is there even a market for a new Danielle record out there anymore?"

Ryan's expression got serious quickly. "Honestly, Dani, I don't know. It's a different scene from when you started. The rappers and song-and-dance girls run the world now. Rock, especially the kind you do, it's barely hanging on, pushed out into the periphery."

"Great," she whispered.

"But," Ryan teased. "I can tell you that the world *needs* a new Danielle record for that very reason. Real, organic music played by real musicians with real instruments needs to come back. I'm tired of this push button, program a computer shit. If anyone can bring it back, it would be you. You saved the guitar hero once. Don't see why you can't do it again."

Danielle slumped against the door frame. "And what if I fail? I don't know that I could handle that. I heard this DJ make fun of me on the air recently. He was talking about how I was washed up and wasn't cool anymore. It cut me. Deep."

Ryan stood, circled the counter, and took her shoulders in his tiny hands. "Danielle, I say this with all sincerity. If they don't get you, fuck 'em. They don't deserve you."

Danielle chuckled. "Okay."

"Seriously. I can't believe I'm having to say this to the baddest woman in all of rock'n'roll. The Queen of Blues-Rock, the Siren of the Strat. When do you let other people dictate things? You always set the standard; you didn't try to live up to it."

"Yeah, but I'm not that girl anymore. She died a long time ago."

"No, she didn't," Ryan said, dismissing her comment with a wave of his hand. He tapped her lightly on the chest. "She's still in there. You just gotta take the chains off. Let the beast loose, Danielle. You'll be amazed at what it will do for you."

CHAPTER THIRTEEN

Danielle headed west down Ben White Boulevard and then turned northwest onto the Capital of Texas Highway, speeding northwest toward Milam Miles Studios. Danielle felt no more at peace now than she had before, Ryan's attempt at a pep talk falling far short of her expectations.

The studios were in the converted ruins of an old K-Mart, and though it was obvious from the outside, inside things looked nothing like the soulless department store it once was. Steve was pacing nervously in the lobby and working his phone when Danielle arrived. It didn't take long for her to find out why.

"Why will you not answer your phone? I have been calling you for a half hour."

"I threw it in the glovebox," Danielle said as she carted her guitar and amp into the building. "Had the radio up loud, so I didn't hear it. Sorry."

"I spent good money on that phone in the expectation that you would actually use it. You have to stay in touch with me, Danielle. Things aren't like they used to be. You can't just go —"

"Yeah, I know, things are different, blah blah. Where am I going?"

"Oh, yes. Follow me."

Just like that, the issue was dropped. Steve led her around a central desk to a small studio in the back corner of the lot. Inside, Shannon was sitting on a burgundy couch, legs crossed, wearing a shockingly conservative black dress with jade flowers. A balding Hispanic man sat in an office chair at the big soundboard, twirling one way and then the other.

"She's here, everything's fine," Steve announced as he entered the room. Danielle followed, slogging her equipment along with her.

"Glad you could make it," Shannon purred. "I was afraid you skipped town on us."

Danielle set her burden down with a huff. "Not yet." A ripple of worry shot across Steve's face and Danielle took a subtle pleasure in it. "But I want to make something clear. The fact that I'm here is not me accepting this proposal. This is strictly a test run to see if this will even work. That's it."

"That's all I'm asking for," Steve assured her. The Hispanic man stood and approached Danielle, holding out his hand. "This is Alejandro Garza," Steve said. "He's going to be our engineer today."

"Ma'am," Alejandro said quietly.

"Nice to meet ya," Danielle answered as she gave him a hearty handshake. Across the room, Shannon smirked. "Well, let's get this show on the road." Danielle regathered her things and headed for the main room where she and Shannon would perform. She held the door that connected the two rooms open with her foot and looked back at Shannon. "You coming or what?"

Shannon sighed and stood slowly, taking the time to straighten her dress before crossing the room and strutting through the door Danielle held for her.

The recording room was simple enough. Acoustic tiles covered the walls and ceiling, while boom mikes hung suspended from metal rails. An upright piano was pushed off to the right side of the room.

Danielle went directly to the spot she always occupied in rooms such as this, just to the left of center and roughly a quarter of the way into the room. She could never explain why, but that was the position she felt the most comfortable in. Shannon sat on the piano bench as Danielle hooked up all of her gear and adjusted the tuning on her Strat.

When she was ready, Danielle said into her mic, "Alejandro, you're just gonna run tape and see what happens. Right?"

"Yes, ma'am," his voice crackled over the loudspeaker in response.

Danielle turned to Shannon. "All right, princess. It's your show now. Whaddya got?"

Shannon rolled her eyes and turned to the piano. "This is my newest. I call it 'Tamarind.' Steve doesn't like it." She began playing a surprisingly good, ascending piano riff, and after two passes started singing. Her voice was silky and soft, her vocal control excellent. Danielle was instantly jealous of the quality, as she had always felt her own voice was too deep and too rough. Shannon sang through the first verse, pre-chorus, and chorus and was looping around for the second verse when she suddenly stopped and whipped her head around. "Are you going to play something? I've already recorded a version of this. I don't need to play it again."

"I'm getting a feel for the song, Your Highness. Pick up where you left off."

Shannon reset herself and started the song again. Now Danielle began to mimic Shannon's piano riff on the guitar, plucking single notes in time with Shannon's finger. She felt the pre-chorus coming back when Shannon again stopped.

"All you're doing is copying my part. I thought you were some kind of guitar genius. I could have done this."

Danielle looked to the ceiling and let out a long breath. "I was getting there. Quit stopping." She rubbed the back of her neck with both hands. "Can you just give me the lead into the pre-chorus again and quit stopping?"

"Fine."

Shannon started up again, playing four bars of music before singing again. Just as she started into the bridge, Danielle replaced her single note runs with a ringing power chord, playing on the deep end of the register to offset Shannon's lilting vocals. Out of the corner of her eye, she saw Steve pump his fist in excitement. Shannon shot her a dirty look but kept playing. Danielle was stretching out, mixing short runs between the chords, playing in the empty spaces of the song. She executed a quick fill before Shannon started in on a bridge Danielle didn't see coming. She stuck to the main chords, and once the bridge was done, she lit into a solo that was more Richie Sambora than Jimmy Page but felt right.

As the solo was winding down, Danielle noticed that Shannon had stopped playing and was watching her. To prompt her back to the song, Danielle started singing the chorus. Shannon recovered quickly, and they finished the song, Danielle bringing it back down with some soft single note lines, letting the song fade away slowly.

Steve was in the room instantly. "Yes! That is what we've been looking for. Awesome."

"Was that a lesbian love song?" Danielle asked Shannon.

Shannon turned and shrugged. "It's a love song. What does it matter who is singing to who? It's about looking for the missing piece. One half of a soul longing for its other half. Doesn't have to be specifically lesbian. That's just how I wrote it."

"Huh. That's fine," Danielle said. "Just doesn't seem very — "

"Mainstream," Steve finished the thought for her. "It's not mainstream. Change a couple of words to make it sound like you're singing to a guy, and we've got radio gold."

"I don't want to change the words. That is how I wrote it. That was what I wanted to say."

"But you said yourself that it doesn't specifically have to be one woman to another, so change a few words. All we really need is one irresistible song to get on the radio, and that could be it. Don't waste it on account of a few words."

"That's not what I'm trying to say," Shannon said to him. "I don't want it to be about a guy. Those songs are a dime a dozen."

Steve, clearly flustered, turned to Danielle. "What do you think? You've written a dozen Top Forty hits. Should she change it?"

She didn't want to be in the middle, but now both of them turned to her expectantly. Danielle looked from Steve to Shannon and back, deliberating internally. She knew Steve was right from a business standpoint, and she knew how Shannon felt from an artistic standpoint. Finally, she arrived at her answer. "I think its fine the way it is."

"Yes!" Shannon clapped once. "Thank you. She gets it."

"It'll never make it on the radio," Steve lamented. "Shame to banish such a beautiful song to life as a deep cut."

"You don't know that," Danielle said. "I mean, if The Divinyls can have a hit song about masturbation, then why couldn't a lesbian love song be a hit?"

"It's not a lesbian love song," Shannon protested.

"So what if it is? That's not the point. It's the song you want to sing the way you want to sing it. That should be all that matters. I never changed any of my lyrics to make them more radio friendly."

"Yeah, but you weren't...." Steve stopped and glanced at Shannon.

"Weren't what?" Danielle asked.

"Openly bi-sexual," Shannon finished for him. "Steve thinks it will keep me from being a true star. He's been after me from the beginning to put on a more straightforward public face. But I refuse. I will be who I am." Danielle stifled a laugh. "Why are you laughing?"

"I don't know, 'Rikka Olausson,' you tell me. You say that you're going to be who you are while you're pretending to be somebody you're not. If you're already putting on an act, why stop now? Why are you choosing to draw the line at your sexuality?"

Steve shifted so that Shannon couldn't see his lips and mouthed "thank you" at Danielle. She rolled her eyes in return.

"So, you agree with Steve that I should hide the truth about myself?"

Danielle slid the guitar over her head and place it gently on a nearby stand, then crossed the room to Shannon, crouching in front of her. "What I'm saying is, make up your mind. If you want to be yourself, then I'll support you because Steve tried to get me to be someone else too. But if you insist on putting on this fake front, then I don't see the point. What do you want? Do you want to be yourself, or do you want to be a star? If stardom's all you care about, do what Steve says. It'll be easier."

"I see," Shannon whispered, dropping her head. Danielle lingered for a second, then stood and turned to Steve.

"So is that it? We just nail this one song down, and I'm done?"

"No," Steve said. "Let's see what else you can do. I mean, you came up with that off the top of your head. Imagine what you can do if you sit down and really work together. I think I'm going to lock the two of you in a kitchen and not let you out until you have a hit."

Instantly, Ryan's warning popped into Danielle's head. "Shouldn't that be up to her?"

Steve took Danielle's arm and led her away. "Shannon doesn't know what she wants. She's not a producer. She needs guidance, and I think she'll take it from you more than she will anybody else. This is what needs to be done. Take the reins on this thing, and by the time the album's in the can, I'll have a new band assembled for you, and we'll get on with the real business."

Danielle pulled her arm away. "Goddamn, you've turned into a cold son of a bitch."

"We all do what we've gotta do, Danielle. You did it, and I've had to do it. Do we have a deal?"

Danielle looked back at Shannon, who sat with her elbows on her knees, head still slumped. She knew what Shannon was feeling.

"I'll do it...." Steve broke into a big smile, but Danielle wasn't finished yet. She pointed at the slumped Shannon. "If she wants me to. This will all be under the table and very, very quiet. Shannon gets all the credit, songwriting, producing, the whole nine yards. It's non-negotiable."

"It's a deal," Steve said eagerly.

"Not till I hear it from her, if not. I'm going home now."

Danielle packed her gear quickly and stopped only to pat Shannon on the back on her way out the door. She still hadn't looked up.

On the ride back into town, Danielle couldn't shake the vision of Shannon sitting there with her head in her hands, but she didn't feel bad about it. Everything she had told Shannon was true, and it was up to Shannon to decide what she wanted. Danielle had drawn her own line in the sand early in her career, even though it was a risk. Shannon had to make this call herself.

It was only the strange sight of a television crew on the side of the road that snapped Danielle out of her thoughts. Probably just a news crew, she thought, but then she looked around. The images began to flash in front of her eyes of this same stretch of road at night, emergency vehicles everywhere lighting up the scene. The world fell away, and Danielle could clearly see the crumpled metal cocoon that had once been her car, sitting in front of the hulking form of a Dodge truck. She'd seen the picture on the news in Oklahoma City. She had been so focused on other things that she hadn't realized where she was.

Danielle's foot came off the gas, and traffic began flashing by her, angry drivers honking and cursing her as she rolled up on the scene. The television crew was standing off to the side, shooting towards the scene of the wreck. A well-dressed man held a microphone in front of a pudgy middle-aged woman.

With a gasp, Danielle realized who it was. As she rolled up

on the scene, the woman turned, looking right at the Camaro. Danielle looked right into the eyes of Nicole Moore, the widow of the man who had hit her. She didn't know if Moore saw her, but she was in no mood to find out. Danielle slammed on the gas and sped away, but her mind was running even faster. It was one thing for the woman to peddle her stupid book on the talk show circuit, but what was she doing here?

Garrett had said the word was out on the street, despite Danielle's best attempts to stay under the radar. Had the word somehow filtered back? Or was it mere coincidence that they both wound up in town at the same time? Danielle did her best to control her breathing as she drove. She could feel another panic attack coming on. Her hands shook so badly that she had to keep both hands on the wheel as she drove.

For whatever reason, Nicole Moore was in Austin, and Danielle was certain she didn't want to be anywhere near her. She needed to get out of town.

Fast.

CHAPTER FOURTEEN

The day was fading fast as Danielle pulled into the driveway. Teri had just returned from a trip to the grocery store and was struggling to cart two overloaded bags of groceries in through the backdoor. Despite her panic, Danielle tried her best to compose herself before hustling to Teri's side. She took the groceries and followed Teri inside.

Danielle set the bags down on the kitchen counter and looked around. "Where's Randy?"

"He's taking a nap. He always gets tired in the afternoon," Teri said as she began stowing groceries. "He doesn't have much stamina anymore. If it weren't for you, I don't think he'd be around much longer."

"What do you mean by that?"

Teri turned away from the open refrigerator. "He'd given up. He was tired of trying to take care of himself, and he felt like he was a burden to me. He was ready to go. Then you came back, and now his whole outlook has changed. He even told me this morning that he doesn't want any more bacon and eggs for breakfast. He wants to lose weight and get his cholesterol under control. He wants to do physical therapy again so he can get out of the chair. You inspired him."

Danielle saw the tears running down Teri's cheeks and went to her, wiping them away with a finger. "I had no idea."

"You've made a big difference," Teri said as she walked around Danielle to grab more groceries. She discreetly wiped more tears away. "Said that by the time you have your big comeback concert, he wants to be walking again. Can you imagine?"

Danielle stood, holding the refrigerator door open, grappling with what to say. Before she found anything, Teri started up again.

"You never understood that, and you still don't."

"Understood what?"

"How you inspire people." Teri waddled to the fridge with a bag full of fruits and vegetables and filled the crisper drawer. "You never saw it because the lights were always in your eyes, but everybody else did. All the little girls who saw you as a role model. The musicians who admired not just your talent but your courage. The friends that watched you hurting and suffering, and yet you just kept going." Teri took Danielle's hands in hers. "You can still inspire people. So don't do what you're thinking about doing."

Danielle pulled her hands back and spun away from Teri. "I'm not thinking about anything."

"Bull," Teri snapped. "You've got that look in your eyes. That spooked look you get when you want to run. I saw it the second you came up to me."

Danielle meandered around the tiny kitchen, but wouldn't look directly at Teri. "I'm not spooked. I've just had a busy day.

Got lots to think about still." As she stood and looked out the backdoor, Danielle felt Teri's hand on her arm and turned.

"Girl, don't lie to me. I know better. Sit down." Teri nodded toward the kitchen table, and Danielle did as instructed. Teri retreated to the fridge again, and when she came back, she brought two bottles of Coke and sat them down in front of Danielle. "A little treat," she whispered. "Don't tell the mister. He can't have these anymore."

"Gotcha," Danielle said, twisting the top and taking a long drink. She savored the burn as the Coke worked its way down her throat.

Teri got herself a glass of ice before she sat down and started pouring her own drink. "So tell me. What has you so startled? Was it something Steve did?"

"Nah, I can handle Steve. This is something else. I have no idea what to do about it." She glanced over at Teri, who sat expectantly.

"Go on."

Danielle took another drink, delaying the inevitable. There was no way Teri was letting her out of this conversation. "When I was driving back down here, I caught a segment on the news about the widow of the man who hit us. She's got a book out."

"I'm aware. I've seen her promoting that pile of trash on all the talk shows. Playing the victim, boohooing about her perfect husband. Makes me sick."

"She's here. In Austin. I saw her on the drive back in. She was with a TV crew, and they were filming by the accident scene. Totally freaked me out. I don't think I can face that."

"That woman," Teri said with a scowl. "Listen to me. This is just a coincidence. That's all. She doesn't know you're here, and she doesn't have to. She'll probably just be in town for a day or two and then move on."

"Maybe. But even still, when I do come back, everybody's going to want to talk about the crash. I'm going to have to go through it all again." Danielle stared down at the table. "I don't know if I can handle that, having to relive Kyle's death. It freaks me out to just think about it."

"So, you ran so you wouldn't have to face it." It wasn't a question, but rather a statement of fact. "As long as you weren't around, you could avoid reminders and pretend you were okay. I bet in the whole time you've been gone, you avoided almost all personal interaction, didn't you?" Danielle didn't answer, because Teri already knew. "Dani, the best advice I can give you is to deal with it now, while you can still do it in secret. Once you announce your return, people are going to bring it up, and you won't be equipped to handle it. You'll blow again if you don't face this."

"How do I do that?"

"Lots of ways. See a counselor, join a support group, cry your eyes out for days, stuff your face full of ice cream, and watch sad movies. Go to the gravesite and say your peace. I don't think you've ever been there."

Danielle stood up and took her bottle. "No, I haven't, and that's one thing I will not do. I won't go there. I don't do cemeteries. As for the rest of it, I'm beyond things like that now. I'll be okay. I'll deal with it. I can prepare myself for it when the time comes. But this woman, her presence just blindsided me, that's all. I'll be fine." She held her bottle up. "Thanks for the Coke. I'm going to go upstairs and get comfy, maybe work on some songs."

Teri eyed her suspiciously but didn't push the issue. "Okay.

I'll call you when dinner is ready."

Back in the apartment, Danielle slipped into a tank top and shorts and began working on some songs. She was thankful for the pep talk from Teri, but Nicole Moore still lurked around the edges of her mind. Coincidence or not, she was still in Danielle's town and was likely to stir up trouble one way or another. How deeply would she dig into Danielle's past? Would she find out about Randy and Teri? As she played, Danielle frequently glanced out the window, each time expecting to see a news van pulling up to the curb.

They never came, and Danielle enjoyed a nice meal with Randy and Teri. After dinner, she took Randy up on an invitation to join him in the bedroom, where they plopped in front of a forty-one-inch screen to watch the San Antonio Spurs basketball game. Danielle was not a sports fan, but Randy seemed to delight in educating her on the finer points of the game, and she enjoyed the time. At ten, Teri made them switch to the news, which was fine since the Spurs were winning easily anyway.

Danielle was ready to excuse herself for the night when the anchor teased an upcoming story about a distraught widow looking for answers. She and Teri locked eyes, both suspecting who it might be. When the broadcast came back, there was Nicole Moore, standing by the side of the road with an attractive female reporter, speaking in trembling tones about her dear deceased husband. Danielle sat stone-faced, even as her mind raced with a thousand different responses to every teary sentence the woman uttered.

Had the story remained like that, she would have been fine. She was willing to let Nicole Moore publicly grieve her husband and grab her fifteen minutes of fame at the same time. Up until the reporter asked her the last question.

"Mrs. Moore, you're not here in Austin just to view the site of your husband's death, though, are you? There is something else that has brought you down here, isn't there?"

"Yeah, book sales," Danielle spat. Neither Randy nor Teri reproached her for the comment.

"There is," Nicole answered as she wiped a tear away with one hand.

"Look at those nails," Teri whistled. "I bet she dropped a pretty penny on those. She didn't get a mani like that at the local mall."

"I came down here because I want to see the woman responsible for this. I want to sit across a table and look her in the eyes and tell her what she has cost me and my children. I want her to know the pain and the sorrow she is responsible for."

"Have you had any contact with Danielle or her representatives?"

Nicole glared at the camera. "No. We've been after her manager for two years, and he refuses to return our calls and our emails. Danielle is hiding. She doesn't have the guts to come out and face me, but I'm through playing nice. I will get my meeting, and I won't stop until I do."

The reporter turned away and looked into the camera with a put-on smile. "Strong words from a strong woman. Rest assured, this story isn't going away any time soon. Back to you in the studio, Michael."

Danielle shot up off the bed without a word.

"That woman's egg ain't just cracked, it's scrambled," Randy said. "Blaming Dani for what her husband did. What a crock of shit."

Teri was concerned about Nicole Moore, though. "Dani, honey, you okay? Don't let what she said get to you."

Danielle remained silent as she paced the tiny bedroom, her hands balled into tight fists at her sides. She breathed heavy and loud, almost like a raging bull snorting before it charges. Nicole's words echoed in her memory.

"Yeah, Dani, you can't let her get in your head," Randy chimed in. "That's what she wants. She's trying to goad you into coming out or doing something stupid. She's just trying to sell books, darlin'."

"I'll shove those books up her fat ass for her."

"That's what she wants. Just ignore her, sweetie," Teri said. "Eventually, she'll go away. She can't stay down here forever. Nobody knows what you look like now, and Randi and I are unlisted, so she won't find you here. Give it time, and this will blow over."

"Yeah," Danielle muttered. "Sure, it will. I'm going to bed." She didn't give either of them the opportunity to change her mind.

On the short walk from the house to her apartment, Danielle waited for some mystery reporter to spring out of the bushes at her, but again no one ever came.

She took up the guitar and started playing, not to write but just to clear her mind. Her notes were loud and aggressive, and Danielle pushed it hard as she attempted to drive Nicole out of her head by hate and force of will.

She'd been at it for a half hour when she realized that something, somewhere in the room, was buzzing. Danielle put the guitar aside and listened as the buzzing continued. It sounded like it was coming from the floor. She wandered around her room but could see nothing that would be causing the noise. In fact, there was nothing on the floor except her shoes and the clothes she had worn earlier in the day, including her jeans—with her cellphone in the pocket.

She dug out the phone and discovered exactly what she'd expected. Steve had been calling and texting her frantically. Before she could even begin to answer, he called again. "Yes, Steve?"

"I know you don't watch the news, and that's good, but I need to give you a heads up about something."

"I know, I saw it."

"You did?" There was a pregnant pause. "Well then, don't worry about this. I've been dodging this woman for a while, and I'll continue to dodge her. Building security has been instructed not to let them up if they come to the office. They won't find you at the Holder's. Just continue to lay low. I'm sure she has another TV appearance scheduled somewhere very soon."

"Yep. Sounds like a plan."

"Huh. Glad we agree on that." Again he paused, but Danielle was offering up nothing more to him. "So, moving on to other matters, I'm not sure where we're at with Shannon. You really messed her up today. I'm not even sure she wants to continue at this point. She seemed really confused when she left."

"She's got a lot of things to sort out. Probably best if you leave her alone for a couple of days and give her a chance to think."

"Well, I was hoping you would go talk to her. You know what it's like to have an identity crisis. Maybe you could help her, bond with her a little bit."

Danielle finished his thought for him. "And then convince her to continue with the album."

"Hopefully, yes. We all need this, Danielle."

"Not all of us," Danielle answered. She plopped down on her bed and peeked out the window. No news vans in sight. "I'm not the one staring bankruptcy right in the face."

Steve went dead silent on the other end. Danielle wondered if he had hung up, but finally, he responded. "I'm not sure where you heard that, but it's not true. Times are tough, but not that tough. The label does need a hit, though, and it would help me tremendously if it came from one of my acts. Can you please do this for me?"

"I really think you need to give her time to think."

"Last time I did that, my star client ran away for six years. If nothing else, just go check on her. See if you can find out where her head is at."

"Fine. Where is she staying?"

"The Marriott by the river. Room 442. Thank you, Danielle. I really do appreciate you doing this."

He hung up before Danielle could give him a suitably snarky response. She peered out the window once more, then forced herself up off the bed and threw her clothes back on.

Traffic was light, and Danielle easily made her way to the hotel, where she left the Camaro parked by the front door. One way or another, she wasn't going to be there long. She marched right past the desk to the elevators, where she shared a ride up with some soaking wet kids who had been taking advantage of the indoor pool. She roamed the halls until she found room 442. Danielle pounded on the door, wishing that it was Nicole Moore's face she was hitting instead.

Shannon yanked the door open, wearing nothing but a sheer green nightgown, and she smelled vaguely of lavender. Her hair was limp and damp, framing her round face. "Yes?"

"When something's bothering me, and I need to clear my head, I like to go for a drive."

"Thank you for sharing that," Shannon said. "But I'm afraid that little tidbit of information doesn't help me because I don't drive."

"Good, because I don't ride. Get dressed and come on." Shannon stood statuesquely in the doorway. "Well, are you going to get dressed, or are you going to come downstairs like that? Doesn't matter to me."

Finally, Shannon backed out of the door. "Come on in."

Danielle shook her head. "I can wait out here for you to get ready. Just don't take all night."

Shannon chuckled, propped the door open with her foot, and with a quick flick of her fingers slid the straps of her nightgown off her shoulders, and it flittered gently to the ground. "There. Now you've seen everything there is to see. Quit being a prude and come in."

"Wow," Danielle said. "I guess I will." She stepped carefully past the nude Shannon and into the room. Shannon let go of the door, and it closed quietly as Danielle followed her deeper into the room. She had a south facing room with the curtains pulled wide open to reveal the night lights of Austin, glittering like jewels off the dark water of the river below.

Shannon looked over her shoulder. "Don't suppose you'd be interested in a game of I'll Show You Mine If You Show Me Yours, would you?"

"I don't think so."

"That's too bad." Shannon whirled to face her. "Because I have to admit I'm intrigued by the little sneak peek I got the other night."

"That's all you're ever going to get. Now can you please get dressed? I left my car in a bad spot, and I don't want to be in people's way."

"Oh, is that why you're so uncomfortable?" Shannon slithered up next to her. "Is that the only reason you're uncomfortable?'

Danielle wanted to step back, but she wouldn't let Shannon get the better of her, so she stood her ground. "You're wasting my time. Throw on some jeans and come on. We've got things to talk about."

Shannon held her gaze a few moments longer, then gave up with a shrug and turned away. "So Steve sent you to check on me, huh? How nice. Let me find something to slip into. I don't wear jeans. I don't even own a pair."

"How do you not own a pair of jeans? That's weird. Jeans and T-shirts are all I wear."

"I noticed," Shannon snickered. "You hide your beauty too much. But I guess that's why you were a virgin until you were thirty." Danielle felt herself make a face, and Shannon noticed. "I've been reading up on you. Honestly, I had forgotten about that whole brouhaha until I read your Wiki bio." She took a scarlet dress out of the closet and held it up to her body. "What do you think?"

"It's fine. We're just going to be in the car, we're not walking down a catwalk."

Shannon studied the dress, then carefully put it back on the hanger. "I don't want to go out. Let's just stay here and talk. Or can you only think behind the wheel of a car?" She crawled up on her bed and lay seductively on her side.

"Would you at least put on a robe? You're making me

uncomfortable laying there like that."

"I know, that's why I'm doing it. I like to see people squirm. I love to wear low cut blouses when I meet with Steve, and then watch as he tries his damnedest not to steal peeks. He has a hard time with it."

"Oh God," Danielle muttered under her breath. She noticed a chair by a built-in desk and drug it over, sitting on the chair backward where the back was between them.

"What a strange pair we are," Shannon purred. "I'm here buck naked, and you won't even take that jacket off. The Slut and The Puritan. That's what we should call the album."

"So, you're going to do it?" Danielle felt her spirits lift slightly. Maybe she was going to get out of this conversation faster and easier than she anticipated.

"That's all he cares about, isn't it?" Shannon's cocky demeanor never changed, but Danielle saw the flicker of pain in her blue eyes. "He talks about you and him like you were a team, or a family even. He looks at me like a tool. I might as well be a screwdriver in a junk drawer to him."

Maybe it wasn't going to be that easy. Danielle laid her arms on the top of the chair and rested her chin on her arms. "He looks at me like that now. Doesn't matter. If you're not doing this, what are you going to do? What's your plan B if this doesn't work out?"

"Marry rich?"

"Well, you could probably do that. I doubt you'd have a hard time finding the right guy, girl, whatever."

Shannon cracked a genuine smile, and it only made her prettier. "It's not as easy as it sounds, but I guess I don't have to tell you that. Looks like you had your share of romantic missteps along the way."

"I'm not here to talk about that," Danielle said. There was Nicole again, sniffing around. What would she say about this little scene? The woman already considered Danielle a devil woman. "I'll help you with your album if you want. We'll do it your way, I don't care what Steve says about the lyrics being radio friendly."

"But what about my public image? If we do it my way, how is he going to sell it?"

"I don't care," Danielle said. "That's between you and Steve. Y'all work that out. I'm here for the music, that's all. I've already told Steve my contributions will be uncredited."

"That's very altruistic. Yes, I want your help. After you left, I listened to the playback, and it gave me chills. You have an intensity when you play, almost like you erupt into flame. I don't have that."

"Not everybody does," Danielle admitted. "That kind of intensity has some drawbacks too." She absent-mindedly rubbed her right cheek where a broken string during a performance had left her cut and bloodied, and left a thin scar behind as a reminder. "I'll tell Steve so he can set up some studio time."

Danielle turned to leave, but Shannon hustled up off the bed and caught her before she got to the door. "What do you think I should do? Should I be Shannon or Rikka?"

"I can't—"

Shannon put her finger to Danielle's lips. "I know you can't tell me what to do. I'm asking, if you were in my shoes, what would you do?"

"I would be me, and I wouldn't apologize to anybody for it, even if it meant sacrificing my career. If you can't look at yourself in the mirror each day, why bother?"

An impish grin crept across Shannon's face. In a flash, she cupped Danielle's face in her hand and planted a firm kiss on her lips. Danielle was caught off-guard by the speed with which she did it, and Shannon broke the kiss before Danielle could fight her off. "Tell our boss that all is good and I'm ready to work." She reached around Danielle, opened the door, and gently pushed Danielle out into the hall. "Have a good night."

Danielle stood in the hallway with the feel of Shannon's kiss lingering on her lips. "Strange girl," she muttered. On her way back down the hall, she called Steve, who picked up on the first ring. "I just talked to Shannon, and we had an...interesting conversation."

"I want to hear all about it. Come over to the apartment, and I'll buzz you in." He read off the address, which was for a high rise condo a few blocks to the northwest of the hotel. "See you in a few minutes."

As promised, Steve met her at the door in a pair of plaid pajama pants and a plain gray T-shirt. "Wow, this is quite the night. I actually get to see Steve Redus in a, in a...T-shirt." She let out a fake scream.

From inside the apartment somewhere, a female voice said, "That must be Danielle."

Danielle gasped. "Is that the sound of an honest-to-God female in your apartment? At this time of night? You scoundrel."

"Get in here," Steve barked.

Steve's apartment was the antithesis of the Holder's place. Where Randy and Teri's house was warm and inviting, Steve's apartment was stark and modern and felt more like a museum than a home. What it did have, though, was a stunning view of the capitol and the UT tower out of the north facing windows.

"Nice view, huh. I've asked the landlord if there are any vacancies. We need to get you out of that ridiculous garage apartment."

"It's not that bad," Danielle said as she wandered around his living room. "Besides, I don't think I want to live in the same building as you. That would be like moving back in with my mom, only without the physical abuse. But where's the fun in that?"

She heard footsteps padding down the hardwood floors and turned to find a middle-aged brunette woman emerging from the back. She wore shiny periwinkle pajamas and had her hair up in a messy bun. She was a little on the plump side, but it didn't take much imagination to see her as a very attractive woman in her younger days. She greeted Danielle with a pleasant smile.

"Danielle, this is Aja. She's my partner, as well as one of the most acclaimed artists in the Southwest."

"Pleased to meet you," Danielle said. Aja returned the favor. Danielle turned to Steve. "Stevie has a girlfriend," she whispered.

"Partner," he corrected. "We're both too old for that boyfriend/girlfriend business."

"It's okay, don't be embarrassed," Danielle said with a grin. "Apparently, I have a girlfriend too. It's been that kind of a night."

"Shannon?" Steve and Aja said simultaneously. Danielle nodded an affirmative. "She's a bit of an odd duck, isn't she?" Aja said. "Would you like some coffee or tea?"

"No ma'am, thank you," Danielle answered. "I won't be long." To Steve, she said, "Shannon said she's ready to work, and she wants me on board."

"That's great," Steve said. "That's excellent. I knew you could do it."

"Oh, I did it," Danielle answered. "But we are in agreement on something I don't think you're going to like. We're going to do the songs her way, and she's going to do it as Shannon. The Rikka Olausson thing is dead."

"Good for you," Aja applauded from the attached kitchen, where she was steeping a teabag in an oversize mug. "I've been trying to get Steve to drop that ridiculous routine for months."

Steve rubbed his bald head. "It won't work. I'm telling you. She'll be a darling on the coasts, but Middle America will shun her, and that's where most of the buying public is. Coming out is career suicide."

"Don't make it about her sexuality," Danielle said casually. "Just don't make it an issue. I wouldn't even address it. If people make a big deal, just be cryptic about it. Sometimes you say more by saying nothing."

Aja sauntered up next to Steve and swatted his arm. "I don't think she even needs you. This girl had got things down. I thought you said she was a walking train wreck."

"Oh, just wait. This is together, Danielle. You haven't seen her in meltdown mode yet."

"This is true," Danielle said in his support. "So anyway, as soon as you can get us some studio time, we'll get to work."

"Good," Steve said. "Because she already has time. In fact, she's been burning time, and I need her to get back to work. I'll make the necessary arrangements in the morning. Plane tickets and such."

Danielle's blood ran cold. "Plane tickets?"

"Yes. She's been living and recording in California for the last five weeks. I rented her this gorgeous little house on the beach in

Malibu. It's just her as far as I know, so she'll have room for you. It'll save us money on a hotel. I can probably have you a flight out of here tomorrow afternoon."

"No, no, no," Danielle said. "No, on so many levels. You know I don't fly, and there's no way I'm staying with Shannon. She's a predator."

"Yes, but you're a big, strong Texas girl who can take care of herself. Though you're not as big and strong as you used to be. We need to beef you up some, by the way—you look sickly. And as far as the plane tickets, you will fly. She's only got three weeks of studio time left and a whole album to be redone. I can't afford for you to take three days to drive out there. This is one of those 'put on your big girl panties' moments."

Danielle looked to Aja for help, but she just sipped her tea and watched. "Listen, if I left first thing in the morning—"

"It's still a full two days drive out there, and then you'd need a day to recover. Can't do it. We just don't have time. Besides, there's another reason this is to your advantage."

"What would that be?"

"Nicole Moore won't be able to get to you in Malibu. She thinks you're hiding around here somewhere, and I'm very happy to let her think that. You need to get out of town and fast. This is the best way, I promise."

"I fly all the time," Aja offered. "I've never had a problem."

"You're not a musician," Danielle responded. "God hates it when musicians fly."

Steve laughed and led her to the door. "Go home, pack, and get some rest. I'll get with you in the morning." He pushed her out the door. "And thank you. I really do mean that."

Aja called out, "It was nice meeting you," just before Steve shut the door in Danielle's face and locked it. Danielle stood in the hallway, feeling sick to her stomach. She wasn't sure what was worse, the certainty of her impending death, or the thought of living with Shannon for three weeks if she didn't die.

CHAPTER FIFTEEN

The next morning Danielle had breakfast with the Holders, though it felt more like a last meal for her. They ate in silence, Teri's attempts at making pleasant small talk failing badly. Finally, Danielle pushed her plate away.

"Well, that's it, I suppose." She looked at the two people that were the closest thing she had to parents. "I love you guys. Just remember that."

"Would you stop?" Teri said. "You're going to be fine. This whole superstition you have about flying is just absurd."

"I'm sure that's what Stevie Ray thought, too," Danielle responded.

"Lynyrd Skynyrd," Randy chipped in brightly.

Danielle snapped her fingers. "Randy Rhodes,"

"Patsy Kline," Randy responded, ignoring the nasty look Teri gave him.

"Buddy Holly."

"Otis Redding." Randy was having entirely too much fun.

Danielle nodded and began softly singing. *"Sittin' in the*

morning sun…." Randy immediately joined in his deep baritone, a perfect complement to Danielle. *"I'll be sittin' when the evenin' comes. Watchin' the ships roll in. Then I watch 'em roll away again."*

Teri picked up a dishtowel and launched it at her husband. "Stop this. You're feeding into her irrational fears."

"Ah man," Danielle fake pouted. "We didn't even get to the dock of the bay."

Teri answered by jabbing a bony finger at her. "You quit stalling and get going. People are counting on you, and you're not going to let them down. Got it?"

Danielle leaned toward Randy. "Bossy, isn't she?"

"Tell me about it."

With a laugh, Danielle stood and circled the table to give Teri a hug. "We're just yanking your chain a bit. I'll call you when I get settled." They hugged a minute longer before she started for the door. When she got there, she turned around. "Unless, of course, I'm a charcoal briquette on the ground, in which case—"

"Get. Out."

Randy rolled up to her as Danielle was about to step outside. She leaned over, and Randy pulled her in close to whisper in her ear. "Wait for the other girl to board and then haul ass to the rental counter. They can't stop you that way."

Danielle giggled. "I already thought of that."

After breakfast, Danielle headed out for some last minute supplies. She pulled into an area AxeMasters location with a shopping list in hand but never got out of the car. Instead, she decided to return to her roots and drove to Ty's shop on South Lamar.

Inside, very little had changed from when Danielle and Ty had worked there together as teenagers. The front of the store was still dedicated to band instruments, pianos, sheet music, and assorted necessities, with a separate room off to the side for guitars and other "rock" instruments. The counter was still in the middle of the room and raised slightly. The counter itself had been updated with all new cash registers, new Plexiglas cases with LED lights inside, and the old tile floor had been changed out for a gray stone polished smooth. The walls were freshly painted a matching gray, giving the room a darker, but somehow warmer feel.

Behind the counter, a pleasant woman in a Cincinnati Reds hoodie introduced herself as Maxine. Danielle explained what she was looking for, and Maxine enthusiastically pointed her toward the side room.

Again there had been some subtle changes, but not many. Recessed lighting had replaced the old fluorescent lights, and the walls and ceiling were covered in black acoustic tiling. The room was empty except for Ty, who sat on a stool fiddling with a blue Ibanez guitar.

"Times must be tough if you're slumming it on an Ibanez," she said as she entered the room. She said it with a smile, though she instantly doubted her idea to approach with him with a smart ass remark.

Ty barely looked up from his playing and showed no reaction to her presence. "A guitar is a guitar. Nothing wrong with an Ibanez."

The counter with all the strings, picks, and other goodies was to her right, and these cases had also been upgraded. Danielle leaned on the counter casually. "There's nothing wrong with driving a Ford Escort either. It'd just be a lot cooler if you didn't."

Ty groaned and set the guitar down easily on a stand.

"Danielle—"

"Easy. I'm here on official business. This is strictly a customer-businessman transaction. I think you both made your personal feelings very clear the other night." She pulled a folded up piece of notebook paper out of her back jeans pocket and held it up with two fingers. "I need the stuff on this list, and I need it pronto. I have a flight to catch."

Ty furrowed his brow as he walked up and took the list from her. "You're flying? Where are you flying to? Didn't you just come home?"

"Yeah, that's the real bummer. I just got here, and now I've got to leave again." Ty made a face, and Danielle guessed what he was thinking. "I'm not running. This is a business trip, therefore, the list. Time to get back to work."

Ty unfolded the paper and looked it over. "You know, you could get all of this stuff at AxeMasters a hell of a lot cheaper. I can't compete with their prices."

"Yes, but I hate AxeMasters. No soul. I prefer to give my business to small, home owned establishments." Over his shoulder, Danielle saw a guitar hanging on the wall that piqued her interest. "Is that a Danelectro?" She pushed past him, plucking the black and white guitar off the wall.

"It's a reissue," Ty said. "A fairly good copy of a '59 DC. They're pretty solid guitars, not great. Give you a nice, deep tone."

Danielle turned and pointed to the amp Ty had been plugged into. "Do you mind if I take her for a spin?"

"Go ahead." He waved her list in the air. 'I'll get the rest of this stuff." He started to go, then stopped. "You know I'm not going to give you any sort of old friend's discount or anything, right? You're paying full price."

Danielle looked up with a grin as she plugged in the guitar. "Like I can't afford it?"

Ty smirked and went on, leaving Danielle to fiddle with the Danelectro. She liked it well enough but determined that it didn't have quite the sound she was looking for. She hung it back on the wall and strolled the floor, sizing up the rest of his selections.

"Are you looking for something in particular?" Ty asked from behind the counter, where he was ringing up items and putting them in boxes for her. "A certain sound?"

Danielle kept inspecting the instruments on the wall. "Yeah. I'm looking for something that will give me a good crunch. Something really meaty and hard. What I'm doing is going to be harder than what we did, and I don't really want to use the Strat for it."

Ty edged up next to her. "You know, most guitarists have collections of hundreds of guitars of all types, and they switch off from song to song and sometimes use several different guitars for one song. You are the only guitar player I've ever heard of that just wants one or two guitars."

"I've never been much of a gearhead, you know that."

Ty nodded and moved to his right, where he used a special tool to pluck a purple and black Gibson Les Paul from high on the wall. "If you're looking for a hard rock sound, Les Paul is the best of the best. Give it a run."

She took the guitar with a devilish smile and plugged in. "Don't suppose you'd want to grab one and join me for a little jam session. For old time's sake?"

Ty drummed his fingers on the countertop but ultimately shook his head. "No. I don't think so. Let me finish getting this boxed up for you. Besides, you have a plane to catch. Remember?"

Danielle was disappointed but focused on the new guitar. This one was much more of the sound she was looking for. After just a few passes, her mind was made up. Ty was still adding up her bill as she walked over. "Throw this on there with it. I like it."

"Will do."

Danielle reached into her back pocket and pulled out a simple black credit card, which she slid over to Ty. He raised his eyebrows when he saw it. "Black card, huh?"

"I always kept one, just in case of emergencies. Like this."

"Must be nice if this is an emergency." He read off her total and ran the card for her. Once the transaction was complete, he picked up a box. "Let me carry this to the car for you."

"How very chivalrous. Right, this way." Danielle took the guitar as well as a brand new Orange Crush amp and led him to the Camaro, where she popped the back hatch. They quickly stowed the new equipment, mainly replacement strings, cords, and effects pedals.

"You must be working on something big," Ty said as he slammed her trunk shut. "I'm interested to hear it."

"We'll see how it goes. Stepping way out of my comfort zone, but maybe it's a good thing." She held out her hand for a shake. "Thanks for your help."

Ty looked at her hand, then pulled her in for a hug instead. "Be patient," he whispered in her ear. "Things will change."

Danielle pulled out of the hug but laid her palm on his cheek. "I'm glad to hear that because I miss you guys. I always did."

She turned away and jumped in the car. She had packing to do, and time was running short. She noticed that Ty stood in the parking lot and watched her until she was out of sight.

Danielle's soul felt lighter as she drove home. Ty's last words had given her reason to hope that things would eventually return to something more normal. That hope made the rest of the day tolerable.

She pulled up to the front of Bergstrom Airport to find Steve and Shannon had already arrived. Steve was helping an attendant load an ungodly amount of luggage onto a cart. Shannon, wearing a navy blue pants suit with silver trim, stood by watching.

Danielle left the car idling and hopped out. "That is a lot of luggage. We're only staying for three weeks."

Steve slammed a suitcase on the cart and glared up at Danielle. "This is just what she brought with her from L.A. This is a couple of days worth of stuff."

"I don't travel light. I'm sorry."

"This is going to be fun," Danielle muttered under her breath. "Let me get one of these things," she said, referring to the cart. Another attendant hustled to help her as Danielle loaded her box of goodies, two amps, and two guitars on the cart.

"That's all gear," Shannon said. "Where are all of your clothes?" Danielle grinned as she popped open the passenger door and pulled out a single black duffle back stuffed to the gills. "You can't be serious. That's all you're bringing?"

"Danielle does travel light," Steve said, not even trying to hide his smirk. "She's a fantastic traveler."

Danielle approached him. "What are we going to do about my car? I hate to leave it in an airport parking lot for three weeks."

"I took care of that." Steve knocked on the trunk of his car, and the passenger door opened. Aja nearly ran down the length of the car and enveloped Danielle in a bear hug.

"You take care out there," Aja said sternly. She leaned in

close to whisper in her ear. "Keep an eye on that girl, and don't let her do anything to you."

"I can take care of myself. Do you think you can handle my baby here?" Danielle asked, jerking her head toward the Camaro. "She's pretty powerful."

"Please. I learned to drive on a '67 Cuda. I can handle that." Again she leaned in close. "I'm not an old fuddy-duddy like Steve. I like to have a little fun."

"Well then," Danielle whispered in return. "Let 'er rip."

Aja hugged her again. "I promise I'll keep it under a hundred."

"Why?"

Aja simply smiled bigger and put her arm around Danielle's waist. "I love this girl, Steve. Have I told you that?"

"More than once," he answered. To Danielle, he said, "I don't know how I feel about this. I think my girlfriend likes you better than she likes me, and I'm almost positive the two of you together will be the death of me."

"Ah, ah. She's your partner, not your girlfriend. Remember?"

Steve and Aja said their goodbyes. Steve handed her the tickets and a manila envelope to go over while on the plane. With that, they left, leaving Danielle and Shannon to embark on the journey alone.

Heading into the airport, each pushed their own cart. "I see that you've won the Mrs. over," Shannon pouted. "She doesn't like me at all. She barely said two words to me when I met her."

Danielle was in no mood to spar with her and just left it at that. Once they got all of their bags checked in and made it to the boarding area, Danielle felt the nervousness creeping in. She sat on the edge of her seat, bouncing both legs like pistons and wringing her hands non-stop. After a few minutes, she bounced up and paced the area, sometimes staring out the windows and longing to go outside, only to turn away when a plane either took off or landed.

Shannon sat back in her own seat, casually flipping through a fashion magazine. After fifteen minutes of watching Danielle bounce all over the airport, she patted the seat next to her. "Will you please come sit down and relax?"

With a jagged breath, she sat on the edge of her seat and started bouncing her legs again until Shannon reached out and stopped her. "Why exactly are you so afraid of flying? Did you have a bad experience or something?"

"No," Danielle answered as she kept up the hand wringing. "I never had a bad experience—I just don't like it. You're in this tin can way up high in the sky, and if it falls…." Danielle shuddered. "If something goes wrong, there's nothing you can do but sit up there and kiss your ass goodbye."

"So it's a control issue? Like the other night when you said that you don't ride. You don't like being in a situation you can't control."

Danielle kept looking around, not even sure what it was she was looking for. "Yeah, I guess. Maybe." She went back to bouncing her legs and breathing heavily.

Shannon snaked her right arm around Danielle and forced her head down onto Shannon's shoulder. "Relax," she whispered as she ran her fingers through Danielle's hair and over her scalp. "Just relax, breathe easy. Don't think about it. Just focus on my touch. Let everything else go."

She began humming softly, an indistinct tune. Danielle felt the vibrations as much as she heard the sound, and it was soothing. Slowly Danielle began to feel herself relaxing.

"I like seeing you like this, to be honest," Shannon said after several minutes. "When you're not trying to be such a badass. I was beginning to think you were a robot or something. You always seem so cold."

"Don't get used to it," Danielle whispered. She kept her eyes shut tight, focusing completely on Shannon's touch. "Once we hit the ground in L.A., it's business as usual. Unless we hit the ground in Colorado, in which case —"

Shannon laughed lightly. "We're not going to crash. Quit worrying." Danielle went silent, and Shannon continued to stroke her head until her cellphone started ringing loudly. Danielle sat up as Shannon dug the phone out of her purse and answered it. "Yes. Right here. One second." Shannon held out the phone. "Steve on the line for you."

Danielle took the phone but didn't have a chance to say anything. "Turn on your damn phone," he barked. "I've been calling you for a half hour. Now listen, I called the label and gave Rico an update. He wants to stop by on Monday and check on your progress, so when you get to L.A., don't dawdle. Get right to work and keep Shannon focused."

"He's only giving me two days to get this done?"

"No, no," Steve tried to assure her. "He doesn't expect a completed product. He just wants to see some progress. He wants to be sure you're on the right track before you waste any more time. I think he has some doubts as to how well this is going to work."

"Steve, Rico Cardenas can climb up on a step stool and kiss my ass. I give zero shits about what that soulless piece of trash has to say about it."

"That soulless piece of trash is the head of the label and

controls the purse strings, so you're going to have to care. Need I remind you, this isn't your record and your future we're talking about, it's Shannon's. Don't let your pride sabotage her chance at a career." Danielle merely grunted in response before Steve shifted gears. "Now, I'm texting you all the necessary info: the address of the studios in Santa Monica, the names of the people you'll be dealing with, et cetera. I'm also sending you some wave files of the songs they've been working on so you can give a listen while you're on the plane. I thought it might keep your mind off of…things. I'm going to have a driver meet you at the airport. You'll have full use of a car service for the full three weeks, take advantage of it. I'll see you in two days when Rico comes."

"'Bye, Steve," Danielle muttered as she rang off. She gave it back to Shannon. "Steve sends his love and reminds us that time is of the essence, so no fucking around. He wants us working as soon as the wheels touch down."

"Well, there went my evening plans," Shannon said. She seductively licked her lips and gave Danielle a wink. When she responded with disgust, Shannon broke out into laughter. "I'm kidding. Jesus, loosen the chastity belt a little."

Thankfully the plane finally boarded. Even Shannon's best relaxation techniques didn't help Danielle during takeoff, as she nearly pulled the arms off her seat from the stress. Once the plane was airborne, she released her death grip and started to breathe a little easier. She had dug Steve's phone out of her carry on, and Shannon loaned her some earbuds so she could listen to the files Steve had sent her.

The music did help. Soon Danielle was lost, her mind swimming with ideas as she listened to each track multiple times. She began to realize that Steve hadn't been giving

Shannon enough credit. There were moments when she heard real potential in Shannon's work. What she needed was guidance and support. She began to wonder if Shannon's flippant attitude was natural or a defense against being constantly that she wasn't good enough. She would have to find out.

Landing was almost as bad as take-off, except for the knowledge that as the plane got lower, it meant the inevitable fall from the heavens wouldn't be quite so long. However, the plane failed to explode into a fireball or plummet from the sky, and they landed safely. As the plane taxied to the gate, Shannon smirked at her.

"See? Nothing at all to worry about. That was a picture perfect flight. Now, let's go grab some dinner, do a little shopping, maybe a nightcap, and do it up right."

"We're supposed to get to work."

"Oh, forget that. We can't do anything tonight. Nobody will even be in the studio. Besides, we have three weeks."

"We have two days." Danielle registered the shock that crossed Shannon's face. "That was what Steve called about. Rico is coming by Monday to check our progress. By that, I take it to mean that if he doesn't like what he hears, he'll just pull the plug. So we need to really get cracking on this."

Shannon looked away, seeming rattled by the new news. It passed after a few short moments. "Be that as it may, we're still not getting anything done tonight." The plane reached the gate, and the passengers all stood to begin unloading. "Let's go to the house, clean up, and have ourselves a nice night. Come on."

They gathered their bags, and Danielle began looking for directions to the car rental agencies.

"I thought Steve hired a driver for us," Shannon said as

she struggled to keep pace with Danielle. "He always gets me a driver."

"You've got me, you don't need a driver."

"Yeah, but I figured if we had a driver, you could just sit back and relax. Maybe we could make out in the back seat."

Danielle stopped on a dime, forcing Shannon to swerve to avoid running into her. "You are impossible. Do you know that? I am not into women."

"I am persistent, thank you. Besides, how do you know if you've never tried? I bet I could change your mind." Danielle rolled her eyes and walked away, leaving Shannon to play catch up. "If nothing else, it's funny just seeing how riled up you get. Steve and I both think it's cute how I intimidate you."

"Intimidate me? Don't make me laugh."

"Deny all you want, but we both see it. You are so uptight. You're going to keel over from a stroke by the time you're forty. You gotta understand, it's a new world now. You need to let go of your old fashioned ways and embrace the freedom."

Danielle slowed enough for Shannon to finally catch up. "You need to learn to focus on the job at hand. We're here to work, not mess around. What I need right now is a car."

She finally found directions, and they caught a shuttle to an Enterprise Car Rental. Their selection wasn't great, but they did have a royal blue Dodge Challenger, and Danielle jumped on it. Shannon wasn't sure the car was big enough to hold all of their luggage, but Danielle made it fit, and soon they were out on the road.

Cruising down the Pacific Coast Highway, Danielle felt better. She had an objective in front of her now. Better still, Nicole Moore was still back in Texas, where she could make as big a scene as she wanted to. With any luck, she'd get bored and be gone before Danielle returned home.

Shannon pointed out the house when they got to Malibu, a surprisingly underwhelming home with a semi-circular drive in front and lush hedges to provide some privacy from the cars speeding by outside. Danielle grabbed as many bags as she could while Shannon jumped out and held the door open for her. Danielle stepped into a pleasantly cool foyer that opened up into a spacious living room.

"Nice digs."

"Thanks. Rent is a bitch on it, though. One day I'll be able to buy a place like this. Right now, I'm subletting from...." Danielle glanced at her expectantly. When Danielle didn't offer any sort of speculation, Shannon continued. "A certain Hollywood celeb who is going to be spending some court ordered time away from home, if you get my drift." She snorted to drive her point home.

"I really don't care about all of that celebrity business. I never got caught up in all of that. Ruinous if you let it get to your head."

"You sound like you speak from experience."

Danielle was non-committal. "I've seen some things. So do I have a room, or should I just toss this stuff on the couch?"

"Of course you do. This way." Danielle followed her out of the living room and down a short hallway. "My room is there," Shannon pointed. "And yours is right here across the hall. Just in case you need something. If you have a nightmare and need to cuddle or anything," she said with a wink.

"I don't have nightmares." Danielle poked her head in the room. It was simple enough—a queen size bed, a pair of nightstands, and a chest of drawers with a flat-screen TV on top. "This will work." She stepped in fully, tossed her duffle bag on the end of the bed, and gently laid down her guitars before moving to the window and opening the drapes to let some light in. Shannon had followed close behind and sat on the edge of the bed. Danielle studied her in the light.

Shannon came and stood next to her and began fiddling with Danielle's hair. "I need to take you somewhere and get your dye job updated. You haven't been maintaining it, and now your roots are showing. It looks terrible. If we're going to be palling around in my town, you have to look sharp. I know a girl who can do it. I'll even pay for it."

Danielle scoffed and walked past. "I don't want to mess with it. Sitting in a chair for two hours while some stranger puts her hands all over me? No thank you."

Shannon wasn't about to let Danielle resist, taking her by the hand. "Come on, treat yourself. Let's have a girl's night out, pamper ourselves a little bit, and just kick back. I know you don't think you do, but you need it. I promise, you will survive, and you'll still be every bit the tomboy when you wake up in the morning. Let me do this for you."

Danielle looked down into Shannon's eyes and saw how desperately she wanted this and decided it wasn't worth fighting her on it. "Fine, we'll go do your girl's night. Give me a few minutes to call all these people and tell them to meet us tomorrow." Shannon exclaimed, but Danielle wagged a finger at her. "This is a friend thing, there's nothing romantic or anything behind it."

Shannon stood on her tiptoes and planted a quick kiss on her lips. "I'll take it. In fact, where's your phone?" Danielle retrieved it from her jeans pocket, and Shannon snatched it away. "You're probably awful at texting, so I'll do it. When do you want to meet? Nine?"

"That's fine."

"Perfect. I'll text everybody, you unload the car, and then we'll go." Shannon was bouncing with excitement. "You're going to love this. I promise."

CHAPTER SIXTEEN

Shannon had a ball taking Danielle around town. They met with her personal beautician, a tall and beefy woman with blonde and black streaked hair who worked out of a portable building in the backyard of her house. Shannon paid an ungodly amount for hair, manicures, and pedicures for both. Danielle sat in pained silence as the other two women chattered on endlessly about men, women, celebrities, beauty, and everything else under the sun.

After that, it was a trip to a local mall, where Shannon insisted on upgrading Danielle's wardrobe. She also insisted that Danielle purchase some workout clothes so they could run together in the mornings. She had to admit she had allowed herself to get lazy over the years, and agreed that getting in better shape was a good idea, which just spurred Shannon on more.

Then Shannon insisted that they eat dinner at a seafood place not far from the beach house. Eventually, Shannon spotted the place she was looking for, an overgrown wooden shack just off the highway. There were neon beer signs shining through the windows, and a parking lot full of motorcycles and sports cars. The sound of loud rock music punctured the air.

They were seated at a window seat for two by a guy who'd listened to too much Jimmy Buffett in his life. Shannon ordered a Corona with lime and a plate of oysters, while Danielle ordered a Coke. The faux pirate came back minutes later with their drinks, and Danielle watched as Shannon squeezed the lime into the bottle of beer. "Corona, huh? I figured you'd order white wine or something prissy."

Shannon stuck her tongue out. "I'm not as prissy as you like to think. You don't grow up in a Minnesota farming town without getting at least a little tomboy in you. It's in our DNA."

"I spent some time up there a couple of years ago," Danielle said. "It was pretty in spring, but still cold. Down here, spring usually hits about late February or early March. It was late April, and I was wearing jackets. I decided it was time to move on."

"You Southerners are weak," Shannon kidded. "A little cold snap in the air, and you all want to go running for the equator. Try spending a winter up there some time."

"Not on your life," Danielle answered with a smile.

Their waiter returned with the plate of oysters. Danielle cringed at the sight of them. "I got these for us to share, by the way," Shannon said, oblivious to Danielle's reaction.

"No, thanks," she answered. "Not my thing. I tried once. Spent a summer up in Oregon living on a houseboat around Bandon. Ate a crap ton of seafood. Can't say I developed a taste for those things."

"Don't know what you're missing." As Danielle watched, Shannon shucked the oyster, salted it, and sucked it down her throat. The whole process made her want to vomit.

"So, what's your deal?" Danielle asked to take her mind off the display. "How did you become Rikka Olausson?"

"Oh, you want my life story? Do I get yours?"

"Whatever there is left to tell," Danielle said. "My life is pretty much an open book, and you've already read it."

"I have a good idea of what you did up until six years ago. Your Wiki bio stops at 2003. I know that you went traveling. So what did you do?"

"My life since I left has been pretty unspectacular. Moved around a lot, worked a lot of odd jobs, and kept to myself. I thought I was going on a grand adventure, but it didn't work out that way. I spent the last several months in Kansas, of all places. Your turn."

Shannon shucked another oyster. "I'd probably still be up there in Minnesota and married to some husky, fourth-generation farmer, spitting out kids like a Pez dispenser, if it hadn't been for Kaia."

The waiter interrupted her story for a food order. Shannon ordered a bowl of lobster bisque and a salad, while Danielle went for shrimp linguine. When he moved away, Danielle prompted Shannon back to her story. "Who is Kaia?"

Shannon looked away, her eyes tracking out over the darkened ocean on the other side of the highway. "Kaia was a foreign exchange student from Albania. She was unlike anyone I'd ever met. She had these designer clothes and listened to this obscure European club music. The other kids treated her like a freak, but I befriended her. She exposed me to...so much."

Shannon broke out in a big smile, and Danielle was sure of what the smile meant. Shannon caught her staring and confirmed Danielle's thoughts. "Oh yes. That too. I was totally in love.

After that, no Minnesota farm boy would ever be enough. So we hatched a plan to run off to New York after graduation and start a band. We both sang in the choir," she threw in as an afterthought. "My parents found out and disowned me. I spent the last three weeks of my senior year sleeping on my school counselor's couch because no one else would have me. Then we ran off. Like you, I thought I was on a grand adventure, but it didn't work out so well for me either."

Danielle felt herself being pulled into Shannon's story. For the first time, it seemed like she was dealing with a real person, and she was intriguing. "What happened?"

"Kaia had some extended family that lived in Yonkers. We crashed there and would slip out at night to explore the city. We met a bunch of wild people, did a bunch a wild stuff. Sex, drugs, the whole bit. Then one day, her parents showed up and took her home. I was so stupid."

"How so?"

"I never stopped to question why she was spending her senior year away from home. Never wondered why we didn't have any classes together. I never thought it weird in the least. Turns out that she wasn't graduating. She was only a junior, and she'd basically gone rogue. Her parents were pissed. Once they took her, I was out on the street. I had no money, no job, and nowhere to go. Couldn't call my parents."

"You don't think they would have come for you? Even if you explained what had happened? Even if you'd been lied to?"

Shannon stared down at the table and sucked on her lip as she thought about it. "Probably," she finally said. "But I was still hurt and too proud to go begging them for help. The next several months of my life were very unpleasant. I did a lot of things I wasn't proud of just to make it from one day to the next. Things a country girl from Mankato never has to think about. They were dark, dark times."

Shannon paused, and Danielle took a deep breath. It occurred to her that her story could have been very similar had she not stumbled upon Randy Holder and found a friend and father figure. Danielle realized how lucky she'd been, how fortunate she was to have avoided so many of the pratfalls that come with pursuing a life in show business.

"Finally I tried out for this band that was doing club music and got the job. They had this whole shtick about being a Swedish export. I came up with the name Rikka Olausson and rolled with it. I buried Shannon Henderson and intended to keep her buried."

"So Steve found you in New York?"

"He was up there on business, and I was moonlighting, performing in coffee shops during the day for extra cash when he happened in one day. He came up to me when I was done, gave me his card, and asked if I wanted to come to Austin with him. I turned him down."

"You turned him down?" Danielle was incredulous. "Good God, why?"

"I felt loyalty to the band. Plus, after everything I'd been through, I was a little afraid it was a scam. That maybe he wanted me to come down for other purposes, you know?"

Danielle nodded, yes.

"A girl can't be too careful," Shannon continued. "Anyway, I kept doing what I was doing, but I held on to his card and kept thinking about him. This late winter storm blew through, and I was trapped in my apartment for a few days. I remember looking out over this gray, decrepit city and how everywhere I looked, all

I could remember were bad things. So I called him up, completely expecting him to blow me off. Most of the time, those offers are one time only, you know. I called and told him I'd changed my mind, and Steve said, 'pack your bags, and I'll be on a plane to get you tomorrow.' That was it."

Danielle was studying Shannon and realized instantly what had happened. Yes, she was talented, but Steve had seen beyond that talent. He'd seen the spirit of a young girl in need of help. She wouldn't tell Shannon that theory, but she knew in her heart that Steve was playing the white knight.

"He did everything he promised he would, too," Shannon continued. "I became this phenomenon on the World Music charts. He got me gigs at all these fancy clubs. We went to Europe. It was fantastic."

"All right then. If you're such hot shit on the World scene, why not just keep doing that? Sounds to me like you could have a pretty solid career just doing what you were doing."

Emotions arched across Shannon's face and flashed in her eyes, and Danielle knew that she'd touched a nerve in Shannon. Her jaw tightened as she resumed her story. "Because he booked me a show in Minneapolis and I went back home a couple of days before. I wanted to see my parents and my friends from high school and show them what I'd made of myself. I thought I'd impress everyone, and instead what I got was, 'Have you been on Letterman or Leno?' Or 'Does MTV play your videos?' When the answer was no, then everybody was like, 'You must not be too big then.' Even my parents were like that."

"Wait a second," Danielle exclaimed. "You're telling me that this whole project is just so you can fulfill some ego trip? So you can show up the folks back home? You gotta be kidding me."

"No," Shannon answered defiantly. "I'm doing this because I want to know it has all meant something. That being deserted in that hellhole town and all the times I sold my body and my soul for a couch, a shower, and some cold takeout food had a point." Danielle had never seen her more animated than Shannon was at the moment. "If I died tomorrow, it would be a one paragraph blurb in *Rolling Stone*. To the people back home, I'd just be another cautionary tale of the dangers of running off to the big city. I want to make a statement. I want to *be somebody*."

Danielle sat back and took her in. Shannon was breathing heavy and staring daggers at her. Out of the corner of her eye, she saw the waiter coming with their food. "Then I'll help you," Danielle finally said. "But understand something. Even if you make it, it's not going to do what you want it to. As long as you're trying to impress somebody else, even your victories are going to feel hollow. The only way you'll find what you're looking for is to do it for yourself. Forget everybody else."

As the waiter sat the food down between them, Shannon looked Danielle in the eyes. "Let me worry about that."

Lying in bed later that night listening to the waves outside, Danielle thought a lot about Shannon's story. Could it be that Rikka Olausson and Renae Tucker were one and the same? Both were inventions of damaged women designed to insulate themselves from a world that had beaten them down. Danielle didn't necessarily approve of how Shannon went about it, but she did understand the reasoning.

It felt like she'd just fallen asleep when suddenly Shannon was on her, sitting on the bed, straddling her. "Get up, Danielle. Get off your ass. Come on."

Danielle tried to rub the sleep out of her eyes. "What are you doing? I just got to sleep."

"Morning jog," Shannon responded gleefully. "Best way to wake up. Come on, let's go. Get up, get up, get up."

Danielle rolled and shifted and tried to get Shannon's weight off her legs between lengthy yawns. "If you want me up, get off me." Shannon did as asked, and Danielle forced herself up on her elbow. "You're annoying in the morning."

"You always think I'm annoying. Come on, I laid out some clothes for you. Hurry up and get dressed and meet me in the kitchen."

Shannon bounded out of the room, leaving Danielle in bed. She wanted nothing more than to roll over and go back to sleep. The mattress had fingers that were wrapping around her, pulling her back down. The mattress promised tranquility. She felt herself falling over....

"Don't go back to sleep." Shannon had popped back into the doorway.

With a groan, Danielle swung her legs out of bed. "You're evil. You know that?"

Shannon just smiled and disappeared down the hall. Danielle shuffled around until she found the workout clothes Shannon had laid out, and slowly got dressed.

She finally stumbled out of the bedroom and made her way to the kitchen, where Shannon was waiting with a tall glass of disgusting liquid that looked like it had been bottled in a swamp. Shannon pressed the glass into her hand. "Veggie smoothie. Best way to start your day. Drink up."

Danielle took a sip, gagged, and started to put the glass down, but Shannon wouldn't allow it. "Finish it up. All you're drinking is nature's best stuff. Get your motor running the right way. Come on. Unless the big strong Texas girl can't handle it."

Danielle stared at her from under heavy eyelids. "You're challenging me?" She looked again at the putrid concoction in her hand, sighed, and proceeded to choke it down. The entire time, Shannon was cajoling her. Danielle finally finished and managed not to throw it all back up.

"That's a good girl," Shannon kidded her. "Now, let's get to it. I'm usually already on my way back by now. Come on, let's go."

Danielle followed her out to the beach, and they began to jog. It quickly began weighing on Danielle, who hadn't done much in the way of physical fitness in years. Shannon kept pressing, urging her to run just a little farther.

Danielle was convinced she was dying and was ready to welcome the reaper's sweet release when someone started applauding her. Still running, Danielle turned her head to follow the sound, but her legs were done and buckled, sending Danielle tumbling to the sand.

Shannon yelped and stopped to circle back around, but the other person got there first and extended a hand. An embarrassed Danielle took the hand and looked up into the face of Adam.

"Fancy meeting you here."

Danielle yanked her hand out of his grasp. "How? Of all the miles of beach in this state…."

Adam just gave her his infamous snarky grin, the one that had made him famous. "Destiny keeps trying to push us together. One of these days, you'll understand that."

"Excuse me." Shannon stepped between them, a fine sheen of sweat making her exposed skin glisten in the early morning light. "Are you bothering my girl?"

Adam did a double take, and instantly the game was on. "Good morning." He took Shannon's hand gently in his own. "I'm Adam. Danielle and I go way back. And you are?"

Shannon sounded like she was purring as he gently kissed the back of her hand. "I'm Rikka. I'm trying to whip Danielle here into shape, and apparently failing." She glanced down at Danielle, still prone in the sand. She sighed. "It's a real chore sometimes."

"You will find that Danielle is exhausting even in the best of circumstances. So what brings you lovely ladies to my stretch of the beach?"

Shannon edged closer to Adam, who noticed and took a step toward her as well. The sexual energy coming off the two of them could have powered a small town. "I run this beach every morning I'm in town," Shannon said. "I rent a house down that way. Jordie Cruz's place."

Adam inched ever closer. Their shoulders were almost touching. "Then how is it I have never seen you before? Because I definitely would have noticed an exquisite creature such as yourself."

"I run earlier. I'd usually be in the shower by this point, but Danielle here has been slowing me down."

"Ah." Adam glanced down at Danielle, who was still sitting on the sand, watching the two of them flirt. "I'm sorry she's holding you back, but if I can be selfish, I'm glad she did. We might never have met if it hadn't been for Danielle." He stepped even closer, close enough that their arms grazed each other. "So do you need any help with that shower? Because I'd be happy to oblige if you do."

Shannon started to purr. "That sounds like fun."

Danielle jumped to her feet. "But we have work to do, and we're wasting time." She nudged Shannon in the ribs. "Remember, suits are coming Monday to check our progress. We need to get to it."

"Is she always this big a buzzkill?" Shannon asked Adam.

"Bigger most of the time. If you ever want to join me for my run, or for a shower, my house is that one right there," he said, pointing at his house just up the beach from where they stood. "Mine's a lot nicer than Jordie Cruz's."

"Sounds like a date," Shannon answered.

Danielle grabbed her arm and pulled her away from Adam. "All right, enough of that shit. Let's get back to the house so we can get cleaned up and get on the road." Shannon glanced back over her shoulder and waved at Adam as Danielle yanked her down the beach. "You probably want to stay away from that. He's not too particular about where he parks his car if you know what I mean. Besides, I thought you were a lesbian."

"Oh no, sweetheart," Shannon grinned. "I'm Bi, remember? Actually, I'm into anybody that makes my lady parts vibrate, and he's got me buzzing like a hyperactive bumblebee."

"Ew." Danielle risked a quick look back, and Adam was still standing there, hands on his hips, watching them walk away. "Still, he's bad news. Adam loses interest in women quickly. He's always looking for the next piece of ass to come along," she said as they resumed their walk back to the house.

"That's okay with me. I'm not the settling down kind myself." They walked on for a few steps before Shannon spoke again. "So I take it he's parked in your lot a time or two?"

"Oh God, no. Not for lack of trying on his part. We were actually engaged once a long time ago. He freaked out at the prospect of settling down, started drinking too much, and did something stupid. I've tried to keep my distance since then, but he keeps coming back."

"I'm still not sure how you can be engaged to someone and not have sex with them. How does that even work?"

"Didn't Wiki cover this?" Shannon told her no, and Danielle sighed, amazed that she had to relate the tale for her. "I kind of made a big deal about my being a virgin, and it became this huge thing. So I felt like I had to have a solid commitment before throwing that away. Adam proposed, but he never would give me a date or even a general idea of when we were actually going to get married. So since he wouldn't commit, neither would I. So we never got there."

"You poor thing." Shannon paused. "You're not still a virgin, are you?"

"Is that any of your business?" Shannon started to answer, but Danielle cut her off. "See, that's why I came out and admitted to it back then. The attitude that saving yourself for the right person was a negative thing. I wanted to show girls it was okay to wait, that you didn't have to drop your panties for every swinging dick that walked by just so you wouldn't be considered uncool or something. I thought I would do some good, but I guess those attitudes haven't changed."

"Or is it that people like you place too much emphasis on the concept of virginity and the sanctity of sex, to begin with? Maybe it was your attitude that needed adjusting. Just saying, not trying to offend you or anything."

"I don't know," Danielle said. "Maybe you're right. But no, I'm not still a virgin. I found the right guy."

"The one who died?" Danielle kept walking, and Shannon

dropped the conversation. When her house was back in view, Shannon broke the silence. "You know, just a thought here. If you want Adam to leave you alone, and he loses interest after he has his fun, and if your virginity is already lost, maybe you should just sleep with him. He gets what he wants, you get what you need — because honey, you're in need of a release — and then you can both go about your business."

"You're suggesting that I have sex with someone as a method to drive them away?"

"Could work."

"Not a chance. My relationship with Adam is complicated enough without introducing sex to the picture. He had his shot, and he blew it. I'm not in the habit of giving second chances."

"Okay then," Shannon said as they climbed the steps to the back of the house. "So you're not big on forgiveness. Then you wouldn't mind if I hook up with him sometime, right?"

"If you want Adam, he's all yours."

~*~

Danielle and Shannon strolled into Kingdom Sounds in Santa Monica just a little after nine that morning, Danielle carrying her guitar and amp while Shannon brought a gym bag filled with Danielle's effects, pedals, and other devices. They were met by two men in the control booth — a pony-tailed young man with double chins in a Pokemon T-shirt, and a shorter, older man who was bald save for a ring of wispy gray hairs along the side. The older man rolled his chair over to the two of them when they walked in.

"You must be the hired gun. Redus told me you were coming. Leo Friesz. I'm the producer. The brain surgeon over there is Roy Davis, he's the engineer. And in there," he said with a sweep of his hands, indicating the main room. "Is the latest iteration of the Rikka Olausson band. And you are?"

Danielle froze. Did they know who she was? She had no idea what Steve had told them. She decided to play it safe. "Renae Tucker. Hired gun." She held up the guitar case with both hands. "Have guitar, will travel."

"Well, if you can figure out what those yahoos at the label are going for, we'll all be happy to have you here. We've been busting our butts for months, and nothing makes those weasels happy." He rubbed his bald head. "I looked like Roy over there when we started this project."

Danielle laughed. She liked him so far. "I've got some ideas. Do you mind if I step in the studio and introduce myself?"

"Have at it, Renae."

Shannon tapped her on the shoulder. "I'm going to go to the bathroom to freshen up while you handle all the introductions. I'll be back in ten minutes," she said as she laid Danielle's gym bag down.

"Have at it."

Danielle excused herself and entered the studio. Shannon's band was bigger than Danielle was used to. There was a drummer in the back center of the room in a small Plexiglas encasement, three backup singers and a bass player to the right, a percussionist, and a keyboardist to the left, and front and center was another guitar player. He was a good looking guy, lean but muscular, with a three day beard and a gold top Les Paul slung around his neck. He stood and approached Danielle as she entered the room.

"The mystery guest." He extended his hand. "I'm Derek. I'm the leader of this band of reprobates. I understand you're our savior."

"Renae Tucker," she said, taking his hand. "Y'all seem so happy to be here."

Derek retreated to his stool, sat, and began fingering the strings on his Les Paul. "Working with Rikka is like…." He rolled his eyes skyward, thinking deeply, nodded, and looked back at her. "Like being balls deep in a snowman. It's cold, uncomfortable, and if it doesn't stop soon, your dick is going to fall off."

Danielle tried and largely failed to suppress a laugh. "Let's see if I can do something about that." She sat her equipment down. "Just give me a minute to set everything up here." She didn't say that Derek was in her usual spot, though she wanted to. She was just going to have to deal with it. "The faster we get started, the faster we can all get out of here, and you can take your dick out of that snowman. What do you say?"

This time it was Derek who failed to suppress a laugh.

Ten minutes later, they had sufficiently rearranged the room, and Danielle began drilling the band on the new direction for the song "Tamarind." When they had it down, she instructed Leo and Roy to start recording. They were wrapping up a third take when Shannon finally strode in wearing a curve hugging black dress with gold sequins that she had somehow smuggled in without Danielle noticing.

"The peacock is here," Derek murmured.

Danielle removed the guitar from around her neck and left the studio for the control booth, where Leo was apprising Shannon of what had gone on in her absence. She pivoted when Danielle entered the room. "You started without me," she said in a fake pout.

Shannon may have been playing, but Danielle was deadly serious. "Your ten minutes was more like an hour. Why the hell did you change clothes?"

"I have to get in the right mindset. I can't just roll in here wearing jeans and a T-shirt and perform. I need to become Rikka Olausson."

"I thought you decided to drop that nonsense."

"I have," Shannon said defensively. "But this is how I work. I have a process that I go through. Don't tell me you don't. I never met a musician that didn't have some sort of ritual."

Danielle decided not to press it. "Okay. So we're doing 'Tamarind' just like we did it back in Austin. We got a pretty good take with the band. Roy, can you que that up?" Roy acknowledged and went to work. "We just need to get you in the booth to lay some vocals." Roy let her know the song was ready, and she instructed him to play it. "Now, I'm singing as a guide, but we'll bury that in the mix, so don't worry about it."

"Actually," Leo said from his seat at the mixing board. "I think it would sound good if we layered you underneath Rikka. The girls do a good job, but they're all the same basic range. The contrast in your voices could be great."

Danielle had already thought that but feared that suggesting it would be a step too far. Leo seemed to be on the same page, which was a good sign. She looked from Shannon to Leo and back. "It's your album, so I'll leave that up to you. Let's just get a couple of takes, and we'll go from there."

"All right," Shannon answered. She dropped her fancy pretense and began concentrating on the song as it played back, mouthing the words. When it was over, she started for the booth. "Let's do this."

~*~

Danielle was a taskmaster, keeping the band and Shannon

working steadily into the night. It was only when everyone started to drag that she decided to call a stop to the day's work. As everyone stood up, Danielle leaned over to whisper in Leo's ear. "Do we have exclusive use of the studio?"

Leo kept his eyes on his work but responded. "Yeah, for the next three weeks. Why?"

"Just wondering." Shannon had excused herself to the bathroom, so Danielle slipped into the studio and sidled up next to Derek while he packed up his gear for the night. "How would y'all feel about doing a little side work? Just with me, no Rikka. I'll make it worth your while."

Derek eyed her suspiciously. "How worth our while?"

"Whatever she's paying you, I'll double it. But keep it quiet. It'll be after hours. Probably just a couple of hours a night. Talk to your guys and let me know tomorrow. If they agree, I'd like to start next week." Derek said that he would, and she left it at that, put away her own instrument, and started for the parking lot. Shannon caught her on the way out the door.

"So, what do you want to do with the rest of the night, bestie?"

"I figured we'd grab some takeout on the way home and stay in for the night. Especially if you're going to insist on getting up at the crack of dawn again."

"That's fine," Shannon said with a sly smile. She produced her phone out of midair. "A nice night at home sounds like fun. Let's get to it."

Danielle had the impression she was up to something, but it had been a long day, and all she wanted was a warm meal and a soft bed. If Shannon wanted to slip off, that was up to her.

They got in the car and headed back to the house. It had been a productive day, and she felt confident that things were trending in the right direction. She would dare Rico to disagree with her.

Chapter Seventeen

"I thought that went fairly well today," Danielle said as she munched on a club sandwich. They were sitting in the kitchen, where she and Shannon ate sandwiches and chips off paper plates. "I was expecting more resistance from your band, but everybody seemed to be on board."

"That's not my regular band or even my touring band. Steve threw that collection together." Shannon sat casually in a chair with one leg pulled close to her chest. She was nibbling on a stray piece of avocado that had escaped from her sandwich. "Better be nice to them. Some of those guys may be in your band next."

"Not a chance. Those guys can't hang with me. Besides, I'll put my own group together when I get a chance. I won't just play with whatever mercenaries Steve can cobble together. I have to have a real band behind me. It's going to be hard."

Shannon peered out the sliding glass door that led to the beach. "Do you really think we can pull this off? I'm afraid that when Rico comes Monday, he's going to hate it."

Danielle pushed her meal aside. "Are you happy with what

we're doing?"

Shannon slowly brought her gaze back into the room. "Yes. I think what you've done is amazing. When you put everything together on 'Tamarind' today, I almost cried. I never thought I could do a song like that."

"Then that's all that matters. Rico Cardenas can go suck a garden hose for all I care. At the end of the day, you are the only one who needs to be pleased. People like Rico, they don't know what it's like to create something, to put your soul into something. All they care about are spreadsheets and profit margins. You can't base your personal fulfillment on what The Suits say."

"I hope you're right. I get what you're saying, but The Suits can decide if my career goes on or not. If Rico doesn't like what he hears, he could just pull the plug on me."

Danielle shrugged. "He could. I think that's a decision a lot of musicians have to make eventually. Do I stick to my guns, or do I chase the gold ring? Very few are the acts that can do both. I think you have to be prepared to walk away from it." Danielle saw Shannon's eyes get wide. "Truth is, a lot of musicians either wind up in regular jobs or still plugging away in the little clubs and small labels for whatever they can get. It's a possibility you have to consider."

Shannon wrung her hands and then shot up out of her chair and walked to the patio doors. "I don't have a clue what else I would do. I never knew what I wanted to do. I just figured I would fall into something."

"With your looks, you could model in a heartbeat. I'm kinda surprised no one's brought that up to you before."

Shannon turned and fixed Danielle with a warm smile. "You think? That could be interesting." Her phone vibrated on the table, and Shannon rushed to get it. It didn't take a detective to see that the text she received wasn't good news. Danielle eyed her as she quickly typed a message and sent it. "I think I'm going to go to bed," Shannon said as she gathered up the remains of her dinner and threw them away. "It's been a long day."

"Gonna be another long one tomorrow," Danielle agreed. She was watching Shannon's reaction, but there wasn't much to watch.

Shannon slumped her shoulders on the way by. "I know. See you in the morning, boss."

Danielle picked at her meal a little longer as she wondered about Shannon's mystery text. She hadn't said anything about having a significant other or any plans, but there was definitely something wrong. She debated going to Shannon's room and asking her to talk, but being a shoulder to cry on was not Danielle's role. She'd never been particularly good at it.

She passed, deciding instead to work on some of her own songs until she was too tired to go on. She shuffled off to bed, no longer thinking about Shannon at all, but about how she was going to produce her own album.

The incessant buzzing of an alarm clock woke her the next morning. Confused, Danielle rubbed the sleep out of her eyes as she searched for the clock. She knew she hadn't set an alarm, instead depending on Shannon to get her up for another morning jog. She finally spotted the clock on the dresser across the room, and it had definitely not been there the night before.

Danielle killed the alarm and made her way across the hall. Shannon's room was empty, her bed carefully made. Still too tired to make too much of it, Danielle stumbled down the hall into the living area, which was also deserted, as was the kitchen.

She did find a handwritten note taped to the refrigerator door.

Something came up, and I had to leave early. Go on to the studio, and I'll be there as soon as I can. – Shannon.

"Great," Danielle muttered.

Instantly, Ryan's warnings of Shannon's questionable work ethic started bouncing around her head. As she rooted around in the fridge for something to eat, she began to worry that the pressure was too much. She felt a trickle of disappointment in that thought because she liked the work they had done so far. On the other hand, if Shannon did bail, it opened up more time for Danielle to focus on her own music. With strong doubts as to whether or not Shannon would show up, Danielle dressed and headed out for the studio.

Leo was pacing the control room and rubbing his bald head when Danielle got there, carrying a Burger King bag and a Coke with her. "Oh, thank God," Leo said when he saw her. "You're here. We've been waiting."

Danielle checked the clock on the studio wall. "It's ten after. I'm not that late. There was a line at the drive-through."

"Shannon texted us all and told us to be here at eight. We've been sitting and twiddling our thumbs for an hour. What was that all about?"

Danielle sat her lunch on a table at the back of the room. "That's a really good question. I haven't seen her today. She was gone when I woke up." She noticed Leo and Roy give each other knowing glances, and knew exactly what they were thinking, not that it mattered. She took out her cell and quickly called Steve, who assured her that he had not heard from Shannon either, but not to worry because she frequently got distracted and showed up late. He wanted to talk more about the next day's big meeting, but Danielle put him off and hung up.

"Steve says not to worry; she does this sometimes. So I guess we go on."

"What do we do without our star?" Roy asked.

"Well, I've got some songs we can work on. I wouldn't mind a little help bringing them to life if everyone is agreeable." Leo and Roy were all for it, and after a quick show of hands, the band also bought in. "All right, give me a minute to eat, and let's do this thing."

All thoughts of Shannon evaporated as the group began working on Danielle's music instead. Her assertion from the night before that they couldn't hang with her was valid, but the band did the best they could. The first song they did was one Danielle had started writing back in Wichita, a bluesy ballad called "Already Fallen" that was inspired by Adam's movie. It took most of the morning, but they were able to produce a demo that Danielle was happy with.

She dismissed everyone for a long lunch and started working her phone again. Shannon still wasn't answering, and Steve was already on a plane to Los Angeles and out of pocket. She started to worry. She knew nothing of Shannon's life in L.A., none of her friends or hangouts. If something had happened to her, Danielle had no way of helping.

So she stuck to the only thing she could do, working on the album. As she waited for everyone to return from lunch, Danielle began going over another one of Shannon's earlier demos called "Heaven." The song was a sappy ballad about a woman who died young and now waited for her lover to join her in the afterlife. The production on the original version was as sappy as the words were maudlin, but the song inspired her.

By the time everyone was back and ready to record, the song had been changed to "Walking Through Heaven," and now told the story of a woman who found herself in Heaven knowing she shouldn't be, desperately searching for her love before she got kicked out. But when she finally found him, he couldn't hear her because it was not her time yet, and she was banished back to the world of the living.

Derek, the guitar player, whistled after reading the rewritten lyrics. "This is pretty deep stuff."

"It's personal," was all Danielle said in response. They set about recording the demo and spent the better part of the afternoon doing so. The entire time Danielle had to keep reminding herself that this was going to be Shannon's song and adjusting to meet her higher vocal range.

They finished up with some minor tweaks to the songs they had done the day before, and then Danielle sent everyone home. The Suits would be there in the morning, and she wanted everyone, including herself, to be as well rested as possible.

Back at the beach house, Shannon was still nowhere to be found. It was coming up on twenty-four hours and still no sign of her. Danielle's legs went weak with the sudden fear that something terrible had happened to her. Immediately she snatched her cellphone out of her pocket. Steve answered on the first ring.

"Tell me that Shannon has called you today."

"No," Steve muttered. "Why should she?"

"Shit." Danielle turned in circles, trying to will her presence into existence. "I still haven't heard from her. I'm afraid something has happened. Do you know any of her friends, or where she hangs out? Anything?"

"I really don't. We don't have that kind of relationship. You know, I'm sure she's fine. She probably found herself a guy or a girl, and just doesn't want to pull herself away. She does that. I'm sure she'll show up tomorrow, looking like she just stepped off the pages of a magazine. Don't worry about it."

"I am going to worry about it. You know what can happen to a girl, especially if she likes hooking up with strange people. She's gotta be somewhere. You gotta know something."

"I don't. I'm sorry. You've spent more time with her out here than I have."

Danielle sighed. "Yeah. Okay. I can try the couple of places she took me to. Maybe I'll stumble across her."

She hung up and headed back to the car and raced to the restaurant they'd had dinner in the first night. Carefully picking her way through the late shift diners, Danielle struck out on her search there. Next, Shannon's personal stylist was none too pleased to be awoken by Danielle's banging on her door. Again no luck. The shops they had visited were all closed, and Danielle was out of ideas.

~*~

Steve and Rico were already at the studio when Danielle got there the next morning. As soon as she parked the car, she jumped out and rushed up to Steve. Rico, a short and skinny Hispanic man with round-rimmed glasses, watched her from a distance as she approached, his hands tucked into the pants pockets of his navy blue suit.

"Where's Shannon?" Steve asked before Danielle could even speak.

"I was hoping you could tell me that," Danielle answered. "I went to the few places I could think of last night and nothing.

Steve, something has happened to her." Danielle was aware that she was talking fast and probably sounded panicked. "She could be at the bottom of a canyon for all I know."

Steve listened intently. "Let me make some calls," he said, his voice soft but earnest. "I'm sure she's fine, but we do need to find her. She needs to be here. This is her moment. The fact that she's not here sends a bad message."

"I'm not worried about what kind of message it sends." Danielle felt herself start shaking. "Steve, if something happened to her…. I should have kept an eye on her. I was focused on coming up here and working on my own thing."

Steve had already fished his phone out of his pocket. He froze. "You've been recording on your own?"

"Just some simple demos with Shannon's band. Doodles, really."

"You know I've got people for you to meet. I told you about this. Now's not the time for you to be going rogue and doing your own thing."

"I don't care about that," Danielle snapped. "We need to find Shannon. Make your calls."

"You're right. Take Rico inside and let him start listening to the tracks. You know how these meetings go. Just tell him she got hung up, and she's on her way. I'll see what I can find out." Danielle nodded and started off, but Steve stopped her. "Gather yourself. Don't let him see you nervous. Everything is fine. She does this."

Danielle agreed and went on to greet Rico, who did not hold out his hand when she reached him.

"Danielle Regan, nice of you to finally come out of hiding."

"Rico. Nice suit." She made an exaggerated motion of looking around on the ground. Confused, Rico asked her what she was doing. "Well, that suit looks new, so I was wondering where your old skin was. Isn't that what snakes do, shed their skin for a new one?"

"Cocky for a girl staring down the barrel of a lawsuit."

"You don't scare me. You may be sitting in the catbird seat now, but you're still the whiny little Yes Man I met a long time ago. You'll get your albums, but you'll get them on my terms. You will never get the best of me. Never." Then she smiled brightly at him. "For now, let's go inside and give Shannon's album a listen, though. That is why you're here today, isn't it?"

"Where is the lady of the hour? I would think this would be an important enough day that she could see her way to being here."

"Shannon got hung up, but she'll be here just as soon as she can. Circumstances beyond her control." She held her arm out toward the front doors. "Why don't we go inside and start listening? I'm sure she'll be here before we get through."

Rico grumbled skeptically but followed Danielle's lead. Just before she ducked inside, she saw Steve still pacing in the parking lot, working his phone. Not a good sign.

In the control booth, Leo and Roy sat casually in rolling office chairs, making some last minute adjustments on the mixing board. The band had the morning off and was on a holding pattern until they knew what the label wanted to do. Danielle took the time to introduce Leo and Roy to Rico, who shrugged instead of offering handshakes.

Once the pleasantries were out of the way, Rice settled onto a couch in the corner. Danielle took that as her cue. "Leo, whenever you're ready, let it rip."

They had managed to record four strong demos during the course of their two days, and Rico sat quietly and patiently while they played. He made no notes, showed no reactions. Halfway through, Steve finally joined them. She caught his eye, and he responded with a subtle head shake. Danielle backed into a corner and started gnawing at her thumbnail as she tried not to think about her wayward partner.

As the last of the songs faded out, Rico stood, put his hands back in his pockets, and said, "Meh. It's all right."

"All right?" Danielle said. "Just all right? That's it?"

"That's it. Honestly, I was expecting more. Maybe you've been out of the game too long now. What I just heard doesn't excite me." He turned to Steve. "I still don't hear crossover potential. I'm going to ask, one more time, to give me more of what she does best. If she doesn't want to play ball, and it doesn't look like she does judging solely on the basis that she couldn't even bother to show up today, we'll cut her loose. World Music hits, even Number Ones, don't make money."

Steve's face went ashen, and his jaw went slack. Danielle had never seen him look so thoroughly shocked and defeated. Rico wasn't done yet.

"As for you," he said to Danielle. "If you wanted to beat me, you just did. If that's the best you've got after six years, you're useless to me. You could give me a dozen albums of that bullshit, and I couldn't sell it. You're a Has Been. It'd cost us more than it would be worth to even try and sell that."

"But Rico," Steve stammered. "What about the label? You told me—"

"I know what I told you. That's my problem, not yours. There are things we can do. Avenues. One thing is for sure, this partnership is over."

Danielle stood in her corner with emotions swirling inside her. She wanted to lash out and defend her work, yet the thought of being released brought with it a certain comfort. She could truly be free and take full control of her career and her life. She stood, indecisive, as Rico reached for the door.

"Hang on," Leo called out. "Wait, just a second." Rico turned, and Leo wheeled his chair over to him. "Let me play you something. A different mix that Roy and I have been working on. Give me one song, and if you don't think its better, then I guess we're done."

Rico smirked but agreed, and Leo wheeled back to the mixing board. He and Roy quickly reset their board. "I think you're going to like this." Soon the strains of "Tamarind" started up again; only this time, Danielle's contributions were front and center. They had layered her voice with Shannon's, making it sound like they were singing harmony, and brought her guitar playing up in the mix.

As Danielle watched, Rico's demeanor changed. "Is there more of this?"

"Yeah," Roy said as he concentrated on the board. "We did every song." They played another, again, with a radically different mix than what Danielle had come up with. She and Steve exchanged worried glances as Rico seemed to get more excited.

Rico stood at the board, peering over their shoulder as the songs played. Danielle noticed a small yellow legal pad sitting on the edge of the board. Rico was giving it a good once over. As the current song ended, he pointed to a line on the legal pad. "What's this 'Already Fallen' about? Can I hear this?"

"Sure," Leo said.

Danielle intervened. "No. That's my song, not Shannon's. I was working on that in our downtime. I'm not finished with it. We don't even have a band for me yet."

Rico grinned at her, and Danielle saw the devil in his eyes. "Play it," Rico repeated. Leo obliged, and moments later, her song came on the loudspeaker. "Ah, there it is. You've been sandbagging me. This is what I've been looking for. This is our lead single, right here."

"I'm glad to hear that," she started. "But like I said, I'm not finished with it. We're here for Shannon's album."

Rico shook his head. "No. There is no Shannon's album. She alone doesn't have what it takes. From this point on, it's a Shannon *and* Danielle album."

Steve, who had been sitting out the conversation, finally pushed away from the wall and spoke up. "Rico, I share your vision here. However, I don't think you can lead with 'Already Fallen.' If it's a Shannon and Danielle record, then the lead single needs to feature both. So I say we start with 'Tamarind' and then follow it up with 'Fallen.' Gives you two strong singles right out of the gate."

"What?" Danielle was incredulous. "You can't possibly be condoning this. He's hijacking the whole project."

Rico was having none of it. "Steve's a smart man. He knows when to fight, but he also knows to shut up when a gift horse shows up at his doorstep." He turned the other way and spoke to Leo. "Play the rest of it. Let's see what other nuggets of greatness are on there."

"Steve," Danielle pleaded.

Steve cast one worried glance her way, then leaned in toward

Rico, and they began to whisper between them. She pushed away from the wall and stormed across the tiny control room, shoving the two men in different directions when she got there. Steve and Rico both stumbled over their own feet but managed to stay upright. She turned on Steve and wagged a finger in his face.

"Don't you stand there and act like I'm not here. Don't you do that shit to me. This is wrong on so many levels, and you know it. Don't you turn your back on me now."

Steve put his hands up in a defensive posture. "Danielle, I know it doesn't seem like it right now, but this is a smart move. Just let me—"

"No. It's a chickenshit move. It's stealing Shannon's album. It's taking songs I'm not even done with. It's wrong, and you know it's wrong. I won't do this."

She saw something flash in Steve's eyes, and his defensive stance evaporated. He stood straight and tall and squared up to her. "Danielle, shut up. This is a good deal, a great deal, for everyone involved. Now, I have never steered you wrong before, and I'm not now. I will make Shannon see the beauty of this. You leave that to me. I need you to shut up and let me do what I do."

"I won't—"

"You know what I won't do? I won't let you ruin everything for me, for my employees, for all the people who need this to happen. I won't worry that the next time you have a meltdown, you won't come back at all. I won't worry about financial ruin any longer, and I won't go back to living out of Motel 6s and scratching and clawing to survive. If you can't see that, and if you're not willing to bend, just a little, to help out everyone else, then we don't need to do business anymore. If you can't do this for me, *I* don't want to do business with you." Danielle stood stunned, her mouth open, but no words came out. She backtracked, wondering what to do next. In all of their years, Steve had never spoken to her like that. She knew he was right, but in her heart, it still felt wrong, and she still wanted to fight. "Was this your plan all along? Is this what you were hoping for when you put us together?"

Steve didn't need to answer—the look on his face said it all. He turned away from her, and Rico jumped into the void. Deliberately straightening his tie first, Rico spoke slowly. "What was that you were saying to me earlier about I'd never get the best of you? Guess you were wrong."

"Ah, shit," Steve groaned.

Danielle's doubt faded as the rage reignited. "You know what, Rico? You take those songs, you take this album, and you shove them straight up your ass. If this is the way you guys want to play it, fine. You got me. I hope you're happy." She turned away from him and marched up to Steve. "I was going to stay and try to go back to the way things were, but if this is what you've turned into, then you're right. We are done. So you find Shannon, if she's not dead in a ditch somewhere, if you even still care about her, and you explain this. You tell her how you sold us both out. I'm done. And this time I won't come back."

She wheeled back around to Rico. "I hope you enjoy this because I can tell you, that second album you thought you were going to get ain't gonna happen. You wanna sue me, fine. I'll see you in court, and I'll fight you to my last dime. I'm done with both of you."

She paused just long enough to shoot Leo a Go to Hell look that would have sent a lesser man cowering, turned, then pushed past Steve and out into the brilliant sunshine of the day. Her car sat waiting. The open road was just a short drive away.

"Danielle, wait," Steve called from behind her. "Just wait." She turned sharply and planted her hands on her hips. "Danielle, please. If you will just take a minute and think about this. Calm down. I know Rico's being an ass, but if you just stop for a minute, you'll see how this is a good deal for everybody. I'll sell it to Shannon."

"Maybe it is a good deal, Steve, but it's the principle. You just unilaterally make this decision, without Shannon, without me. Maybe Rico's got you licking his boots, but not me. Not now, not ever." She paused, and they looked each other in the eye. "You've changed. You never would have done something like this before."

"Maybe I have," Steve said solemnly. "Unfortunately, you haven't. You're still the same selfish, stubborn, reactionary pain in the ass you always were. You always want things your way. You never want to give, never want to compromise, and you can never see past your own wants." He waved his hand at her car. "You want to go? Go. When Rico sues you for breach of contract, I'll join him, to protect myself. You should understand. Looking out for number one is all you've ever done."

Steve walked away. Danielle stared after him for a second, then with a growl, turned and stomped off to her car. In a minute, she was back on the street. A few minutes after that, she was racing up the PCH toward Shannon's beach house. Her heart ached, and tears threatened to break free from her eyes. Only Danielle's steel trap resolve allowed her to keep things together, to be able to see through the tears to negotiate the mid-morning traffic.

She jerked the car into Shannon's circular drive and slammed on the brakes, the Challenger fishtailing as white tire smoke filled the air. She didn't even bother to turn off the engine. What she needed to do wouldn't take long.

As she ran into the house, Danielle berated herself for ever believing she could go back home. All the things she feared were true. The life she had lived was gone forever, and it was far too late to get it back.

She stomped through the house to her room, threw her clothes in her duffle bag, and tossed the two guitar cases on the bed. What to do with them? Take them with her? Leave them? As she stood and debated, the wind carried the sound of breaking waves in through the still open front door, and she knew. Leaving the duffle bag behind, she picked up a guitar case in each hand and started for the beach. A funeral at sea, the perfect way to say goodbye to Danielle Regan once and for all.

CHAPTER EIGHTEEN

Danielle struggled on her way down to the beach, trying to walk too fast for the conditions. She was aware of everyone around her, and that most of them were staring at the strange girl carting the guitar cases down to the water. There were sounds all around — people talking, seagulls, waves — all blending into a chaotic symphony, the schizophrenic soundtrack to her final act.

Her jade eyes were locked on the water, though. The finish line. She gripped the handles of the guitar cases harder, squeezing so hard she thought they might break in her hands. Someone close by was yelling, but Danielle blocked it out. Let people think what they wanted. In a few more seconds, it wasn't going to matter anyway.

She reached the water's edge and thought about tossing the instruments in from there, but that wouldn't be enough. She wanted them gone forever. Danielle started to wade out into the water, her shoes and socks and jeans instantly getting drenched. Maybe she would just keep walking. The thought came to her like lightning. She could just carry her burden out until the water swallowed her up too. Then she would truly be done with it all.

Danielle didn't even have time to shake the thought out of her head before strong hands were clamping down on her arms and twisting her around.

"What the fuck are you doing?" Adam was behind her, shirtless, sunglasses pushed up on his head. "What are you doing?" He wrestled the cases out of her hands. "What is going on here?"

"Just trying to fix a mistake," she snarled. "I never should have come back. I knew better. Now give me those so I can end this."

Adam pulled the cases back and stepped away. "I don't think so. You're freaking out, Dani. You need to calm down. Let's go inside, and you can tell me what's going on."

"Seriously, Danielle. What the hell?"

Danielle looked over Adam's shoulder, and there stood Shannon in a tiny purple bikini, the water gently licking her polished toenails, looking like the golden goddess she was.

Danielle's eyes got wide with shock. "You." Danielle shoved Adam, who barely managed to keep his balance and keep the guitars out of the water. She saw the fear on Shannon's face as she got closer, stomping through the waves. Shannon was backing up, but not fast enough. Danielle slammed both palms into her shoulders, and Shannon went down hard.

"Where the fuck were you?" Shannon looked up at her with terror etched in her eyes. "You were supposed to be there. I thought you were dead in a fucking ditch somewhere. You were with him? You blew off the biggest day of your career for Adam? How unprofessional can you fucking be?"

Adam stepped between them, allowing Shannon a chance

to crab walk away from the seething Danielle until she got back to her feet. "Ladies, let's take this inside, huh? We're drawing a crowd."

"Go fuck your crowd, Adam," Danielle snarled. "And fuck you while you're at it. I should have known that if something could go wrong, you'd wind up in the middle of it somehow."

Shannon, scared and confused, shouted at Danielle. "I thought you'd take care of it. You know how to handle these guys, I don't. I trusted you to take care of it. Why are you freaking out at me?"

"Why? How stupid are you? Do I really have to explain why?"

"Ladies, please, let's take it inside," Adam insisted. He started nudging Danielle with one of the cases, trying to guide her back to the house. "We can sort it all out there. Come on."

Danielle took two more angry steps toward Shannon, who backed up accordingly. "You've got explaining to do." She started off, stopped, and turned to Adam. "Throw those things in the water and quit lugging them around."

"I don't think so. Just go inside and let's figure this out."

Danielle begrudgingly went in and made her way immediately to the bedroom so she could take off her wet clothes. She heard Shannon and Adam talking quietly, but didn't try to listen in on their conversation. She came out of the bedroom to find the two of them lounging on the big sectional couch in the living room, looking at her quizzically.

Adam popped up when she entered the room. Danielle noticed the twin guitar cases leaning against the wall near him. "There's no way I'm tossing those," he said with an earnestness that was out of character for him. "I know how quick you are to fly off the handle, Dani, but this is ridiculous."

"You don't know your dick from a bean sprout, so shut the fuck up."

Adam could find no smarmy come back for that and sat down, looking confused.

Shannon was watching them with eyes wide open. "I don't think I understand the dynamic between you two."

"Neither do I, honey," Danielle answered quickly. "Just know that wherever Adam Quisenberry goes, trouble is sure to follow." She approached Shannon, who tried to push herself into the couch. "Quit that," Danielle said. "I was worried about you. You were gone for two days."

Adam recovered from her barb enough to chime in. "Yeah, because two days is totally worse than six years, am I right?"

Shannon looked over at Adam. "What does that mean?"

"Nothing," Danielle snapped.

Adam laughed. "Saint Danielle here just got up one day, changed her name, and walked out of everyone's life. No letters or phone calls. Didn't say goodbye to her band, her friends, or her surrogate parents. Just left."

"And you're mad at me for two days? You don't even like me."

Danielle threw her head back in frustration. She was getting tired of everyone teaming up against her. "I don't not like you, Shannon. You're frustrating. You're extremely unprofessional. Unreliable. You come on too strong. You emit sexual energy like a...like...I don't even know what."

Shannon licked her lips and winked up at her. "You feel sexual energy between us?"

Danielle growled and grabbed at her hair. "Like that. Stop that."

Adam tapped Shannon on the shoulder. "Our girl here gets all kinds of nervous when you bring up s-e-x. It gives her the willies."

"Why are you still here? Get the fuck out." Danielle turned her attention back to Shannon. "Could you two stop thinking about sex for ten seconds? While you were banging each other's brains out, Rico was busy hijacking your album."

Shannon cast a worried glance at Adam, then looked back at Danielle. "What do you mean by that?"

"Exactly what it sounds like," Danielle said, incredulous. "Rico hated the mixes that I did for you. He said you didn't have what it takes to be a star and called me a Has Been. Then that little bald asshole Leo played his own mixes with me singing harmony with you, and Rico flipped for it. Now it's not your album anymore, it's *our* album. They're going to release a song that I wrote, a song you didn't even sing on, as a second single. And Steve just stood by and let it happen—agreed to it, no less."

Shannon hunched over with her hands between her knees and intertwined her fingers as she made a humming sound in her throat. Adam and Danielle shot each other a questioning glance as Shannon seemed to meditate on the whole situation. After a minute of introspection, Shannon looked up into Danielle's face. "Okay. If that's what they feel they need to do, I'll go with it."

"What? After all the work you've done, you're just going to let them take it from you?"

Shannon sighed and stood, meandering her way over to the patio door to look out over the ocean. "I've worked at this for two years now," she said, her voice sounding dreamy. "I've worked with three producers, two bands, and now you." Shannon turned slowly, sadly. "Nothing's been good enough for him, for them. If this is what it takes, then I'll go with it. I just want to taste the big time, Danielle. Just once. If I have to ride your coattails to do it, then I'm game. It's not optimal, but it's the way things are."

"It's not optimal? That's all you have to say?" Danielle crossed the room to stand beside Shannon. "Two years of putting your heart and soul into something, and all you can say is 'it's not optimal'?"

Shannon threw her hands up in the air. "What are my choices?"

Danielle took Shannon by the hands. "Fight. Stand up for what you believe in, for what you've worked so hard for. Don't let them push you around."

Shannon pulled her hands back and proceeded to brush Danielle's bangs away from her face. "What's the point if it's a losing battle? It may not be exactly the way I wanted it, but something's better than nothing. I don't see the point in making a big deal about it if there's nothing I can do to change it anyway. It could be worse."

"How could it be worse?"

"I could have nothing at all," she said sweetly. "Besides, you and I make a great team. Why not see how far we can ride that?"

Adam came up behind Danielle and began to rub her shoulders. "Shannon's right. We all have to make compromises sometimes—even the great Danielle Regan doesn't get what she wants all the time. I've had to do it. A script gets changed, a director gets fired, a new costar gets cast. I don't like it, but it is what it is, man." He turned Danielle around. "Are you honestly going to tell me that it would be better to never play again than have to share an album with Shannon?"

"It's not about sharing an album with Shannon. That's not

what this is about at all. It's about how they just took it. They just made this decision and didn't even want to listen to me. They're just going to cram it down our throats. It's not right."

"No, it's not, but The Suits always win in the end."

"Not with me, they don't. I've never lost to them before. I don't like it."

Shannon wrapped her arm around Danielle's waist and laid her head on Danielle's back. "Don't look at it as a loss. We can still take control of the situation. If this is what they want, let's give it to them. Let's go back to the studio and fully embrace it, and do the best album we can together. Let's blow their socks off. "

Adam stepped away and studied the two of them, Danielle still wrapped up in Shannon's arms. "You know, so many nights, I imagined something just like this."

"Oh!" Danielle tore away from Shannon and punched Adam hard in the arm. "You jackass. We're having a moment here, and you go and Adam all over it."

Shannon laughed. "He 'Adamed' all over it?"

"Yes," Danielle said firmly. "Adaming is when you take something so good or pure or beautiful and fuck it up with your stupid mouth. I'm pretty sure it's in the dictionary. You can look it up."

Adam rolled his eyes while Shannon giggled. "Well, the Adaming he gave me last night was a beautiful thing, and I had no problem with his stupid mouth." Shannon gloated. "Completely worth missing today's hysterics."

"I don't want to know," Danielle said with disgust. She spun to look at Adam. "So you corrupted another one. Congrats."

"I think she corrupted me," he answered. "The lady knows

things, special things, that only a few have mastered."

"I don't want to know," Danielle repeated more strongly. She walked away from them both. "So, what am I doing?" She asked Shannon while staring at the phone. "Am I quitting, or are we going to do this?"

Shannon crossed the room slowly and spun Danielle around. "Let's go own this bitch and show Rico and Steve and everybody else how badass we both are. We'll give them all something they've never heard before."

"That sounds like a great idea," said Adam. "I say we take the day, and everybody chills out, and then you guys can get back to work in the morning. I'll take you girls out for a day on the town. What do you say?"

Danielle slipped away from Shannon and ambled deeper into the room. "I don't know. This still feels wrong." She wouldn't look either Adam or Shannon in the eye for fear that they would see the other thought that was running through her mind. She instead kept her eyes glued to the floor.

"Well, it's my album," Shannon cooed from behind her. "And I want to do this. So if you're my producer...."

Danielle's head shot up, and she glared over her shoulder at Shannon. "Don't even try to give me an order." Shannon just responded with a smile. The house phone began ringing as Danielle stared across the room at Shannon. "You're annoying. Do you know that?"

"Whatever it takes to get what I want. Come on, let's do this. We can have fun with it."

The house phone continued ringing, driving Danielle nuts. She turned to Adam. "Do you think you could get that, or are you too Hollywood to answer a phone?" He shot her a nasty look but hustled to the phone while Danielle returned her attention to Shannon. "Is this really what you want? Forget everything else — Steve and Rico and the label — and just tell me what's in your heart. Are you really okay with this? Because if we do this, I'm not going to let you guilt trip me over it later. Or make me out to be the bad guy."

Shannon paused, and Adam filled the void, holding one hand over the mouthpiece of the phone. "You better decide something because Steve's on the line. He wants to talk to one of you."

Danielle shook her head at Shannon. "If I talk to him right now, things are going to get nasty in a hurry."

"He's probably pretty mad at me though, blowing off the meeting and everything. It would be better if you did it. Besides, we're all waiting on you."

Reluctantly, Danielle made her way back into the kitchen and plucked the handset from Adam's grasp. Before answering, she closed her eyes and took a deep breath. "Yes, Steve?"

"So, it sounds like our wayward star has been located."

"Yep."

Steve paused, but Danielle was in no mood to give anything away. "I imagine that wasn't a pleasant conversation." Danielle remained silent. After several more awkward seconds, Steve continued. "Did you discuss the new direction with Shannon? Is everybody on board? I need to know what to tell everybody."

"She's aware," Danielle said, careful to keep her voice as monotone as possible.

"So what did you two decide? I can't keep people in a holding pattern forever. I need something out of you, Danielle."

Danielle looked over her shoulder at Shannon, who was creeping towards her, clasping her hands in front of her. Danielle could read the hope all over her face. Danielle was ready to answer when Steve spoke first.

"I'll tell you this if it helps you make a decision. Rico and I had a conversation after you left. If you say no to this, he's going to cut you loose from your contract. No lawsuits, just a mutual parting of the ways. You can go back to doing whatever it was you were doing. One thing, though—if you choose to do that, our relationship is over as well. I just can't continue to have you hanging over my head."

"Oh really?" She pivoted away from Shannon and lowered her voice. "And if I take this out that you're offering me, I could still pursue my career?"

She heard the air go out of Steve's balloon. "Yes. But you'll be starting completely over. No record deal, no management. You'll be back to square one."

Danielle's eyes shifted to Adam, who had edged closer to her. "That's okay. I've got somebody here with me that could probably hook me up with new representation very easily." Adam wasn't a good enough actor to cover up his shock.

"Is that it then? Is that your decision?"

Danielle glanced back at Adam, then turned to look one last time at Shannon. The two of them were mouthing words back and forth. "If I bail, what happens to Shannon?"

"She's gone. She's not worth the time or the money at this point."

"I see." Adam had hustled to Shannon's side, and Danielle registered the defeat creeping across Shannon's face. Despite her flippant attitude, somewhere deep inside, Shannon did want this, and that was really what Danielle wanted to see. "Well, Steve, we talked it over, and Shannon's agreeable to the new direction, so we're going to do it."

Steve breathed a sigh of relief as Shannon leapt into Adam's arms in celebration. Seeing the joy on Shannon's face, Danielle knew that she was doing the right thing, but all wasn't forgiven.

"One thing, though. You told me that Rico wants two new albums out of me. This is one. If I have time, I'll probably record enough songs for two albums, and once that's done, I'm looking for a new label. I won't work with him anymore."

"Done," Steve answered.

"This also doesn't mean you're completely off the hook either. We've got some things to straighten out if we're going to continue on, but that's a different discussion for a different time."

"That's fair. So when should I tell everyone to be back in the studio?"

"Tomorrow morning," Danielle said. "We're going to take the rest of the day off, and then we'll hit the ground running tomorrow."

Steve agreed and rang off. Shannon immediately rushed Danielle.

"I thought you were going to sell me out for a minute," she said. "Scared me to death."

"Ah, I just wanted to make Steve squirm a little. And I might have been watching your reaction a little bit too. So tomorrow, we get back to business. No more blowing me off, though. Agreed?"

"Agreed."

CHAPTER NINETEEN

Adam and Shannon decided they should all celebrate their victory with a day on the beach. Danielle was against the idea, preferring to spend her time working out some new songs, but Shannon wouldn't let it go. When Danielle used her lack of a bathing suit as an excuse, Shannon swarmed her with a number of her own. They were all bad fits in one way or another, but Danielle grudgingly accepted a baby blue and black two piece that wasn't too revealing or uncomfortable.

As she stepped out of the back of the house and into the living room, Adam's eyes got wide. "Wow. Reminds me of the time we shot that video on the beach. You remember? You had that little yellow number?"

"I remember," Danielle said as she constantly fidgeted and adjusted the bikini. "I hated that almost as much as I hate this."

"Oh, you're fine," Shannon chastised. Shannon was wearing a shimmering purple suit that was more like four snippets of fabric held together with string. "Quit thinking about it. Let's just go down to the beach and have some fun. Come on."

Adam, being eternally Adam, couldn't hide his appreciation of the two women in front of him. "So many images in my head right now," he said as he watched Shannon make some last minute adjustments to Danielle's suit. "It's a good thing you're a string bean now," he said to Danielle. "If you were still built like you used to be, you'd pop that thing off in a minute."

"Lucky me."

Shannon stepped back to give Danielle a good once over. "Adam tells me you used to be a lot more...." She struggled to find the right word to finish the sentence.

Danielle did it for her. "Muscular. I was a lot more muscular."

"Yeah, she was," Adam agreed, which brought a disapproving glare from Shannon. "I'm just sayin'," Adam said in response. "Come on, ladies, let's hit the sand."

Danielle spent the afternoon reclining on the beach and watching Adam frolic with Shannon in ways he'd never done with her. As she watched them play, Danielle felt herself getting jealous, even though she knew it made no sense. She was not the frolicking type, and she knew full well that Adam's attention span would soon expire.

She found herself thinking back to her last few months with Kyle. Those precious few months after he had come for her were the most carefree times of her life. She was supposed to have had years, or even decades, of that, and instead had been restricted to mere weeks. Danielle felt the tears forming and slammed her fists into the sand. She'd seen enough and stormed back to the house in order to avoid witnessing any more public affection between Adam and Shannon.

He kept Shannon's attention through dinner and into the night. Danielle kept pushing for him to go home and for Shannon to go to bed, but they couldn't be torn apart. She was ready to go to bed and give up the fight when Adam received a text and slunk away.

Danielle took advantage and darted to Shannon's side. "We've got work in the morning—you need to send him home."

Shannon bit her lip. "I was going to have him stay over. I'm not that concerned about sleep."

"You will be if you can't perform in the morning. We've got a limited number of days left to get this done. I need you focused. Adam is the worst person in the world to have around when you need to get things done."

"Don't worry about it. I won't let you down again. Just go to bed if you're tired. I'll take care of—"

Adam came flying back into the living room, phone still to his ear, as he desperately looked for something. "Where's the remote to the TV? I need it."

Danielle and Shannon both shrugged. "We don't watch TV," Shannon said. "I've haven't turned it on since I've been here."

Danielle sat up on the edge of the couch. "Why? What happened?"

Adam stopped his searching to glance at Danielle, and that look was enough to stop his search. "I'll call you back," he said into the phone. "All right, give me a second." Adam hung up and forced his way on the couch between Shannon and Danielle, who was watching Adam work his phone. He brought up YouTube and soon had a video queued up.

"Steve flew home tonight," Adam said, a rare edge of tenseness in his voice. "He landed in Austin a little while ago."

"And?"

Adam didn't answer, instead holding his phone high and

playing the video. There was Nicole Moore, camera crew in tow, harassing an obviously distressed Steve as he tried to hustle his way around her.

"Where is Danielle Regan?" she asked. "Why won't you return my calls? I have a right to talk to her." The woman matched Steve's strides and stayed in his face. "Do you know what it's like to lose the love of your life? Don't you have any sympathy at all? Are you even human? Do you have a heart?"

Steve refused to say a word or even look at her. Danielle felt her anger percolating again as she watched him endure the barrage. As angry as she was with Steve, he didn't deserve the third degree from a woman that Danielle was beginning to suspect was psychotic in her own right.

"What is this?" Shannon asked innocently. "Why does this woman want to talk to you so bad?"

"Don't worry about it." She reached up and hit the pause on Adam's video. "I've seen enough. I'm going to bed now." She stood, looking to beat a quick retreat.

"What are you going to do about this?" Adam called from the couch. "This woman, she's popping up all the time. Sooner or later she's going to get a line on you."

Danielle stopped with her back to the others and debated that. Slowly she turned and focused on Adam. "If she pulls that with me, I'll kick her fat ass back to Wisconsin. The nicest thing I can do for her is avoid her because nothing good will come of it if we do meet."

"She may not leave you a choice."

"You better hope not, because I've got six years of rage to let loose on someone, and she's looking like a damn good candidate. Good night."

Danielle hurried through her nighttime routine, thankful that no one tried to intervene. She laid in bed with her phone in her hand, debating if she should call Steve. His refusal to talk was quite a show of support. Given the rocky status of their current relationship, Danielle wouldn't have blamed Steve for throwing her under the bus. Yet he stayed strong.

She had fallen into a restless sleep when Danielle was suddenly aware of a pressure on the bed. Instantly, one of Shannon's skinny arms snaked around her waist as she cuddled up. "Are you okay?" Shannon whispered in her ear.

"I'm always okay."

Shannon didn't immediately respond, but finally, she whispered, "You're a liar."

It struck Danielle that those three words were perhaps the most observant words Shannon had spoken since they met. It wasn't Danielle's style to burden others with her feelings, and that wasn't about to change. "I'm fine."

"You can talk to me about it. I'm your friend. I won't judge you. I know what it's like, having a storm raging inside you all the time. Talk to me."

"Nothing to talk about," Danielle snipped. "You should go to bed. The morning will be here before you know it."

"I am in bed. Even if you won't talk to me. I'm going to stay right here beside you because I want you to know you're not alone anymore. Eventually, you're going to understand that. I will help you because we're really not that different. Push me away all you want, I'm not going anywhere."

Shannon's words almost broke through, but Danielle was in no mood for an emotional catharsis. "If you insist, but please be quiet and go to sleep. I'm tired."

"How long has it been since you weren't tired?"

Danielle craned her neck, but all she could see of Shannon was a gray lump lying beside her in the dark. She didn't know how to answer that question. Shannon's arm tightened around her waist, perhaps anticipating an attempt to pull away. Instead, Danielle laid her head back on the pillow. She thought about it for several minutes, hoping that maybe Shannon would fall asleep before she finally answered.

"A really long time."

CHAPTER TWENTY

The next morning began with Adam joining them for their morning run. He jogged between the two women and kept routinely bumping into Danielle as they ran. Whether it was just a consequence of running on a beach or if it were intentional, Danielle couldn't quite figure out.

Once they were cleaned up, Shannon bid Adam goodbye with a lingering kiss that forced Danielle to pull them apart. Then it was on to the studio. As Steve had promised, everyone was there bright and early and ready to work. Danielle smiled as she entered the control room and noticed that Leo and Roy had everything set up.

"Hey guys, looks like you're both ready to go. Mics all set up?"

Leo beamed at her. "Sure are."

"Good. Get the fuck out." Behind her, Shannon gasped as Leo and Roy's faces dropped. Leo stammered, and Danielle decided not to make him ask. "I didn't appreciate that little stunt you pulled. I can't do anything about it now as far as the label goes, they've got my back to the wall, but you little shits have no leverage over me, and I'm not going to work with a couple of backstabbers. You're fired. Get lost."

Roy slumped in his chair and seemed ready to go, but Leo found a reserve of courage. "Mr. Cardenas loved *my* mixes, and he promised me producer credit."

Danielle gave him a predatory smile and stepped up to the smaller man. "Mr. Cardenas made *me* the producer, and as a producer, I get to determine who my assistants are. If you think you're a big man, give him a call and see what he says. But if it comes to you or me, who do you think Rico is going to side with?"

Leo tried to stare her down and failed. "I'll talk to the union."

"I'll tell them to shove it up their ass too. This is my studio now." Leo saw that he wasn't going to win the battle and bowed his head in defeat. Together he and Roy made their way to the door. Danielle waited until they were almost out before calling to them. "Bad thing about being a backstabber; when you need help, nobody's going to be there for you."

Leo shot her one last go to hell look before leaving. Once they were gone, Shannon rushed to Danielle's side. "Are you sure that was a good idea? I think we need those guys."

"Nah. I texted Steve this morning and told him what I was going to do. He said we'd have a new engineer by lunchtime. I can produce. I produced all of my albums. Besides, I'm not holding back now."

"You were before?"

"Yeah," Danielle snickered. "I could have done what those guys did. I thought about it, but it was supposed to be *your* album, not ours. Now things are different, so I can play with the mixes more. It's time to have fun. "

Danielle patted Shannon on the shoulder and then made her way to the studio. "All right, guys," she announced upon entering the room. "Leo and Roy have been relieved of their duties. If anyone wants to go with them, now's the time to do it. For everybody else, we've got two more weeks to get this album done, so we don't have time to piss around. I need you focused and at your best. Questions?" She was met only with silence. "Good. Let's make some music."

Shannon laid a hand on her shoulder. "Why don't you warm the boys up while I get ready?" Perhaps anticipating pushback, Shannon spoke first. "It won't take me an hour. I promise."

"Fine. Go." Danielle grabbed her new Les Paul and stepped into the studio. "While we wait, let's get in the groove a little bit. I came up with this the other night, and I wanted to see if we could do something with it." Danielle started playing a fast run of single notes. On the second pass, the drummer picked up the beat, and soon the band was jamming to a fast, aggressive tune, freeing up Danielle to lay down some of the hardest rocking parts of her life. When they were done, Danielle noticed Shannon in the studio watching them. "You ready?"

She sauntered into the room and up to Danielle. "That was fabulous. I've always wanted to do a straight ahead rock song like that. You could write me some words?"

"Why don't you write them? I'm not the only songwriter here. The song made you feel something. Write about it."

"I just might," Shannon answered. "If I do, you'll let me have the tune?"

"Might," Danielle teased. "You gotta write the words first. For now, let's work on the songs we do have. Okay?"

Danielle ran the session with an iron fist, pushing everyone, including Shannon, to perform beyond their own expectations. By the time the sun was going down, Danielle felt confident she had things on the right track.

As Shannon's backing band made their way out, Danielle heard one of the background singers complain to a bandmate. "Is every day going to be like this?"

Danielle stopped the girl dead in her tracks. "It will be if you want to be on this album. If you don't, just don't come in tomorrow. Doesn't bother me."

Shannon sat on a piano bench and waited for everyone else to leave. "You're a real hard case in a studio. Have you always been like this?"

"Not usually." Danielle sat down at the control board and began to que up one of the songs they had been working on. "Recording was always the fun part for me. My band and I, we knew each other so well that I didn't have to be hard on people. We worked well together. These people…it's just a job for them. If I don't push them, they'll half ass their way through it. They're studio hacks and not even top flight ones. I'm sure Steve got them on the cheap."

"Still, you keep pushing that hard, they'll all leave."

Danielle met Shannon's gaze quietly before turning back to the board and starting the playback. As the air filled with music, Danielle shrugged. "I'm through worrying about it. This is about you and me now. If this album sucks, it falls on us, not them."

Shannon checked her phone. "Save that for tomorrow. Adam wants to take me out. Let's just go home."

Danielle swiveled in her chair. "Y'all are really into each other, huh?"

"We have fun together, and there's no pressure. We're both live in the moment type of people who keep getting into relationships with people who have their eyes on the future. It's refreshing to break that cycle."

"You know that I was one of those eye on the future type of people?"

"Yes, I know. Adam talks about you all the time." With a sigh, Shannon knelt in front of Danielle. "He still has a thing for you. He denies it, but I see it."

"Aren't you worried about that?"

"No. I would be." Shannon stood and straightened out her skirt. "But you don't look at him the way he looks at you. That, and the knowledge that you're emotionally constipated, gives me complete confidence that you won't steal him away from me, intentionally or otherwise."

Danielle laughed. "Emotionally constipated?"

Shannon cocked her hips. "Tell me I'm wrong."

"Oh no," Danielle answered, still laughing. "Guilty as charged. I've just never heard anyone put it that way before."

"Glad I could amuse you. Come on, let's get out of here."

~*~

Danielle relaxed in the living room of the beach house while Adam cooked up a special dinner to celebrate the end of the recording process. There was one day of studio time left, a day that Danielle intended to spend refining mixes before sending the tracks on to the studio. As she waited for dinner, Danielle kept fiddling with the guitar, constantly tinkering with parts that she thought were already done.

She was thankful the project had worked out. As much as it pained her to admit it, Steve had been right—not that she was going to be volunteering that information to him. She was still nursing an unhealthy grudge against her manager and had no intention of letting him off the hook anytime soon.

She was sprawled on a plush sectional couch and on the edge of sleep when her cell phone starting ringing on the oak coffee table where it rested. She lifted her head slightly, stared at the device, then laid her head back down.

"Aren't you going to answer it?" Shannon asked from the bar that separated the kitchen where she was hunched over a piece of paper.

"Nope. It's just Steve, probably calling to stress out over the last day. I don't need the headache." Shannon didn't push, and Danielle let herself edge back into the mist.

Almost instantly, Shannon's phone went off. She snatched it up on the first ring. Danielle soon felt a nudge and forced open one eye to find Shannon standing over her, extending her phone. "Steve insists on talking to you."

Danielle moaned and sat up. "Yes, boss?"

"I just thought I would give you a heads up. Rico is coming to the studio tomorrow to review the mixes. It's supposed to be a surprise, but I know better than to let him sneak up on you. I'm hopping a red eye out there now."

Danielle sat up straighter and felt her muscles tense up. "I'm not done with the mixes, Steve. That's what tomorrow is for. Does he understand that I have one more day?" Steve went silent except for the sound of his breathing. Danielle got tired of waiting. "What's the deal?"

"He's not confident you can pull this off. Apparently, someone has been telling him the sessions are a disaster."

"Oh really?" Danielle immediately thought of Leo and Roy,

whom she'd kicked to the curb so readily. Were they now trying to get back at her through some juvenile stunt? "Let him come. I'll stand behind the work we've done so far. If he doesn't think so—"

"Yeah, that's what I'm afraid of," Steve said, audibly subdued. "Be ready to go to the studio extra early tomorrow. I'll meet you. Say six?"

Danielle chewed on her lip as she thought it over. "Fine. Six it is." She started to stand up but stopped. "Hey, Steve?"

"Yes?"

She froze, suddenly finding it impossible to say the next words. Her pride didn't want to let them go. Finally, she forced herself to say it. "Thanks for the warning."

Steve didn't immediately answer. Surely he was also aware of how strained their relationship had become. She wondered if he knew how hard it had been for her to show that simple gratitude. "Think nothing of it. "

Danielle pulled the phone down slowly and stared at the darkened screen. Slowly she looked up to find Shannon watching her intently. She tossed Shannon's phone back to her.

"Hey, Adam? How's dinner coming?"

"About to dish it out."

"Well, throw it in some Tupperware, because we gotta go." She stood quickly and headed for her room to get dressed.

"Where are we going?" Adam called after her.

Danielle stopped in the mouth of the hallway. She looked over at Shannon, who was perked up like a prairie dog. "We gotta go to work. The assholes are dropping by for a surprise visit in the morning. Rico thinks he can catch me unprepared. I'm going to show him."

"So, we're going back in?" Danielle confirmed it. With a squeal, Shannon snatched up her paper and bounded across the room. "Then can we work on this? I've been working on it for days."

Annoyed, Danielle stepped back into the living room and took the paper from her. Written at the top in fancy script was the title Girls Night Out. She glanced up at Shannon.

"You said I could have that song if I wrote words for it. There they are. It's about you and me, and the night I wish we had together. Still could if you'd loosen up just a bit."

The last thing Danielle needed was yet another song to work on, but the pride Shannon had was unrelenting. "I'm sure we can do a couple of quick takes. I've got the band take recorded at the studio."

"Yeah!"

"And what am I going to do while the ladies are working?"

"You'll be moral support." Danielle saw him readying a response and knew what she needed to do to shut him up. "Besides, maybe we could use you. You could do some vocals or handclaps or something. At the least, your very presence will annoy me, and I'll work harder. You'll get a credit in the liner notes."

"I'll get credit?" The moment when Adam's ego overrode his reluctance was visible to Danielle, who could read him like a cheap paperback. "Fine. I'll gather everything up. You girls go on. I'll bring some coffee and Cokes when I come. Sounds like it's going to be an all-nighter."

~*~

Danielle drove hard through the night, her eyes laser focused on the road ahead. In the passenger seat, Shannon studied her every movement. After several miles of silence, she finally spoke up.

"Are you nervous about this meeting tomorrow? I can't tell. Sometimes you seem nervous, and sometimes it seems like something else."

Danielle kept her eyes on the road. "I feel like I've been challenged, and it pisses me off. Rico got the best of me once. I won't let him do it to me again."

"Um." Shannon turned away, and several more miles passed before she spoke again. "You love it, though, don't you?" Danielle didn't respond. "You love the challenge," Shannon answered for her. "You say it pisses you off, but I think secretly you enjoy it."

Danielle shot her a sideways glance. Shannon remained quiet, letting the statement hang in the air between them. Finally, Danielle spoke. "I do my best work when I'm in a negative mood. Almost all of my songs were written when I was angry or lonely or hurt. Those negative emotions are where my fuel comes from. So when I left, and I shut myself off, I couldn't write."

"Most? So there was a time when it didn't work that way?"

"Once," Danielle nodded. "After Kyle and I got engaged, we wrote an album of love songs together." She felt the maudlin smile cross her face. "Love songs, lust songs, whatever you want to call them. But Kyle wrote most of the lyrics on that album. I couldn't do it."

"Why is that?"

Danielle turned her head toward Shannon. "Because I don't write love songs."

"That's crazy. I can't write when I'm in a bad mood. I have to be at peace. When I write, I go away, somewhere beautiful and inspiring. I surround myself in it and let it soak into my bones."

Danielle grunted. "That's why all of your songs are so fluffy. You need to learn how to tap into your dark side more. If you want to rock, you can't be fluffy."

"I don't need to worry about that anymore." Shannon waited for Danielle to glance her way. "I have you now, and that's your job. I'm the poet, and you're the badass. *You are my dark side.*" Danielle gave her a quizzical look. "That's why you can't get rid of me. I need you to be the bad girl for me."

Danielle laughed out loud. "I'm the bad girl. I'm Snow Fucking White compared to you."

"Only in the bedroom. I can't compare to you anywhere else. Look at how you dress, with your ripped jeans and boots and leather jacket. You've got that dark hair and that smoldering look. I've been watching videos of you on YouTube, and you're terrifying. You're like a vampire rock goddess. It makes me so hot. It's a shame you're so normal."

Danielle laughed again in spite of herself. "I'm so sorry to disappoint you."

Shannon answered with a fake pout. "Don't I know it."

~*~

By the time Adam arrived at the studio with their dinner and drinks, Shannon was at the mic, booming out her brand new song as Danielle ripped a new guitar part. As he stood on the other side of the studio glass watching, Danielle did a double take, because, for a moment, he looked like the shaggy beatnik kid she had met that first summer in Austin. Just like that, she understood Shannon's comment about the way he still looked at her. If only he still was that kid from the streets.

They finished their song and then broke for dinner. Danielle continued to listen to playbacks and fiddle between bites. She was aware of Shannon and Adam carrying on a whispered conversation behind her back, but it didn't matter enough for her to pay attention. Once dinner was finished, they resumed work in earnest.

As a payback to Adam, Danielle did come up with some things for him to do. She let him play various percussion instruments, clap, and even add some background vocals. He wasn't a great singer, but she could bury him in the mix. Shannon made his night by producing an impromptu poem for him to recite, which Danielle then tacked onto the beginning of a song.

Eventually, Shannon ran out of gas and passed out on the control room sofa, leaving Danielle and Adam alone. He sat at her side, watching with rapt attention as Danielle maneuvered the controls, looking for perfect mixtures.

"Who would have thought it, huh?"

"Thought what?" Danielle asked without taking her eyes off the task at hand.

"That you and I would be sitting side-by-side like this again. The way things ended between us? I never thought it. That's for sure."

Danielle was only half listening, trying to focus on the music. "Yeah, I guess life takes you to some funny places."

Adam reached over and laid a hand gently on Danielle's. She snapped her head around as Adam scooted closer. "I came to see you when you were in the hospital. I want you to know that. I wanted to stay. I felt I should have been there by your side when you woke up. Steve didn't think so. He sent me away. That's the only reason I wasn't there."

Danielle stared straight into his crystalline eyes and felt herself starting to buckle. She knew the feeling well—he had done it to her many times before. Suddenly the music fell away, no longer important as Adam slowly monopolized her senses. "I didn't know that," she whispered. "I never wanted to know anything."

"I understand." He drew closer, uncomfortably close, but Danielle found herself powerless to pull away. "I don't blame you for that. I just want to be sure you know I was there for you when you needed me. I always will be."

He came in for a kiss, and Danielle breathed deeply, anticipating the moment. As his lips made contact with hers, she pulled away with a start. "That's not true." Adam pulled back, a question in his eyes. "You weren't always there for me. In fact, you were the one always hurting me. Always pushing me away."

Adam dropped his eyes from hers, but only for a moment. "You're right about that. I did hurt you, and I did push you away. I did that because I was afraid of you." He started to edge in close again. "Because you were the one person who always saw through me. You know the real me, the one I never let anyone else see."

Danielle felt his power pulling her in again. For some strange reason, she wanted this. She craved his lips on hers, to feel his touch again, even as part of her brain screamed out against it. He leaned in for another kiss, and Danielle was ready to meet him when she caught the glimmer of Shannon reflected in the studio glass, sleeping like a baby behind her.

Instead of kissing him, Danielle put her palms flat on his chest and pushed Adam back. "You're with Shannon now, and she's my friend. So this can't happen."

Adam scoffed. "Shannon and I are short term. She knows it as well as I do. When this album is done, she's going to leave, and that will be it. She's a great girl, but our time is up. You—I will follow you. I will drop everything for you if you ask me too."

"Yeah, right." Danielle felt her control coming back, felt herself grow stronger. "We've been down that road. I won't go again."

"I'm different now. I've changed. I've grown up. This Hollywood life, it leaves me empty now. It doesn't fulfill me. Only you can do that."

She wanted to believe him. The old attraction was still there, flickering in her soul. He could almost arouse it into a flame. Almost. She rolled away from him and returned her attention to the board. "I had a healthy relationship once, with a man who really loved me. A man who treated me right. After having something like that, why would I ever want to go back to someone like you? You're still poison, whether you know it or not."

"I see." Adam stood and turned a slow circle. Danielle kept a close watch out of the corner of her eye. "So that's it then. We're truly finished?"

Danielle didn't bother to look at him. "We were finished a long time ago. I can be your friend. That's all I've got for you now." She knew from the feeling still welling inside that wasn't entirely true, but she was betting Adam wouldn't call her bluff.

He didn't.

"Well then, it's getting early, and your boss will be here soon. I think I'll go home now. Thanks for a fun night. Tell Shannon I'll catch up to her."

He hustled away, and Danielle didn't dare watch him go. She wasn't sure she was strong enough to let him.

CHAPTER TWENTY-ONE

Danielle was slumped over in her seat. She felt herself being pulled down, felt her body swaying. The music was still playing, repeating the same song over and over again, but she was unable to pull herself out of the daze long enough to stop it. Her body was slowly leaning forward, further and further, her face on a collision course with the mixing board.

Then came the pounding on the door.

The noise startled her awake and stole her breath away. Danielle looked around, panicked until her mind began to catch up. The pounding came a second time. She tried to rub the sleep out of her eyes as she fumbled for the switch to shut off the continuous playback. The knocks came a third time before Danielle finally shuffled to the door.

Steve stood on the other side in a deep maroon suit and a silver tie with matching maroon stripes. He held a cardboard tray with three tall cups of coffee in it. Danielle fumbled for the lock and finally got the door open.

"Good morning, Sunshine," Steve said, more friendly than

he should have been for the time of day. "Let me guess, you came here as soon as we got off the phone?"

Danielle stepped aside to let him in. "What gives you that idea?"

"Because I know you." As Danielle closed the studio door behind her, Steve picked a cup out of the tray. "This one's for you. I know you don't like coffee but try this. It's a French vanilla cappuccino. I think you'll like it."

"Does it have caffeine in it?" Steve confirmed it did. "That's all I need to know right now."

Steve gestured toward Shannon, still sleeping on the couch. "So how have things gone between you? You're both still alive, so I assume it hasn't gone too terribly wrong."

Danielle shrugged. "She's a pretty good kid, I guess. She's very...."

Steve nodded. "Yes, she is." He crossed the room and sat gingerly next to Shannon's curled up form. Setting the remaining coffees on the floor between his feet, Steve looked up at Danielle. "Tell me straight. How did it come out?"

Danielle shrugged again and sipped at the cappuccino he had brought her. As much as she hated to admit, it wasn't bad. Danielle took her seat at the controls. "I'm proud of it, given that I've never really collaborated on an album before, and that I generally don't play well with others. If I had more time and a better band, it would have been better. If I had my band."

"Danielle—"

"I know, those days are gone. You don't need to remind me." She spun around to face him. "It's going to be hard to find another band as good as they were. I really did screw up when I let them go."

"Yes, you did. Nothing we can do about that now. When this is all over, I have an idea I want to pitch you, just an idea, but it merits your consideration."

"Whatever you say, boss." She pointed at the speakers suspended above the board. "You wanna hear this now or wait until the head asshole gets here?"

"Hang on." Steve softly patted Shannon's bare leg, and when that didn't get a response, he began softly shaking her as he softly called her name. Eventually, she began to stir.

"Steve?" She asked sleepily. "When did you get here?"

"Just now." He plucked one coffee off the floor and held it in front of her nose. She breathed in the aroma.

"Oh, you're a godsend." Shannon snatched the cup out of his hands and immediately took a drink. "That's exactly what I needed." She adjusted into a sitting position and looked slowly around the room. "Where did Adam go?"

"Adam?" Steve asked.

"He went home," said Danielle. "He said he'd catch up to you later. I guess the whole recording process just got too tough for him. Wuss."

"Oh, okay."

"Adam?" Steve asked again. "What Adam? Who's Adam?" Danielle answered him only with a look. "Quisenberry? How did that sniveling little shit worm his way into this?"

Danielle glanced over at Shannon, then smiled. "You know Adam, he has his ways."

"Oh God."

"Don't worry, he was actually on his best behavior over the last couple of weeks." Shannon raised her eyebrows but said nothing, so Danielle went on. "He actually helped us out last night. He's going to be on a couple of these songs. He liked that. Fed his ego."

Steve turned to Shannon and wagged a finger at her. "He's bad news. I'm just telling you."

"Enough about him," Danielle snapped. "Shannon, would you like to hear your final, completed album?" She energetically said yes. "Steve? Ready for this?" He also agreed. Danielle spun back around to the board and readied the playback. "Here you go, boys and girls."

~*~

Rico Cardenas sat on the studio sofa in a navy blue power suit. At his side, a rail-thin, cute brunette sat with a legal pad in her lap, ready to take notes and looking nervous. Across the room, Danielle sat relaxed in her chair at the board. She was exhausted, but her resentment of Rico gave her strength enough to stay awake. They sat, both staring daggers at the other, neither reacting as one song after another played.

Steve and Shannon sat shoulder to shoulder on a love seat on the back wall, their eyes darting from Danielle to Rico and back like they were watching a tennis match. No one spoke, and the only movement was the pretty brunette as she fiddled with her pen.

As each song passed without comment, Rico and Danielle's faces both seemed to harden. Neither appeared willing to be the first to react to anything. Shannon leaned over to Steve and whispered loudly enough that the room heard it. "Is it always like this?" Steve merely shook his head, and the staredown continued.

Finally, the last song faded out. Twelve songs and just over an hour had passed. Still, Danielle and Rico glared at each other.

The brunette finally spoke. "So, Mr. Cardenas, anything I should write down? Anything at all?"

Rico broke his staring contest with Danielle, looking instead at Steve. "So this is what two years and a quarter of a million in production costs buys?"

He stood and straightened his tie, making a production out of it. Shannon buried her face in her hands. Steve fumbled for something to say, but Rico put up his palm, clearly uninterested. He took one step toward Danielle.

"Ms. Regan."

Danielle narrowed her eyes. She was ready to fight and waiting for the invitation. She said nothing.

"It'll do."

"It'll do?" Steve repeated.

"That's it, boss?" asked his assistant. "Just 'it'll do'?"

"I'll have more for you in the car, Maycee. For now, it'll do. Come along." She stood dutifully as Rico started for the door. "Redus, we'll talk soon." He reached the door, but stopped suddenly, almost causing his assistant to run into him. He turned to Steve. "I'll want it out soon. We'll need at least three videos. I want these two in them together. Don't pull any of this splicing shit with me. I want good quality, but don't go crazy on the budget. Be smart. I'll be in touch."

With that, Rico Cardenas had his last word, and he walked away. Maycee, the assistant, stopped and looped back around to Danielle. "I loved it," she gushed, allowing just that one show of emotion before she composed herself and hustled after her boss.

Danielle swiveled in her chair as Steve rose and closed the studio door. "It'll do, my ass," Steve near shouted. "That may be the greatest thing you've ever done. I'm serious. It's like…

Heart from the '80s, only leaner and meaner. Your playing is ferocious. And you." He pivoted to Shannon. "I've never heard you sing like that before. You found a whole new voice. I hope you're ready because this is about to launch your career into the stratosphere. You're going to be a legitimate superstar."

Shannon squeal with delight. "Thank you so much. I wasn't sure about this, but you were right."

Danielle stood, remaining stoic. "Looks like my work here is done."

"Just for the time being. I'll get this mastered, and we'll be on our way. Lots of work to come, though. I have a feeling that Rico is going to want a full court press on this, so be ready for lots of PR." Steve gripped Danielle by the shoulders. "You did it. You saved us. Our careers, the label. This is going to save everyone. I'm so proud."

Danielle wriggled out of his grasp. "I'm glad. I'm going back to the house now, and I'm going to sleep for two days. Don't call me. Don't text me. Don't have Shannon come and bother me. I don't want anyone to mess with me."

Steve nodded and stepped back. "Fair enough. But just two days, and then we need to talk. Lots of planning to do for both of you. I'll set up a meeting."

Danielle held two fingers in front of him. "Two days. I'm serious."

"Can I crawl in bed with you?" Shannon teased as she joined them at the front of the room.

Danielle eyed her suspiciously, then grinned. "Sure, why not?" Steve's eyes widened, and Danielle puckered her lips at him in response before crooking her arm for Shannon, who took it in both hands. "Are you ready, my dear?"

"Yes, ma'am," Shannon beamed.

"Two days, Steve. Remember."

Danielle and Shannon strutted out of the studio together. "You're just messing with Steve with all of this, right?" Shannon asked when they got to the parking lot. Danielle nodded. "Can I really sleep with you?"

"As long as you don't snore, I don't care."

"Awesome. Before that, can we —?"

"Nope." Danielle pulled her arm away so she could get the car keys out of her pocket. "Once my head hits that pillow, it's lights out for me. After that, I don't care what you do."

"You're no fun."

~*~

Two days later and now rested, Danielle and Shannon met with Steve in a conference room at the airport Marriott. It was a small, simple room with a round wood table and a few cloth and metal chairs. Steve was waiting on them, looking more relaxed than Danielle had seen him in a long time. He had no sports jacket or tie, and the top two buttons on his dress shirt were undone. He was ready to do business with his laptop running and a legal pad at his side.

"Look at Mr. Casual here," Danielle kidded when they walked in the room. "No tie? It's scandalous, I tell you."

"Wow," Shannon chimed in. "Give a guy a couple of days in California, and it changes him. In another week, you'll be wandering around in nothing but sandals and swim trunks, with a surfboard under your arm."

Steve, who had been spinning a ballpoint pen between his fingers, slammed the pen down. "I'm a California guy, I'll have you know. And I've been known to catch a wave now and again."

His voice dropped an octave as he looked down at his pad. "I kind of miss it out here sometimes."

Danielle felt a pang of sympathy for him. It was unusual for Steve to give anyone, even her, a glimpse behind his curtain. It made her uncomfortable. "All right, boss," she said, claiming the chair immediately to his left. "What's the deal?"

He seemed relieved to switch gears. "Right. So first things first. Rico loved the album, he just didn't want to give you the satisfaction of knowing it. So expect things to happen quickly on that front. We want the album in stores by the end of summer, earlier if possible. I'm meeting with some directors while we're out here about some video concepts. When I've got some dates lined up, I'll let you know."

"Adam can direct," Danielle said, being completely serious.

"That's not even an option," Steve barked. "Because Shannon is fairly new to the game here in the States, we're going to want you to do some appearances. Of course, you'll have the talk show circuit when the album is close to dropping, but even before that, we want to get you out there. Now Shannon, how are we going to promote you? Do you want Rikka Olausson? Do you want a different stage name? How do you want to do this?"

Shannon didn't bat an eye. "I want to be myself. Dani doesn't hide behind a stage name, so why should I?"

Steve raised his eyebrows. "She's Dani to you now? How do you feel about that? Getting chummy, huh?" Danielle merely shrugged. "Okay," Steve said. "So we've agreed that the first single will be 'Already Fallen.'"

"Why that one?" Shannon quickly turned to Danielle. "No offense, but this started as my project, so I think that one of my songs should go first."

"Three reasons. First, Danielle is the bigger name, and this is her comeback album, so we think it'll get more attention. Second, it's the most commercial of the songs. The label thinks, and I agree, that 'Already Fallen' would be the best song to open the door, if you will, to the rest of the album. Third, everyone who listened believes that it's the best song on the album. If you were an established act, we'd hold the best song back, but we all feel it wise to put the strongest material out first."

Shannon slumped back in her chair. "Fine."

Beside her, Danielle remained quiet. She agreed with the logic but saw how it stung Shannon and felt it best to let the subject pass. "So what about the other singles?"

"Good question. 'Tamarind' will be second up, and that one will probably get the most lavish video of the bunch. You're such a visual songwriter that it lends itself well to a video treatment. I have some big, big ideas for the video that I think you'll love."

"Really?" Shannon sat up a little straighter. "I'll star in the video, right?"

"Absolutely. We'll do a long form version for online, where you can even do some acting. Then we'll have an edited version as well. It's going to be glorious, trust me. Then we'll follow up with 'Walking Through Heaven,' because that's probably the song where you two blend the best. If those songs hit big, we might choose to release more singles. We'll just have to wait and see."

Steve flipped a page on his legal pad and studied some notes before turning his attention back to Danielle. "This is going to be different for you. The industry has changed a lot in the last few years. Digital downloads are the big thing, and they're only going to get bigger. We'll do the standard PR fare, but you'll have to get used to podcasts. You'll need to pump up your social media presence, which I've been managing, but I want to turn that over to you. A lot more fan interaction. Can you handle it?"

Danielle fidgeted in her seat. "If you want me to go on some show and play, I can do that with my eyes closed, no problem. I don't care where it is or for how big an audience. Social media, though? Facebook and shit like that? Tweeter?"

"Twitter," Shannon corrected. "It's called Twitter."

Danielle rolled her eyes and mimed typing into a phone. "Look at what I ate for dinner tonight! Look at this pretty flower growing through the crack in the sidewalk! Look! I took a dump, and it was perfectly round! O.M.G. Fuck a bunch of that."

Steve groaned. "Shannon, can you help Danielle with the social media part? Teach her."

"I can do that. Social media is great. If you just open your mind, you'll love it."

Danielle ignored Shannon and turned to Steve. "I've got a better idea. You said you've been managing this stuff while I was gone, so clearly, you don't need me. If you don't want to do it, let's just hire a staffer to do it. A social media specialist. That way, you don't have to worry that I might have a bad day and say something crazy."

"That's not a bad idea, but you at least have to contribute. People want to see you and to hear your words and converse with you. You have to at least take some sort of role. It's important. Social media is probably the best marketing tool out there. Shannon and I, we'll work with you on it."

"Fine. But as little as possible. I'm not going to live the rest of my life looking at it through a phone."

"Understood. Next order of business. Shannon, is your

passport all up to date?"

"Of course. Why?"

"Because I need you on a plane to Oslo, PDQ. Tonight, if possible. And I need you in full blown Rikka beauty. I need you to be fabulous."

Shannon scoffed. "I can't go to Oslo tonight. That's insane. Why do I need to go to Norway anyway? I thought we were done with all of that. This is my focus now."

Steve let out an exasperated sigh. "Yes, but you've heard of the Norwegian filmmaker Ariq Gustavsson?" Shannon nodded. "He put 'Setting Fire To My Paper Heart' in his latest movie, and now the song is screaming up the charts. It looks like it will be your biggest hit to date. We need to strike while the iron is hot and milk the shit out of this. Just give me a few weeks while we put things together here. Hit a few film festivals, make some TV appearances. You know the drill. This is big."

"I can go...." Shannon stumbled and looked to Danielle for a suggestion. She held two fingers, trying to be discreet, but Steve caught her.

"No, not two days. Twenty-four hours. Please, Shannon. Your team's already assembled and ready to go. I'll take care of the details. Can you be ready to go in twenty-four hours?"

Shannon continued to flail about but finally resigned herself. "Yes. I can do that. I'll need to start packing immediately."

"You live out of a suitcase anyway, honey. I promise this will be worth it. This movie is drawing early Oscar buzz. You could be nominated."

Shannon breathed in sharply. "Wow, really?"

"Great. Now, Danielle, back to you." He reached into a leather satchel on the floor at his feet and pulled out a CD. "I want you to give this a listen. It's an all-female rock band out of St. Louis called The Black Heart Chokers."

"Black Heart Chokers? Sounds kinky," Danielle said.

"It's a thing they do. They all wear these little chokers with black hearts on them. It's a gimmick. Anyway, they're an Indy band that's making some noise, but the sisters who lead the band aren't real keen on being out in front. I've reached out to their management about possibly backing you for your next album and tour, and they're open to the idea. I want you to give them a listen. If you like what you hear, they'll be swinging through Texas in a few weeks, and we could put you together somewhere and see how it goes."

"You really think they're the best option? Are they that good?"

"No. The best thing, what I'd like to do is to build you an All Star team. There's a lot of good guys out there without a lot to do. Michael Anthony of Van Halen? He's available. Hell, I could get you the entire rhythm section of Aerosmith if you wanted. Those guys haven't done jack shit in a decade. I could put together a dream team, but I know how you are about cohesion. Plus, I'm not sure I want to put you in a band where you might be overshadowed by bigger names."

Danielle thought it over. "The other problem is that if you put me with a bunch of guys people think are over the hill, it might come off as an oldies act."

"Good point. So give these girls a listen. If you like, we can take the sisters and augment them with some other players. I think it could be good, a real girl power moment to see you fronting an all-female band."

"Girl power? Oh Jesus. Next thing I know you're going to

have me singing Spice Girls songs, for Christ's sake."

"You scoff, and I know that you never envisioned yourself as a trailblazer, but you don't understand what happened in your absence. There are women guitar players popping up all over the place now. There's this Australian chick that shreds like the demon love child of Dick Dale and Steve Vai. I can name a half dozen really good blues players — not bluesy rock like you do, but hardcore, Muddy Waters style blues players that would knock your socks off. I'm telling you, there's a movement out there, and you can be the queen of it."

Reluctantly, Danielle reached out and slid the CD into her hand. "I'll listen. No promises. That brings me to my next question. Can I go home now?"

Steve smiled at her. "Absolutely."

"Great." She fished the car keys out of her pocket and tossed them at Shannon. "Looks like we've both got packing to do, sis. Why don't you head on down to the car, and I'll be right there?"

Shannon caught the keys, noticed the look between Steve and Danielle, and promptly left the room. Danielle stood and perched herself on the table next to him.

"If you miss Cali so much, why don't you move out here?" She plucked his cell phone up off the desk and waved it around. "Thanks to these godforsaken things, we don't have to be in the same city anymore. I'm sure I could hold down the fort back home. Me and that spitfire of a receptionist you've got."

"I'm actually glad to hear you say that because I've been thinking about it." He stood and circled the table as he tucked his hands in his pants pockets. "I spent so long hoping you'd come home. Now I feel like it's my turn. Don't get me wrong, I love Austin. And Aja's there, but I do miss it out here."

"So go. Aja strikes me as a gal who'd do well out here."

"That she would. I'm just worried about what would happen if I wasn't there to put out one of your fires."

Danielle stood and approached him. When she was close enough, she slugged him in the shoulder, harder than she'd planned. The flesh gave way much easier than in years past when she'd done the same thing. "Ah. My fire starting days are over. I'm a more mature person now."

Steve leaned toward her. "Bullshit." He laughed and started pacing the room. "Shannon told me you tried to drown yourself in the ocean. What was that?"

"I didn't try to drown myself," Danielle defended. "I tried to drown my guitars." Steve stopped pacing and glared at her. "Which would be like drowning myself, yes, but that was just a temporary overreaction. I was pissed."

"But what happens the next time someone or something pisses you off? Without me, no one will be there to stop you. Unless you and Shannon are a thing?"

"Oh God, no." Danielle sat again on the table. "We have gotten close, but no. I just like teasing you with that. It's a little mean because I know she would jump on it if given the chance." Steve continued staring at her. "What? It's nice to have someone look at me that way again. Besides Adam, that is. It's flattering, so I string her along a little bit. It's all in good fun."

"Don't fuck up a good thing. She's good for you. I wouldn't be against the two of you in a relationship. I could spin it."

Danielle chuckled and sauntered over to Steve. "You're a perv. I see you, you got images in your mind, naughty boy. Seriously. I can take care of myself. I don't need a babysitter anymore. If this is where your heart is, this is where you should be. Took me six years to learn that lesson."

Steve reached out and pulled Danielle in for a tight hug and held it longer than normal. When he finally pushed her away, he smiled. "Your girlfriend's waiting in the car for you."

"Oh! My honeybunch! I almost forgot!" Danielle said in a put on Southern accent.

"It's good to have you back, Dani."

She reached the conference room and turned around. In all their years together, she could never remember him referring to her as Dani. "I bet I can make you regret that statement," she said with a grin.

"Get outta here."

~*~

The next morning, Danielle loaded her meager possessions in the trunk of the rented Challenger as she readied for the long drive home. She'd just finished carefully stowing the last of her equipment in the back of the car when Shannon walked out into the brilliant sunshine of yet another gorgeous Malibu morning, wearing a jade tunic top and dark blue jeans.

Danielle faked shock. "Look at you. Wearing jeans of all things."

"They're not ripped," she said sheepishly. "I haven't worn jeans since I was in high school. It's a weird feeling."

Danielle slammed the car trunk shut and approached her. "I don't think you could pull off ripped jeans anyway. You're too foofy for that."

"Now I'm foofy? I'm not even sure what that means," Shannon giggled. "So, I guess you're about ready to go?"

"Yeah. I can stay until your car gets here if you want. I could help you load up."

"No, you go on. You have a long drive ahead of you. Besides, like Steve said, I live out of suitcases. This is nothing for me. I haven't had a real home in so long, I don't know that I could handle it." She glanced over her shoulder at the beach house. "I will miss this place, though. Maybe someday I'll get one like it."

Danielle tucked her hands in her pockets. "What about Adam? Have you talked to him?"

"We mutually broke it off. It was time. He is a good time, though. And a very skilled lover. You really missed your chance there."

"How will I live with myself? Oh yeah, just fine."

Shannon shook her head. "Maybe you should give him another chance. There is still chemistry there. I didn't need to witness that little scene between you the other night to know that." Danielle instantly felt herself blush and started to defend herself before Shannon intervened. "You're my friend," she said, teasing. "That meant a lot to me."

"Well, what can I say? You grew on me."

"Really?" Shannon sized her up, then thrust forward. She cupped Danielle's face in both hands and gave her a lingering kiss. She slowly pulled back, expectant. "Anything?"

"Nope," Danielle said. "It's just not my thing. You're going to have to settle for friendship."

"I could continue to grow on you."

"You're a handful enough already." Danielle pulled Shannon in for a long hug. "You take care of yourself around all those crazy Europeans." She broke the hug, but her hands lingered on Shannon's arms. "I need you with me when we do this thing. It's gonna be a ride."

"I will. You be careful on the road. I really wish you'd fly. It's so much safer."

"I'm fine," Danielle said. "I love to drive. It's when I do my best thinking. I know it's dangerous out there."

"No, I mean, you're the danger. I've seen you drive. You're crazy."

They stood silent, neither one of them knowing what else to say next. As she stood there in the warmth, staring down at Shannon, it struck Danielle just how quickly things had changed for her. All because of a strange, desperate man with a piece of junk guitar. She thought about Sam Beck and hoped that things had worked out for him and his family. Maybe she'd look him up sometime.

"All right. Well, Austin ain't getting any closer standin' here," Danielle said, innately aware that her natural Texas twang had suddenly come out thick.

Shannon wiggled her fingers in a wave. "See you in a few weeks, my friend."

"Yep." She felt awkward as she turned away from Shannon. Suddenly she couldn't hit the open road soon enough. Danielle jumped in the car, started it up, and revved the engine twice, her way of waving goodbye. Watching in the rearview mirror, she saw Shannon step back and blow her a kiss. "Crazy girl," she muttered. She dropped the car in gear and took off without a look back. She soon slipped easily into the traffic on the PCH, winding south. Danielle wished the car was a convertible but had to settle for just rolling down the windows.

Along the way, she popped the CD Steve had given her into the stereo. Austin was three days away. What better way to pass the time than with some music?

It felt good to be Danielle Regan again.

CHAPTER TWENTY-TWO

April 18, 2009

Danielle awoke early after a restless night. The three months since she had left California, had flown by so quickly that she hadn't had an opportunity to get nervous, until now. She made her way in the dark to the living room and pulled back the curtains to take in a sweeping view of downtown, still mostly asleep.

She'd long since left Randy's garage apartment, agreeing to take on the lease for Steve's penthouse apartment when he and Aja pulled the trigger on their move to Los Angeles. The apartment still felt cold and impersonal, but she was working on it, slowing, bringing more of a personal touch to the place.

Danielle hugged herself as a chill shot through her body. For three months, she had somehow managed to fly under the radar. Either people didn't know she was back or didn't care, but that was all going to change. Steve had planned Danielle's return down to a T, and zero hour was fast approaching.

She went over the itinerary in her mind for the thousandth time. Steve, Aja, and Shannon would arrive soon. She would meet them at Mossy Oaks golf course for a special breakfast with the governor and select other Texas dignitaries. After breakfast, the governor would officially welcome Danielle back home by declaring it Danielle Regan Day.

From there, it would be on to the university, where Danielle would hob knob with former Longhorns. She would follow that up by throwing out the first pitch for the Longhorns baseball game against their rivals, the Oklahoma Sooners.

After spending an afternoon in the president's box watching baseball, she and Shannon would reconnect for an invitation only meet and greet with fans. All of that leading to the big moment, the moment when Danielle would officially retake the stage for the first time since before her accident. Steve had assembled his dream team of musicians for the show and lined up several special guests, including Austin legend Jimmie Vaughan. Toward the end of the evening, Danielle would then introduce her official band for their upcoming tour, including the sisters Steve had told her about.

Danielle stood in the window, savoring the last moments of peace, her mind racing with the thrill and fear of what was to come. She knew too well what would follow: interviews, TV appearances, clothes fittings, and so forth. It all felt so routine and yet so intimidating.

After staring out over the sleepy city longer than she should have, Danielle finally drew the curtains and forced herself to start getting ready. The entire time, she was haunted by the feeling that something was going to go wrong. Her return had been too easy, and things didn't work out this easily for people. It felt like she was living a Hollywood movie instead of real life.

Even as the thought bounced around her head, Danielle

could hear the voices of her supporters, all telling her the same thing: that she was just being paranoid. Steve had been assuring her for weeks now that slipping back into the spotlight was as easy as riding a bike, and that she would be fine the second the lights went on.

Danielle showered and cleaned up, then laid out her clothes. Per Steve's orders, she would wear a Western style dress in burnt orange to the morning breakfast and to the ballpark, before changing into shorts and a customized Longhorns baseball jersey with her last name and the number 09 on the back before first pitch. Finally, a third outfit, designer jeans, and plain white blouse with a shimmering seafoam green jacket for the meet and greet that she would then wear to the stage.

For a woman who was used to spending days on end in ratty T-shirts and athletic shorts, that was far too many wardrobe changes for one day. She knew how important this day was for Steve and how nervous he was as well, so she didn't fight. Even Danielle Regan could learn to compromise on occasion.

She slipped into the dress and stowed her other outfits in a garment bag before heading to the parking garage. One thing she wouldn't budge on was the car. Steve had wanted to send a service for her, but Danielle would have none of it. Instead, she'd had her Camaro fully detailed, and it now glittered under the parking garage lights.

It was a perfect morning to put the top down, but Danielle resisted the urge. It was a cool and overcast morning that portended a mild day ahead following rain the night before. She took her time on the drive to the exclusive Mossy Oaks Country Club that lay just southwest of the town. The last time she'd been in a country club had been Kyle's last night....

Danielle growled and squeezed the steering wheel. Not today. She'd mourned Kyle every day for almost seven years now. Today was about her, and he was not welcome to intervene. She hadn't moved on, but she was trying.

Danielle still made it to Mossy Oaks in time and, after a couple of sideways glances from the workers, was shown to a private room. As she stepped in, Steve and Aja and Shannon erupted in cheers, having beaten her there by just a few minutes. Shannon was Shannon, her blonde hair swept up in a perfect bun, sporting a tight white dress with a plunging neckline and a snazzy diamond necklace. She pounced on Danielle, immediately enveloping her in what felt like a never ending hug.

"Oh, I missed you," she said softly into Danielle's ear. She finally wiggled out of Shannon's arms. "Now, do my eyes deceive me, or is Danielle Regan actually wearing a dress?"

Danielle looked away, already feeling self-conscious about the getup. "I can wear a dress. I am fully capable of going full girl on occasion. I just don't like to."

Shannon giggled and hugged Danielle's neck. "My giant Texas tomboy has a feminine side after all. Who knew?"

"All right, enough of that," Aja said, muscling her way between them for a hug of her own. "How are you holding up? Is the apartment working out good for you? I hate you being here all alone."

"I'm not all alone," Danielle assured her. "I eat lunch with Randy and Teri every day. I go into the office at least twice a week and check in on things." She looked up to Steve, who stood across the room with his hands tucked into his pants pockets. "And I'm rehearsing with the new band every night," she said, directing her comment at him. She looked back to Aja. "I get plenty of social interaction."

"Well, it still sounds like you're alone to me, and I don't like it. We never should have left you there."

Danielle started to protest, but Shannon butted in. Resting her chin on Danielle's shoulder, she grinned down at Aja. "I could always move in and take care of her. Somebody needs to watch out for the poor thing."

"Oh, Jesus," Danielle muttered. She extricated herself from the women and approached Steve. "Well, boss, are we going to pull this off?"

Steve didn't hesitate. "We sure are. Everything is going to be perfect, you'll see. Quit worrying."

"I'd feel a lot better if Shannon had been able to come in for some rehearsals. We've never played together live. She doesn't know the band—"

"Hey," Shannon intervened. "I know I come off as distracted, but I am a professional. I know the songs, I'll be fine. If I get lost, I'll just follow your lead."

"We'll see," she said to Shannon. To Steve, she asked, "Any word from Trish and Ty or Garrett? What about DeShon?"

Steve grimaced. "No. No response." Danielle dropped her head, and Steve immediately lifted it. "Today isn't about them. They are the past, today is about the future. Focus on what is ahead of you, and don't let old stuff bring you down."

"Forget about them," Shannon said. "Hey, look at this." She darted across the room and picked through a ridiculously big leather bag, emerging with a CD. She just as quickly returned to Danielle's side. "Look. Steve got me an advance copy!"

Danielle took the CD from her. The cover was split in half with a thinly dressed Shannon on the left side wearing light blue against a black background, while Danielle was on the right side, looking pissed off. Silver metallic lettering announced the album title as *The Fairie Meets The Fury*.

Danielle snickered. "The Fairie Meets The Fury?"

"I came up with that," Shannon boasted. "I think it perfectly sums up the album. Don't you?"

Danielle instead looked toward Steve. "I didn't get a say in this?"

"Well, it did start off as Shannon's album," Steve said, his arm wrapped around Aja's waist. "Besides, like she said, it fits perfectly. That's exactly what the album is. As soon as Shannon suggested it, I knew it was the title. I didn't need any other suggestions."

Danielle bristled at that but knew it wasn't a battle worth fighting and let it go. Glancing back down at the CD, she noticed something else, something that did set her off. "Rikka Olaussaon?" She stepped away from Shannon. "I thought you were dropping that routine. We talked about this. At length."

Shannon backpedaled, the same look of terror on her face as the day Danielle had confronted her on the beach. "The label thought it would make more sense to do it this way since that's my professional name."

"Goddamn it, Shannon. Stand up for yourself."

"Now dear," Aja tried to step in. "Don't get yourself all riled up about this. This was a business decision—"

"Again, made unilaterally. What, I left California, and all of a sudden, I'm not involved in the decision making process anymore? What the hell else did y'all do?"

"It didn't have anything to do with you," Steve said, putting just a little weight behind his words. "We're marketing this as a crossover between you and Europe's reigning pop queen. We can't do that if she goes by Shannon Henderson. Nobody knows who that is. We had to go back to Rikka. Surely you can understand that."

"I don't know why it matters so much to you," Aja threw in. "It's Shannon's choice. If she's more comfortable going by her stage name, then that's her decision."

"Thank you," Shannon said. "Danielle, baby, I'm okay with this. I made this decision."

"After they bullied you into it."

"No, they didn't." Tentatively, Shannon approached Danielle. "They didn't. We talked about it. They explained why it made sense, and I agreed with them. Nobody consulted you because we knew you'd make a huge deal out of it when you didn't need to. This is the way I want it. Can you please just accept it?"

Danielle stared into Shannon's pleading eyes, still wanting to press the issue. With a growl, she looked away. "Fine. Have it your way, Rikka," she said sarcastically. "It's already done anyway. I just thought I was an equal partner in this thing." She turned the case so that the front was facing Steve. "After all, my picture is on it. My name's on it. I would have liked to at least be informed of all of this."

It was Aja who stepped forward. "Little displays like this are exactly why people shut you out of the process, dear. You have no control over your emotions. Have you always been like this?"

"As long as I've known her," Steve said.

"Whatever," Danielle muttered, though the slow burn she felt in her soul wasn't going away anytime soon. "Let's see if y'all fucked anything else up." She studied the tracklisting on the back. "I see 'Girl's Night Out' made it." She glanced at Shannon.

"Good for you."

"I know. Steve said they might even release it as a single if the other songs do well."

Steve eagerly jumped into the conversation. "That's right. I fought with Rico over that. I told him that song was the type of good time, let 'er rip rock'n'roll that nobody releases anymore. I think that alone could make it a hit. She really surprised me with that."

"Yet another thing I wasn't consulted on." Danielle sighed, then turn to Shannon. "But I'm happy the song turned out so well. You did good on it."

"Thank you." Shannon's shoulders slumped as it appeared that the storm had passed. "It's going to be even better when we sing it together on stage tonight."

"Speaking of which. I've been thinking about the set list for tonight, and I think we should make some changes. Just some tweaks. I made some notes—"

"Danielle!" Steve called out. "Baby, please. Everything is set. Relax. This is supposed to be the easy part. Take your victory lap and quit trying to borrow trouble."

"I'm not borrowing trouble I just—"

There was a subtle knock on the door, and everyone turned in that direction. "We are ready for you," a male voice said.

"Perfect," said Steve. He took Danielle's arms and gave her a thorough looking over. "Perfect. You're going to be great. You've got this."

Still not satisfied, Danielle picked at the hem of the dress. "If you had let me wear jeans—"

"You're having breakfast with the governor—you don't wear jeans to something like that. This isn't Dubya we're talking about. He would have been cool with it. Speaking of which, he wants to give you a call later. He wanted to be here, but had other commitments."

"Who?" Shannon asked.

"The former president," Steve answered.

"That W?"

"Yeah," Danielle said casually. "We go way back. I knew him when all he did was own a baseball team. He's a cool dude."

Shannon spun in a circle. "Unbelievable. You're besties with a former president, and all you can say is that he's a cool dude. You always claim to be so uninteresting. Who else do you know? The pope?"

"No," Danielle answered. "But I did bump into Matthew McConaughey at a movie premiere once."

"Really," Shannon said with excitement. "How was he?"

Danielle shrugged. "He was just all right, all right."

Steve groaned at her side. "Enough of that. The governor is waiting. Everybody put on your serious faces. It's showtime."

Danielle couldn't repress her laugh. "All right."

~*~

The breakfast was outstanding and innately Texan, with huge platters of every breakfast meat known to man, pancakes, waffles, eggs, and of course, biscuits and gravy. Danielle wanted to eat until she burst, but her fluttery stomach wouldn't allow it. She sat at the right hand of the governor and engaged in polite conversation with him and his family while they ate.

Once everyone was through eating, she was swarmed with all manner of people, most of whom she didn't know. Lots of people pushed for support in upcoming elections or sought some sort of endorsement for their businesses. Danielle handled it all in stride, though she felt lost without Steve at her side. Even Shannon would have been a valued lifeline, but she was inundated with her own crew of admirers, most young men.

Then came the pubic portion of the morning. The governor conducted his press conference just outside the clubhouse. He spoke eloquently of Danielle's place in Texas's rich musical history before declaring it Danielle Regan Day and presenting her a plaque.

More gifts followed. The head of a Texas-based Western wear company gave her a set of custom made boots and a hat. Despite her preference for Coke, a representative of the Dr. Pepper Company unveiled a series of collector cans featuring images of Danielle through the years, as part of a summer long promotion that would send one lucky winner backstage at her concert in Houston in early September. Fender gave her a Stevie Ray Vaughan signature Stratocaster. The gifts and the accolades kept coming.

The program ended with one last gift. Danielle had noticed when she stepped outside what was clearly a car kept under a tarp in the style of the Texas flag. To the podium went the Head of Marketing for General Motors, a man of youthful middle-age wearing what looked to be the most expensive suit in a crowd full of expensive suits who, after a lengthy speech about Danielle's previous service to the company as an endorser, presented her with a new Camaro.

Attendants quickly pulled the tarp away to reveal a deep royal blue Camaro with white racing stripes. The man held out the keys for her. "I think as we end our festivities here today, it would be all too appropriate for you to ride away in your new Beauty."

Danielle stepped up to the podium to accept the gift. The sheer amount of attention was becoming overwhelming, yet she couldn't deny that it was making her feel loved. She reminded herself that all of this was a show, and most of the people in attendance were using this as an excuse to get their products more attention, but it didn't seem to matter.

She took the keys and said a brief thank you. Off stage, Steve was pointing at his watch. Time to go. The crowd parted as she made her way to her new car. The car started with a roar, and Danielle goosed the gas pedal, revving it up to the roar of the crowd. Out of nowhere, Shannon materialized in the front seat. "Let's go for a ride."

Danielle grinned. "Let's."

She was good, not peeling on the well-manicured grass, but once she cleared the crowd and her wheels hit the pavement, Danielle gunned it, giving the audience a shower of white tire smoke as she drove away.

~*~

Danielle was happy to slip out of the dress and into more casual attire when she got to the school. Steve and Aja caught up, and soon Danielle found herself in an expansive conference room in the Moncrief-Neuhaus Athletic Center, being fawned over by a new group of people.

This meeting was more informal than the first. She didn't follow sports any more closely than she followed politics or business, so many of the names and faces meant nothing to her. Still, she shook every hand and signed every autograph, and swapped stories with some of the more talkative guests.

A nervous young man who identified himself as an assistant athletic director talked to her at length about how the first pitch ceremony would go. It seemed to be a lot of work for what appeared to be a simple thing, but then again that was probably what concert goers thought as well.

The assistant AD began shuffling people out of the room as the time to go the ballpark drew near. One man lagged behind and subtly avoided detection by the school official. He was a tall man, slightly taller than Danielle, with broad shoulders, long legs, and a thick torso, his arms and legs already deeply tanned. He wore a white Longhorn polo tucked into Dockers shorts with burnt orange and white Nikes, and the iconic Texas baseball cap: white with an orange bill and T. Unlike the rest of his clothes, which were immaculate, the cap looked heavily used, the white no longer brilliant after repeated wearing, the bill bent severely, and he wore it low over his eyes. In his hands, he clutched a newspaper.

Danielle watched the man, thinking she should be nervous of him but not feeling any particular caution. He noticed her watching him and stepped forward. She could see his toothy smile beneath the bill of the ballcap. When he was within arm's length, he held out the newspaper and a pen. "Could I please get your autograph?"

"Sure." She took the paper, which was yellowed and frayed on the edges, and turned to a nearby table to sign it. She took in a deep breath when she realized what it was. It was a thirteen-year-old insert from the *Austin American-Statesman* titled "20 Young Austinites To Watch." A much younger Danielle shared the cover with a UT baseball player in full uniform, who held out a ball with a sheepish grin on his face. The cap was the same.

Danielle looked up at the man, who pushed his hat up with a single finger. Danielle pointed at the picture of the younger man.

"You?"

"You remember me?"

"Sure, I do." She let her eyes sweep back over the cover, searching for and finding the photo caption. "Brett."

His eyes followed hers. "Cheater," he said, grinning bigger. "You had to look."

"It was thirteen years ago," she defended. "But, I do remember you. We ate lunch at the little pharmacy with the burger joint in the back. It was a fun day."

"Ah, you do remember," Brett Walls answered. "I was afraid you wouldn't. I've been over here for an hour, wondering if I should approach you. I was afraid I was going to feel stupid. "

"Not at all. I'm glad you came over." She rotated the insert so Brett could see it as well, and started flipping through it.

The assistant AD hustled over to them. "Sir, I'm sorry, but I need you to leave. Ms. Regan is needed elsewhere."

"It's okay," she said, trying to swish him away with her left hand. "Give me a minute."

"Ms. Regan," he replied urgently.

"The game's not starting without me anyway. Just cool your heels for a minute and let me look through this." She turned her focus to Brett. "I never met any of these other people. Did they do anything?"

"Oh, several of them. I mean, nobody made it like you did, but there's a couple of successful business people in there, a software developer, a graphic artist. Most of them are fairly well known locally or regionally."

"Cool." She closed the magazine and quickly autographed the cover for him. "What about you? If I remember correctly, you were supposed to be a real hotshot."

Brett's smile faded just a little. "It's a long story, but I'd love to tell it to you sometime. Would you like to get together and do lunch again? Or even dinner, maybe? My treat."

Danielle was aware of the assistant AD, who was pacing nervously. "I'd love to. I really would, but I'm afraid I'm about to head out of town. Gotta go market myself."

Brett slowly slid the magazine off the table, careful not to touch her signature. "Just like last time, I guess. We always seem to be heading in opposite directions."

Danielle remembered that, as well. She had been about to go on tour, and Brett had a baseball tournament to go to. They had exchanged letters once, but that was it. There had been a spark, but it had been snuffed out before it was anything but a flash. "Tell you what. I still have a couple of days. Give me your number, and I'll see if I can clear up a couple of hours. Would that be okay?"

"I'd like that. You got a phone? I can put my number in for you."

"Yeah, actually." She pulled the cell out of her back pocket and handed it over. Brett did what he needed and pushed it back.

"Thank you," Brett said. "I know you gotta go, but I'm going to the game as well. My seats are down the first base line if you get a chance to walk around."

"Okay, that's good," the assistant AD said, taking Brett's arm and steering him toward the door. "Ms. Regan really needs to go now. Thank you for coming."

Danielle fiddled with her phone as she watched him go. Deep in her soul, she felt the tiny stirring, one she hadn't felt in a long time. One that always seemed to get her in trouble. If she had any sense at all, she'd lose Brett's phone number and let him go.

Nothing good ever came to a man she cared about. But after all this time, Danielle couldn't ignore the feeling, but she also didn't have time to linger on it. Her presence was needed elsewhere, and Brett would just have to wait.

~*~

No rest for the wicked.

The thought echoed in Danielle's mind as she made her way from Disch-Faulk Field to the Erwin Center to prepare for the show. She was ragged, the lack of sleep beginning to catch up to her now. In a way, she was thankful. She was too tired to be nervous or to even think too much about the coming show.

She parked her new car in a special lot reserved for crew members, and a staffer led her through the bowels of the building to her dressing room. This felt normal—the standard pre-show routine. In the first part of her career, this was when everything fell into place and made sense. The two hours onstage were an escape from all of the emotions and pressures that seemed to fill the rest of her days. That escape was a large part of the reason she worked so hard. When she was focused on music, she didn't have to think about herself.

Her dressing room was simple: a dresser, a table, a sofa. Her garment bag hung on a portable rack. Steve had left the boots and hat she'd been gifted that morning, with a handwritten note suggesting that she wear them on stage that night. She took them to the sofa to get a better look. The boots were brown leather with Texas flags on the front and musical notes running up the sides. A little gaudy, but doable. The hat she liked. It was also brown leather, with a braided band decorated with simple turquoise beads and bronze buttons. The hat she would wear on stage, but not the boots. She would stick with tennis shoes for that.

A digital clock on the wall told her that it was already 4:43. The pre-show autograph session and meet-and-greet was scheduled for 5:30. With any luck, she could catch a catnap before Steve and Shannon arrived. She put the hat and boots back where she got them, kicked off her shoes, and laid down, curling into a ball on the sofa. Instantly the sleep began to creep up on her.

The door burst open, and through it stomped Shannon, a young blonde girl trailing behind lugging an overnight case and a garment bag. "There's my girl," Shannon said when she located Danielle on the couch. She'd been shopping, sporting a pink straw cowboy hat that faded to charcoal gray along the brim and pink boots with teal butterflies and silver rhinestones. "Get me set up," she said to the blonde girl trailing her. "Chop chop." Then she pivoted toward the couch and plopped one foot on the table directly in front of Danielle's face. "Like them?"

"They're very…you," Danielle grumbled. She forced herself into a sitting position and tried to shake the sleep out of her head.

"Those that you got this morning were so cute I had to go get some of my own. I don't know why I waited so long." She perched on the couch next to Danielle and placed her hat on Danielle's head. "Pink's not your color," she said after a quick appraisal.

"That's why I don't wear pink." Danielle returned the hat to its rightful owner and then stood and began to stretch, taking some delight in feeling her muscles pulled almost to their limits.

"You better start getting ready," Shannon said. "Showtime before you know it." Shannon kicked off her new boots, sat her hat on the table, and stood. Like magic, her dress fell away and left her in nothing but a strapless slip. She sat in front of the dresser, where her assistant had a make-up case opened and ready to work. "All right, Makaylee, do your thing. Make me shine."

"Oh, good lord," Danielle muttered. She made her way to her bag and took out her show clothes, all neatly put together on a single hanger, and started for the bathroom.

"Where are you going?" Shannon asked.

"I'm going to go change."

"Just do it in here. There's no need to be bashful. I've already seen most of what you have to offer anyway."

"I don't want to give you any ideas. You're bad enough when I'm fully clothed."

"You should hear what she says about you when you're not around," chirped Makaylee, the assistant, without looking away from her task. "It's like being a men's locker room. Kinda disturbing."

"Oh you, hush," Shannon snapped, but she had a playful smile on her face as she did.

"Anyway, I'm going to get out of the way and get dressed. Y'all knock yourselves out." Danielle absconded to the bathroom without further delay and did her part in there. Once she was done, Danielle took a seat on the toilet, laid her head on the toilet paper dispenser, and took a fitful nap, only waking when someone knocked on the door. She awoke with a start. "I'm coming," she muttered as she rubbed her eyes.

"Hurry up," Steve begged from the other side of the door. "The crowd is assembled. Everybody is waiting on you."

"What else is new?" Danielle called.

Stepping out of the stall, she straightened her clothes and stopped in front of the mirror for one last look. When she thought about it, the transformation was shocking. Gone was that stringy, pale, depressed thing she had been in Thrasher. The blonde dye job was finally a thing of the past. She'd put on weight, and a rigorous workout routine was turning it into muscle. She already had the beginnings of a solid spring tan.

Danielle watched her reflection as she ran her hands through her hair. "Well, girl, you asked for this. I hope you're ready."

Steve knocked again, louder and faster this time. "Danielle, come on. People are waiting. We have to go."

Danielle turned quickly and pulled open the door. "All right then. Let's go make some magic."

CHAPTER TWENTY-THREE

The autograph session was set up inside the Lone Star Room, a multi-purpose banquet room inside of the Erwin Center. Shannon and Danielle were set up behind two folding tables. Shannon's was covered with an electric blue tablecloth that read Nordic Ice in jagged silver lettering, while Danielle's was covered in an orange cloth that said Texas Fire on it. Danielle had argued against the Fire and Ice motif for their tour, feeling it too clichéd, but she lost the battle.

Shannon embraced the role of the Ice Queen, coming out in a corset top, mini skirt, and thigh-high boots that were ice blue with silver and white accents. She'd donned a platinum wig, and her makeup gave her features a sharp appearance. Danielle barely recognized her and felt underdressed, though she had to admit that they'd done a good job of matching her jacket to the blue on Shannon's outfit.

The room was already filled with excited fans, and the line extended through the room and out into the hallway. They were crammed in tight, forced into a zig-zag path through the use of portable barriers. When the fans got their first view of Danielle, a roar erupted from the crowd that brought a huge smile to her face.

She'd done similar events dozens, if not hundreds, of times over the years. Sign some gear, engage in some trivial chit chat, stand for a quick photo, and send them on their way. For people who didn't have gear to sign, there were tables set up along the sides with CDs, posters, T-shirts, and more. Staffers in Day-Glo yellow tunics and lanyards chock full of badges circulated, making sure the line moved swiftly, and everyone remained calm. Just in case things got out of hand, two unarmed security guards stood behind the girls at the front of the room.

Danielle had feared that Shannon might be ignored since most of her success had been in Europe, but the crowds flocked to her table as well, and Shannon was brilliant. Danielle sometimes found it difficult not to be mesmerized by the effortless way in which Shannon engaged her fans. She was effervescent, treating each visitor more like a friend than a nameless face. She especially shone when dealing with the surprising number of young girls that were in attendance. Danielle was mildly jealous of how effortless Shannon made it all look.

For herself, Danielle found the praise that was being heaped on her uncomfortable. Every visitor seemed to go on and on about how much her music had meant to them, or what an inspiration she had been. Danielle appreciated the sentiments but was never much good at taking compliments at close range. She could engage the devil himself in a nose-to-nose screaming match and not bat an eye, but heap praise upon her and Danielle's skin began to crawl. She tried not to let it show.

It seemed like the event had drug on forever, and Danielle was feeling the pull of the stage. It was creating an urgent pressure in the back of her mind. Mercifully, the staffers closed the doors as the last of the guests squeezed into the room. It wouldn't be too much longer.

As the guests continued to wind through the room, occasionally, Danielle's eyes would sweep over people who didn't look right. She couldn't define why or what it was that made them stand out. Almost as soon as she noticed one the crowd would shift and they would disappear, leaving Danielle to question if she was really seeing them at all.

Danielle had become so distracted that she had quit paying attention to the faces in front of her, instead watching the line, looking for the ones who didn't fit. The next person in line tossed a book down in front of her. Danielle smiled half-heartedly and pulled the book closer and lifted the front cover when something made her stop. She closed the front. The book jacket was a soft gray and had a picture of a young, average looking couple, both blond-haired and rosy cheeked, smiling into the camera and wearing matching sweaters. The wordmark was in a gothic font, black outline in red, the letters sharp—the Seduction of Alec by Nicole Moore.

With a start, Danielle's eyes snapped up and focused on the face of the woman who had been stalking her in the media for months now. She glowered down at Danielle, dull blue eyes full of hatred, her lips a tight scar across her face. She wore a white shirt and a red and blue sweater over new blue jeans. "You're out of places to run, Ms. Regan."

Instantly several people jumped out of line, each producing either a video camera or a phone. They pushed to the front and spread out in a half circle. Lights went on, spotlighting them and temporarily blinding Danielle.

Nicole planted her fists on the table and leaned down closer, getting right in Danielle's face. "Now, Ms. Regan, you're going to answer for what you did to my Alec, and to who knows how many other husbands out there."

Danielle pushed her seat back to get out of the direct light from the cameras and rubbed at her eyes. Her stomach was churning with a curious mixture of fear and anger she'd never felt before. Her initial instinct was to fire back. She didn't take kindly to being called out, especially publicly. Yet in the back of her mind, she was aware that the woman in front of her was a mourning widow who had been blindsided by her husband's secret desire. They had both lost the men they loved.

"Mrs. Moore...." She started to say, "I'm sorry" out of basic consideration but caught herself. No, she would not apologize to this woman, because she had nothing to apologize for. She took a deep breath and started again. "What happened to your husband was a tragedy. I understand how —"

"You understand nothing, you little tart." Nicole said it loud enough that it caught the attention of the staffers, who started to close in, some calling for assistance on handheld radios. To keep them from getting too close, Danielle held both arms out and put up her palms in the classic Stop symbol. The crowd was rolling behind Nicole, some trying to get away while others pushed forward for a better look.

From the next table, Shannon was pleading with her. "Dani, just get up and walk away. Just leave, Dani."

Danielle heard her words but wouldn't break eye contact with Nicole. "Everybody, just stay cool. She's waited a long time for this, let her have her say."

"Yeah, and you better believe I'm gonna have my say," Nicole continued. "What happened to Alec is your fault. You, with your music and your seductive moves and revealing clothes."

"Revealing clothes?" Danielle chuckled at the words. One of the things Danielle had been known for was her conservative dress. "I didn't really —"

Nicole stuffed her hands in her jeans pockets and pulled out a wadded up paper. She slammed it on the table and undid it. The picture was a professional still of Danielle in her yellow bikini from the "Marina Del Rey" photoshoot.

"Now —"

Danielle started to protest, but Nicole slammed another picture down and unwadded it. This one was a print out of an amateur photo from early in her career when Steve was trying to give her a stage image. The picture showed Danielle in a black leather bustier and mini skirt with stiletto heels.

"This —"

Again, Danielle's rebuttal was cut short by a third picture, unwadded to reveal the cover photo from her controversial *Southern Hospitality* album, where Danielle had worn nothing but a Confederate flag and a come hither smile. She was well aware of the power of that photo. It had been Kyle's favorite of her.

"Look at these." Nicole pounded her index finger onto the top of the pile. "Look. Someone like you looking like that, looking right into the camera and basically saying 'come and get it' to every man, woman, or child who sees it. You're a temptress, and your dark magic cursed my Alec."

There were so many things in that statement Danielle wanted to rebuke that her head spun. "Lady, it's part of the job," she finally managed to say. "They're pictures. Three pictures out of a ten year career."

"Oh, there were more. All over the walls, all over his computer, in his wallet. He watched porn videos with actresses who looked like you. Hundreds of them, all with look-a-likes. Disturbing, disgusting videos."

"That's terrible, I agree, but I didn't make him do these things. I'm a performer." She swatted the pictures to the side. "These pictures, they're just performance. If your husband lost touch with reality, that's his problem, not mine."

She knew the instant the words escaped her lips that she'd made a mistake. Despite the truth of the statement, Danielle knew the last thing she should do was attack either Nicole or her dead husband. In the heat of the moment, she'd slipped up.

Nicole jumped all over it. "You think he was crazy? Alec was the most sane, normal person ever. Until you came along and twisted his mind."

Danielle felt the ring of staffers and security drawing closer. At the back of the room, more security was coming in, and she knew she had to de-escalate the situation quickly. Putting her hands up in a defensive posture, Danielle slowly rose out of her chair.

"I shouldn't have said that." Danielle spoke deliberately, intimately aware of how badly things could go with one more misstep. "I own that. I know you're angry, and you need somewhere to put that rage. I've been there myself. I can tell you from my own experience that the best thing you can do is let it go before it destroys you."

"You already destroyed me! When you took my Alec, you destroyed me!"

"I get that. I lost the love of my life too, and I felt destroyed, just like you do. I wanted to die. I went into hiding for six years because I couldn't deal with it."

"You can do that, you don't have kids. I have to deal with it every day." The hardness in Nicole's face melted as tears began to wet her cheeks. Her shoulders slumped, and her eyes dropped to the floor. Danielle relaxed ever so slightly, confident she had succeeded.

"You're right. I don't have kids, and I never will. I can't even imagine how hard that is. My heart goes out to you, it really does. I can't tell you where to go from here—I'm not trained for things like that. All I can say is that, for me, I had to rediscover myself in order to heal."

"Heal?" Nicole sneered. "I'll never heal."

"No, but we can try. The scars never go away, but life does go on. You have your kids. Live for them. They need you. If I can help you, I will. Just tell me what you need."

Nicole looked up at Danielle through watery blue eyes. "I want you to apologize. I want you to look me in the eyes and say you're sorry for what you did to Alec. That's all I want from you. It's all I've ever wanted."

Danielle licked her lips nervously. Now her pride was riled up. Apologize for something beyond her control? Apologize because this woman's husband killed *her* Kyle? It was a simple thing, a meaningless gesture, but for Danielle, it was a step too far.

The silence hung heavy between them. The crowd was murmuring, and the security staff was whispering in their radios, ready to jump in at the slightest provocation. Off to her side, Shannon chimed in. "Just say it, Dani. Let's be done with this. We have a show to do."

Danielle's delay stoked Nicole's fire again, and the hardness returned. "I'm waiting. Where's my apology?" Around her, the cameramen angled for better views.

"I...won't do that. What I do is seen by millions of people, and I can't be responsible if one guy takes those performances to a dark place. I've been carrying my own cross, my own guilt, for a long time. I won't carry yours too."

"You little tramp," Nicole snarled. "You worthless, two-bit, lying little cunt. You're trash. All these people who came here to worship you, they're trash. You're all just soulless heathens."

"If that's what you think, go ahead. You're going to think what you want to anyway. So if saying those things to me, if calling me names, helps you go on with your life, then go for it. I promise I've been called worse." Danielle saw confusion ripple across Nicole's face, and her mouth dropped open in surprise. "I think it's time you go home now."

Nicole dropped her arms to her sides and shuffled forward, her eyes downcast. She reached for the photos and straightened them up with a shaky hand before dropping them back onto the table. She sighed and looked up at Danielle, her bottom lip trembling.

"If you need to cry, do it. No one will think less of you. I certainly won't," Danielle assured her. "We've both been through the wringer."

Out of nowhere, Nicole's right hand flew up, and she slapped Danielle across the cheek with enough force to rock her backward. She breathed in sharply as her head was driven to the side. The sting in her cheek was immediate and spread, tiny fingers of pain crawling all over her face.

In an instant, Danielle was a little girl again back in West

Texas, cowering as her mother rained down on her. The pain was the same, even with the distance of time. She put her left hand to her face and dug the fingers of her right hand into her palm to keep from losing her cool. Again security tried to move in, only to have Danielle order them to stand down.

She stared back at Nicole, making her face go hard and cold. "Anything else?"

Nicole again seemed confused, then agitated, and finally defeated. She turned to go, and everyone in the room seemed to let out a deep breath all at once. Danielle closed her eyes, thankful she'd managed to maintain her composure through the entire ordeal.

Nicole took a step toward the door before she stopped and turned. "By the way, in regards to your *fiancé,* the only good thing that inbred, hillbilly piece of shit ever did in his whole life was fucking die. I hope you know that."

It took a second for the words to penetrate, but once they did, everything went to hell. Danielle launched herself over the table, slamming full force into Nicole. They both tumbled to the ground as the crowd screamed, and bodies scattered.

Nicole was swatting at Danielle, weak, ineffective slaps as Danielle gathered herself. She glared down at Nicole, but it wasn't Nicole Moore she saw on the ground underneath her. It was twisted, smoking metal, shattered glass, and blood stained sheets. Nicole's slap was still reverberating on Danielle's cheek, and she could hear her mother's voice scolding her for whatever innocuous crime she had committed.

Then Danielle let loose, swinging wild, powerful punches aimed square at Nicole Moore's face. Her fists slammed into her again and again. Too soon, she felt the hands of others upon her, clutching at her arms, her shoulders, her back, her waist, anywhere someone could grab. Danielle shrieked and continued to fire away, each punch accompanied by a guttural profanity.

Someone finally managed to pull Danielle backward, too far away to connect on anymore punches. Nicole began moaning and rolling, begging for help. Danielle swung her legs toward her, wrapping them around Nicole's chest and locking her ankles. Her verbal tirade continued as she insulted Nicole, her husband, her kids, and anything else in an uncontrolled torrent. Whoever had her was yanking, desperately trying to tear Danielle loose. She felt it coming. With one last heave, her leg lock was broken, and she felt herself pulled back. In one last defiant act of rage, she kicked with her left leg. Nicole, finally free of Danielle, leaned up just enough that the heel of Danielle's boot caught her square on the nose. Blood spurted everywhere as the nose caved in, and Nicole Moore went back to the ground, out cold.

The security guards pulled Danielle far away and tossed her face first to the carpeted floor. Immediately someone dropped onto her shoulders to keep her from getting up, while someone else wrenched her arms behind her. She felt cold metal on her wrists and heard the snap as handcuffs locked into place.

Finally, it was over.

~*~

Chaos ensued in the aftermath.

The floor of the Lone Star Room was littered with debris: busted CDs and torn posters, tables overturned, and the barrier knocked on their sides. Around the room, at least a dozen bystanders received treatment for minor cuts and bruises suffered when the fans stampeded. One fan, a teenage girl, received much more serious treatment after she'd been knocked to the ground and trampled by panicked fans.

Shannon sat in a corner, cradling her right arm to her chest, fearful she had broken her wrist when one of the security guards had shoved her out of the way, and she had landed awkwardly. Steve was there, tie loose around his neck and top button undone. He was talking animatedly with someone on his cellphone while almost conducting a much more mellow conversation with a uniformed captain from the Austin Police Department. Two of Nicole's secret camera crew were being interviewed by police, but the rest had managed to slip away in the confusion, no doubt trying to sell their footage to the highest bidder.

Nicole was being loaded onto a stretcher while moaning like a beached whale. "She broke my face. The bitch broke my face. I want her prosecuted. I want her executed."

Danielle sat cross-legged on the floor against the back wall, hands still cuffed behind her back. Her jacket had been ripped in two, and now the pieces hung loosely from her wrists. Several thin lines of blood dried across her back, where she'd been scratched while she was being pulled away. Her hair was disheveled, and her clothes were splattered with blood from Nicole's broken nose. An APD officer stood at her side, just in case she wanted to make another run at Nicole.

"Will someone, please, get that psycho out of here, so I don't have to listen to her fucking stupid voice anymore?"

The officer glared down at her and ordered her to shut up. She looked right, where Shannon just shook her head with disappointment and mouthed the word "why" to her. Danielle looked away.

Once Nicole and the teen girl were wheeled away, they came for Danielle, two officers roughly hoisting her to her feet. Steve saw this and ended his phone call, muttered something to the cop, and rushed to her side.

"Are you happy now? Everything is ruined. Everything we worked so hard for is gone." Steve snarled in her ear. He was close enough and angry enough that another officer stepped in and pushed him back. "You realize you're going to prison for this, right?" he called as the officers escorted her past him. "Not jail, prison. This is it, it's over. There's no coming back from this."

They were approaching the door. Danielle dug her heels in and looked back over her shoulder. "Hey, Steve? Go fuck yourself."

The police led her into the hall and through the Erwin Center concourses and out into the muggy night air. Behind metal barricades, tens of thousands of disappointed fans watched, some in tears, as the woman they had come to celebrate was led away in cuffs. News cameras ringed the scene, capturing and preserving every detail forever.

Danielle chuckled as she took it all in. For the second time, her life was shattered on a spring Austin night, bathed in the glow of flashing red and blue lights. The cops led her to a nearby squad car, and one popped open the back door.

As they shoved her head down and forced Danielle into the back seat, she took in the scene. The last time this had happened, she'd lost years of her life. Now, she wondered if Steve was right if there really was no coming back from this. There was another, much more pressing question on Danielle's mind as the police car pulled away.

Did she even care?

About the Author

Donny Hunt is trying to make daydreaming a viable career while living in working in the Texas panhandle with his wife of 20 years and their four children. Donny is an avid sports fan, music lover and history buff. Already Fallen is his fourth novel and the second in the Danielle Regan series.